本书系汉考国际和世界汉语学会科研基金项目"非洲国际中文 OMO 教育模式研究"(CTI2021ZB07),以及教育部中外语言交流合作中心国际中文教育研究课题"后疫情时代非洲国际中文教育发展研究"(21YH16C)的阶段性成果。

西非民间口头文学作品欣赏
(塞拉利昂篇)

何明清　译著

苏州大学出版社

图书在版编目(CIP)数据

西非民间口头文学作品欣赏. 塞拉利昂篇:汉英对照 / 何明清译著. --苏州:苏州大学出版社,2023.5
ISBN 978-7-5672-4352-1

Ⅰ.①西… Ⅱ.①何… Ⅲ.①民间文学-文学欣赏-塞拉利昂-汉、英 Ⅳ.①I430.77

中国国家版本馆 CIP 数据核字(2023)第 070753 号

西非民间口头文学作品欣赏(塞拉利昂篇)
何明清　译著
责任编辑　朱坤泉

苏州大学出版社出版发行
(地址:苏州市十梓街1号　邮编:215006)
苏州市深广印刷有限公司印装
(地址:苏州市高新区浒关工业园青花路6号2号楼　邮编:215151)

开本 700 mm×1 000 mm　1/16　印张 15　字数 270 千
2023 年 5 月第 1 版　2023 年 5 月第 1 次印刷
ISBN 978-7-5672-4352-1　定价:58.00 元

图书若有印装错误,本社负责调换
苏州大学出版社营销部　电话:0512-67481020
苏州大学出版社网址　http://www.sudapress.com
苏州大学出版社邮箱　sdcbs@ suda.edu.cn

前　言

　　2019年8月27日下午，在位于北京西直门的孔子学院总部办理完离任手续，我正式为自己在塞拉利昂大学孔子学院任中方院长的四年任期画上了句号。这四年有机会为中塞民心相通和文化交流做些力所能及的事，深感欣慰，也很难忘！虽然已挥手道别，但心中依然充满了牵挂。在这四年致力于国际中文教育的日子里，心里堆积了太多的感谢、感恩和感动。感谢各级领导的信任，感恩塞拉利昂各界朋友的支持，感动于历届同仁的通力合作与前赴后继！

　　本书分享了我在非洲工作期间收集到的一些原汁原味的当地民间口头文学作品。这些民间口头文学题材来源于塞拉利昂当地丰富的民间传统文化和民族文化。由于塞拉利昂境内民族的多样性，其民间口头文学也呈现出了文化多样性特征，它们是今天塞拉利昂文化和精神面貌的直接来源和重要体现。

　　不管您此前是否去过非洲，抑或此刻是否正身处非洲，本书都可以从民间文学的视角帮助您了解一个更加真实、立体的非洲，为增进中非之间的相互理解和互学互鉴尽微薄之力。借英国诗人菲利普·拉金（Philip Larkin）的一首诗《一座属于所有人的城市：弗里敦》，向我们一起战斗过的地方——弗里敦致敬，向塞拉利昂的"战友们"致敬！

一座属于所有人的城市：弗里敦

一个产生不了诗歌的地方

却无法阻挡诗歌自发涌现

弗里敦恰恰擅长于此

它的雅致往往出人意料

人们不愿离开这片热土

远行的总是归心似箭

在这里盘桓一年半载的过客

却不禁终生流连忘返

因为他们感受到这座城市的不同凡响

那闹市中的世外桃源

塞拉利昂共和国（The Republic of Sierra Leone，简称塞拉利昂），地处非洲西部，西临大西洋，北接几内亚，东南部接壤利比里亚。国土面积约71740平方千米，总人口约754.87万（2021年），首都为弗里敦。

塞拉利昂属热带季风性气候，高温多雨，全年平均气温约27℃。塞拉利昂一年分为旱季和雨季两个季节，每年的11月至次年4月为旱季，5月至10月为雨季，是西非降雨量较多的国家。受来自大西洋的暖湿季风气流的影响，塞拉利昂与人们印象中炎热、干燥的非洲相去甚远，气候非常舒适宜人。

塞拉利昂境内繁密交错的水道网，为本国提供了丰沛的水资源。境内主要有7条河流：大斯卡西河（Great Scarcies）、小斯卡西河（Little Scarcies）、罗克尔河（Rokel）、章河（Jong）、塞瓦河（Sewa）、莫阿河（Moa）、曼诺河（Mano）。这些主要河流发源于几内亚和利比里亚，基本走向是从东北流向西南，最终汇入大西洋。这些河流为水上交通提供了便利条件。塞拉利昂最早的一批城镇就是在作为水上航运中心的贸易聚集点的基础之上发展起来的。古老的西非民间口头文学便发源于散落在这些纵横交错的河道之间的村镇或居民聚集点。

塞拉利昂主要生活着18个较大的民族，分别为曼迪族（Mende）、蒂姆奈族（Temne）、雅伦卡族（Yalunka）、曼丁哥族（Mandigo）、布洛姆族（Bullom）、林巴族（Limba）、富拉族（Fula）、克里奥族（Krio）、舍布罗族

前言

（Sherbro）、苏苏族（Soso）等。其早期的部落民族中，有些民族已经消亡，如早期生活在海岸的巴嘎人。

塞拉利昂有着丰富且独特的传统文化。从整体上来讲，塞拉利昂传统文化是指以塞拉利昂各民族文化为源头的、由其域内各民族共同创造的、长期历史发展所积淀的文化，它强调的是文化的本源和沿着这个本源传承下来的全部文化遗产，是迄今为止塞拉利昂各民族经过筛选、淘汰，不断丰富又不断发展的人文精神的总和。民族文化是一个不以时代划分的、动态发展的历史范畴。民族文化与传统文化两者之间的关系体现在以下三个方面：第一，每个民族都因地域和发展程度的差异而形成了自己的传统文化；第二，任何一种民族传统文化，在各个历史时期，都要受到其他民族文化的影响，引进和吸纳其他民族文化的成分，这些被引进和吸纳的外来文化一旦与自身的文化相结合，它便成了这个民族的传统文化的一部分；第三，民族文化的丰富和发展是在传统文化的基础上实现的，如果离开了传统文化，民族文化的发展就成了无源之水、无本之木，民族文化就会失去民族特色，失去存在的价值和意义。

要读懂今天的塞拉利昂，读懂非洲，我们非常有必要从这些田间地头的口头文学着手了解。《西非民间口头文学作品欣赏（塞拉利昂篇）》就是这样的一本民间口头文学作品的译编之作。本书融合塞拉利昂的历史与文化，精选和编译了40多篇民间口头文学作品。这些作品主题多样，大致分为四个类别——故事、寓言、歌谣、谚语，揭示了人与世界、人与自然、动物及其世界以及人与人之间的关系，表现了西非各民族的生活经验、社会风俗、文化传统和哲学思想。这些民间口头文学作品通俗易懂，情节曲折，语言保留了非洲方言在语音、节奏等方面的特色，富于音乐性和趣味性，适合各个年龄段的读者，具有较强的文学和文化价值。

塞拉利昂人民教育协会（People's Education Association，以下简称"协会"）为塞拉利昂民间文学的发展做出了积极的贡献。协会是一个志愿机构，在塞拉利昂全国各地设有21个分支机构，主要从事成人教育发展工作。1984年，协会开始着手收集来自全国各地的口头文学素材，包括故事、寓言、歌谣和谚语等。这些口头文学素材来源于塞拉利昂丰富的民间传统文化，是塞拉利昂宝贵的文化遗产。

协会对这些口头文学素材进行收集、整理、转录和出版，其意义是不言而喻的。这将让塞拉利昂的文化圈"久旱逢甘雨"，让在校的学生和成年读者感受到文化的熏染。而且，协会还尝试将这些口头文学素材翻译成塞拉利昂当地不同的民族语言，这也将有力推动该国各民族文化之间的相互交流。对于协会而言，这些口头文学素材的收集、整理、转录、编辑等的工程量非常浩大，在塞拉利昂当时的技术条件下，这几乎是一项难以完成的任务。

本书所选取的这些口头文学作品主要来源于塞拉利昂的13个民族，包括曼迪族、蒂姆奈族、莱蒙族、林巴族、富拉族、基西族、科诺族、柯兰科族、克里奥族、洛科族、曼廷戈族、舍布罗族、苏和亚伦卡族。虽然未涵盖塞拉利昂的所有民族，但是代表了其中的多数，覆盖了该国较大的语言群体。

为了尽可能体现出塞拉利昂文化的多样性，我在收集和编译时，充分考虑读者阅读和感受文化多样性的方式，从一个故事到另一个故事，从轻松娱乐到发人深省，从一个长故事到一首短歌，不拘泥于形式。在编排方式上，也未严格遵循传统的编排样式，比如，没有按照地区、字母顺序、不同的文学体裁、收集日期或不同民族语言等传统的方式来编排。

在阅读时读者能很容易地识别出其中的四种主要的文学体裁。故事或寓言，主要是以动物或人类为主人公的故事，通常带有一定的寓意；歌谣，分属赞美、工作、社会或情歌的范畴，都是一些在当地妇孺皆知、耳熟能详、传唱度极高的热门歌谣；另外一些是人们在日常生活中所熟知、理解和经常使用的谚语。有时，这些不同的体裁会组合在一则材料里：或者从一首歌谣开始一个故事，或者从故事中的一条重要线索产生一首新歌，或者以一个谚语来结束一个故事，抑或在一个故事中间，用一首歌谣来唤醒听众或为即将到来的高潮做准备。凡此种种，形式非常灵活，很符合故事讲述者游走各地时以一种轻松愉悦的方式吸引听众的真实情境。很多时候，以歌谣作为开头，可以起到引人入胜的效果，听众常常会积极参与，为此鼓掌，欢呼雀跃。听众还会不时地对讲述者的调侃和笑话做出反应，而讲述者又反过来用一个接一个的故事对听众的反应做出回应。

塞拉利昂的民间口头文学是当地民间文学的重要组成部分。众所周知，口头文学是与正统文学相对的一个概念，历来是难登大雅之堂的。然而，正是因为它的这一特点，口头文学成为真正属于普通民众的文学。口头文学一般很难确定其具体作者，绝大部分为群众集体创作。在流传的过程中，随意性很强，内容及形式经常会发生一些变化，甚至衍生出许多版本。我在塞拉利昂工作期间参加当地的一些文化活动时，就曾听到过关于同一个故事的不同版本，如《三个求婚者》《那丁与孜克雷》等。诚然，口头文学最本质也最重要的特点就是产生于民间，流传于民间，发扬于民间。从这个意义上来说，口头文学是民众最真实的生命体验，属于"原生态"的文学样式。它不矫揉造作，直抒胸臆，活泼生动，老少皆宜，往往能用最简单的语言揭示最深刻的道理。当然，这种"原生态"的文学样式难免有一些在审美情趣或者价值取向上是我们不认同的，但为了原汁原味地呈现其本来特征，我们也作了最大限度的保留。

这些口头文学的流传时间、地点是随机的、不确定的。或许在一个上午、下午或者晚上，或许在一个休息的走廊、法庭的门口或其他大大小小的公共场所，只要有听众的地方，就是它们流传下去的土壤。大多数讲故事的人都是业余爱好者，但也有著名的故事讲述者或深受人们喜爱的当地艺人，每个人都可以加入其中，成为这些口头文学流传下去的接力者。比如：萨利亚·科罗马（Salia Koroma）、因作品《日历之火》而闻名全国的尼泽、享有派拉蒙至上酋长地位的曼蒂·南库姆·卡巴（Manty Nyankume Kabba）、广为人知的拜斯·康蒂（Bassie Kondi）及喜剧演员克里斯·都灵（Chris During）等，他们中的许多人经常出现在广播和电视等公共媒体。当然，也包括一些夜晚村落里的故事讲述者、职业民间艺术家等。

收集素材的过程是非常烦琐的。从寻找故事讲述者和歌手开始，再到翻译、转录等，每一个环节均要耗费大量的人力和时间。由于素材来源于不同的民族语言，在开始翻译之前必须先把各自的语言从口语转录到书面语。我们在这些口头文学的译介过程中遇到了几个问题。首先，要完成基本的规划和决策，要从海量的素材中选取具有代表性的作品，且要兼顾到不同的文学体裁。其次，是语言问题，由于这些民间口头文学来源于不同的民族、不同的语言，要不停地向塞拉利昂的专家学者求证，尽可能多地进行语言的修正。在此，我要衷心感谢弗拉湾学院的阿里教授和我的同事塞拉利昂大学孔子学院外方院长肯纳斯·奥修先生给予的耐心指导，也要感谢塞拉利昂人民教育协会提供的诸多可供借鉴的素材，为他们对塞拉利昂口头文学的继承和发展所做出的积极贡献表示由衷的敬意。

至于翻译工作，我尽力避免直译、简译或者把故事译成教科书式的文本。这些都不能使原创文学形式发挥最大价值。在保证故事可读性的同时，我将获取到的素材逐行翻译成一定格式的既定模板。翻译中我也遇到了一些挑战，比如：当遇到一些因文化语境的限制而难以翻译的词汇时该怎么办？如何为"Kwa-a，Kwa-o"这样的象声词找到贴切的译文？如何处理意象和双关语？要把一种语言中模糊、平实的意象翻译成另一种语言时应如何拿捏？如何将复杂的阐释作进一步的软化阐述？等等。具体来说，我在处理《猎人》（"Hunter"）的文本翻译时就遇到了难题。如何在一段对话中将单个故事和歌谣分离开来？由于该文本擅长于呈现戏剧化的场面，有许多叙述狩猎者与动物对话的故事情节，一旦处理不好就会与故事讲述者的夜间表演相脱节。诸如此类的困难在翻译中时常出现。另外，在翻译时，我们尤其重视的是最大限度地保留原作的文化特色，尽可能地做到让非母语人员也能读懂并容易理解，这些对于英语非母语的翻译人员而言，是必须面对的巨大挑战。

当然，问题还不仅仅存在于转录和翻译之中。从事语言工作的人都知道，即使是同一种语言，书面语和口语也会有很大的差异。我们要将口头文学这样的"无字作品"转为"文字作品"，这个过程并非易事。长期以来，在现代文学和现代文化中，书面文学一直是文学形式的主宰，口头文学自身的故事讲述艺术则显得微不足道。口头文学在经历了几度的兴衰之后，故事讲述艺术才逐渐被重新发现，希望今后能焕发出勃勃生机。

欧洲殖民势力入侵非洲后，非洲历史是由殖民者等"外人"书写的，对非洲历史多有歪曲，但真实的非洲历史是一直存在的。从大体上说，非洲的历史包括书面历史、考古历史和口头历史等。书面历史包括各种文字记录的历史，如档案、笔记、手稿、书面文献等；考古历史是一种更可靠的无声物证所展示的历史，它包括各种考古成果；口头历史则是保存和传播非洲人民积累的没有文字记载的社会和文化创作作品的历史，它包括非洲各地未被文字记录下来的口口相传的传统和传说。非洲各地的神话、传说、诗歌、寓言、故事等口头历史是构成非洲历史的重要内容。

相对而言，非洲诸多地区的文字资料并不丰富，口头传说在历史与文化的传承中占有突出的地位。因此，加快对非洲口头传说进行挖掘，在非洲历史文化研究中占有尤其重要的地位。有学者称，作为重新获取非洲声音的口头传说方法是非洲研究主动精神复苏的最大突破。因此，加强对非洲口头传说的研究，对非洲历史、哲学、文化的研究而言，显得尤其迫切而独特。

在塞拉利昂民间口头文学的翻译创作过程中，我常常百感交集。如果你曾经参加过塞拉利昂任何一个民族的夜间故事说唱活动，你会被活动深深地吸引。在某个旱季的夜晚，人们围着熊熊燃烧的篝火倾听说唱故事，空气中弥漫着新鲜的棕榈酒和烤花生的香味，男女老少都参与其中。人们随着富有节奏的鼓声扭动着身体，快乐地沉浸在合唱声中，年轻的母亲背上驮着熟睡

前言

的婴儿在尽情舞蹈，故事说唱人旁若无人地发挥着，倾听故事的人时不时地插上几句嘴，不断有人起哄鼓励或挑战讲故事的人……这样，你便能充分认识和欣赏这类活动的创造性。虽然在翻译创作过程中，我极力保留这样的画面，但是，从表演到印刷文字的转录过程中读者难免会感觉到失去了什么，能做的是尽力避免或者减少这种损失。

再次衷心地致敬那些为保护塞拉利昂文学领域丰富的文化遗产而努力的PEA工作者和每一位口头文学的传承者。在塞拉利昂有这样一句话：每逝去一位著名的故事讲述者，就等于失去了一整个图书馆或者至少其中一部分。此书中收录他们所讲述的故事，就是为了供更多的人了解塞拉利昂的民间口头文学，这也将有助于唤醒人们对故事讲述艺术的重视。

在翻译创作这本塞拉利昂民间文学作品时，我并不想把塞拉利昂少数民族的过去浪漫化，但作为一名文化工作者，我希望能从这些口头文学作品中穿越时空看到塞拉利昂过去的许多东西，这些东西将会帮助我们更好地了解塞拉利昂的文化，促进中塞之间的合作交流和民心相通。同时，我们应意识到，塞拉利昂的这些民间文学不仅仅是当地教育的重要资源和主题，也是非洲生活中不可分割的一部分，它们对于我们了解非洲未来的发展将不可或缺。

目　录

三个求婚者 / 1　　　　　　　　The Three Suitors / 2

蒂姆奈谚语 / 4　　　　　　　　Temne Proverbs / 5

这就是你的生活 / 6　　　　　　This Is the Life That You Live / 8

蛇、鱼和松鼠 / 11　　　　　　 The Snake, the Fish and the Squirrel / 13

固执的女孩 / 16　　　　　　　 The Stubborn Girl / 19

死亡是如何进入这个世界的 / 23　How Death Entered the World / 24

猎人 / 26　　　　　　　　　　 The Hunter / 31

服务两位主人的方式 / 37　　　　A Way of Serving Two Masters / 39

忧他人之忧 / 41　　　　　　　　Somebody's Business Is Everybody's Business / 44

哈贝，狡猾之王 / 47　　　　　　Hagbe, the King of Craftiness / 50

碾米 / 54　　　　　　　　　　　Rice Thrashing / 55

军蚁与人类 / 56　　　　　　　　Driver Ants and Human Beings / 58

曼迪族谚语 / 60　　　　　　　　Mende Proverbs / 61

竞争之果 / 62　　　　　　　　　The Rival's Groundnuts / 64

三个文盲 / 66　　　　　　　　　The Three Illiterate Men / 67

我只是来问问 / 69　　　　　　　I've Only Come to Ask / 70

烦恼 / 71　　　　　　　　　　　Worries / 72

再见了，妈妈 / 73　　　　　　　Mothers, Goodbye / 74

被鹿拖走的陷阱设置者 / 75	The Trap-Setter Who Was Carried Away by the Deer / 80
巴·桑吉·班古拉酒店 / 86	Pa Santigie Bangura / 87
忘恩负义的代价 / 88	The Wages of Ingratitude / 90
男孩和他的姐姐 / 93	The Boy and His Sister / 97
三兄弟 / 102	The Three Brothers / 103
谁会为我的死哀悼 / 105	Who Will Mourn When I Die / 108
山洞 / 111	The Cave / 115
陷阱 / 121	The Trap / 124
巴兰基乐手 / 128	The Balangi Players / 130
嫉妒 / 132	Jealousy / 137
饥荒 / 144	Famine / 145
贪婪与懒惰 / 147	Bra Greedy and Bra Beggar / 149
陆上好擒鳄 / 151	Detaining a Crocodile on Land / 156
那丁与孜克雷 / 163	Bra Natin and Bra Zikray / 165
老鹰和母鸡 / 169	Fowl and Hawk / 171
为何鸟儿有多彩的羽毛 / 174	Why Birds Have Different Colours / 175
女仆的仆人 / 176	The Maid's Maid / 178
披着羊皮的狼 / 180	A Wolf in Sheep's Clothes / 182
杧果名字的由来 / 185	How the Mango Got Its Name / 186
穷小子与坏人 / 187	A Poor Boy and a Wicked Man / 188
以德报德 / 190	One Good Turn / 193
狗与影子 / 197	The Dog and His Shadow / 198
老鹰与麻雀 / 200	Hawk and Sparrow / 201
长毛的青蛙 / 203	The Frog that Grows Hair / 205
忘恩负义的男孩 / 208	The Ungrateful Boy / 210
为什么动物会怕猎人 / 213	Why Animals Fear Hunters / 215
三个朋友 / 218	Three Friends / 220

后记 / 223

三个求婚者

从前有一个村子，村里有三个年轻人，他们同时在追求村里一个非常漂亮的女孩。第一个求婚者带着十英镑和一头母牛来向这个漂亮女孩求婚。女孩的父母把钱收下了。第二个求婚者带来了一份类似的礼物，并表达了同样的愿望。女孩的父母也接受了他的礼物。第三个求婚者来了，情况也同样如此。

过了很长一段时间，三个求婚者都决定再一次拜访这个漂亮女孩。第一个求婚者带着四英镑和十个科拉坚果过来，要求女孩父母允许他看一眼这个女孩。父母照例收下了这笔钱，让他回家，两天后带着二百英镑回来再说。这个可怜的年轻人花了二十年去筹集这笔钱。第二个和第三个求婚者也是如此。

某个晴朗的日子，这三个求婚者偶然相遇了。在一次讨论中，他们开始互相询问对方求婚的经验和制胜法宝。

第一个说："我有一条母牛的尾巴，它可以让去世的人复活。"

第二个说："我有一块石头，可以用它来预测未来。"

第三个说："我有一张牛皮，可以带我去任何我想去的地方。"

知道彼此的法宝后，另外两个求婚者央求石头的主人赶紧告知他们远在万里之外的准新娘的情况。可是，当石头的主人使用石头预测时，才发现他们的准新娘早在二十年前就已经去世了。

牛皮的主人立刻把牛皮摊开，让另外两个人和他一起坐了上去，牛皮用最短的时间把他们带回了久别的家乡。

回到家乡后，他们直奔准新娘家里，让准新娘的父母带着他们去了女孩的坟墓那里。牛尾巴的主人用牛尾巴敲了一下坟墓，只见新娘微笑着从坟墓里面走了出来。

从三个追求者在漂亮女孩死而复生的过程中所付出的努力来看，你认为他们中谁最有资格娶她呢？

The Three Suitors

There were once three young men dying for a very beautiful girl in their village. The first suitor came with £10.00 and a cow and asked for the hand of the girl in marriage. The parents accepted the money. The second suitor came with a similar gift and expressed the same wish. The parents accepted his too. A third suitor came, and they did the same.

After a long time, each of the three suitors decided to make a second visit to the girl. The first suitor came back with £4.00 and ten Kola nuts, and asked to be permitted to look at the girl. The parents again accepted the money and told him to go back home and come back with £200.00 in two days. He went away for twenty years looking for the amount. The same happened to the second and the third suitor.

One fine day, these three suitors met together by chance. In a discussion they started to ask each other about each other's experience and achievement.

The first one said, "I have the tail of a cow which I can use to raise somebody from the dead."

The second one said, "I have a stone which I can use to foretell the future."

The third one said, "I have the skin of a cow which can take me anywhere I want to go."

Knowing each other's achievement, the other two suitors asked the owner of the stone to tell them something about their bride-to-be who was miles and miles away. When he consulted the stone he discovered that their bride had died twenty years ago.

The owner of the cow-skin spread it and asked the other two to sit on it with him and be flown home. In the shortest possible time the skin took them home.

When they got to their hometown, they went straight to the home of their bride-to-be and asked her parents to take them to her grave. The owner of the cow-tail struck the grave with it once, and out came the bride, smiling.

Judging from the duties of each suitor in bringing this woman back to life, which of them has the most right to marry her?

蒂姆奈[①]谚语

山药里面有什么,哪有刀子不知道的?[②]
不要朝放瓶子的地方扔石头。
不要咬喂你吃饭的手指。
不要同时追赶两只松鼠。
一根手指抓不住棕榈仁。
如果我把水倒在你身上,不妨梳洗一番。
老人跑不动,但他知道如何躲藏。
空袋子立不起来。
不要从浓烟处跑回火中。[③]
父亲有时需要向孩子学习。
一双漂亮的鞋子合不合脚,只有穿它的人才知道。
不可杀鸡取卵。
不能把花生交给老鼠保管。
沿着河岸行走不等于跨过了河流。
只有等河水干涸了,你才会意识到井的重要性。
不要买装在袋子里的山羊。[④]

注释 ① 蒂姆奈,塞拉利昂的一个民族。塞拉利昂是一个多民族国家,南部的曼迪族最大,北部和中部的蒂姆奈族次之,两者各占全国人口的30%左右。林姆巴族占8.4%,由英国、美国移入的"自由"黑人后裔克里奥尔人占10%。此外,还有约3万黎巴嫩人和少数欧洲及印巴裔人。塞拉利昂官方语言为英语,另有15种民族语言,蒂姆奈语、曼迪语、林姆巴语和克里奥语为四种最为主要的民族语言。

② 用刀子切山药时,刀子是要深入山药内部的,此句意为"你的秘密总会有人知道"。

③ 意为"做事情不能一错再错"。

④ 意为"做事之前需要了解清楚情况"。

> 英文对照

Temne Proverbs

What is in the yams that a knife doesn't know?

Don't throw stones where you keep bottles.

Don't bite the finger that feeds you.

Don't run after two squirrels.

One finger doesn't take a palm kernel.

If I pour water on you, then wash yourself.

An old man is unable to run but he knows how to hide.

An empty bag cannot stand.

Don't run from the smoke into the fire.

Child is father of the man.

If one sees a nice shoe one doesn't know how that nice shoe is hurting the person wearing it.

Don't forego the hen for the guinea fowl.

Don't give groundnuts to a rat for safe-keeping.

Walking along the bank of a river is not crossing it.

You will not see the importance of a well till the river runs dry.

Don't buy a goat in a bag.

这就是你的生活

女士们,别叹息;
停止抱怨和唠叨。
那会给你带来悲伤,让你心碎。
男人不太靠谱,从开始就充满欺骗、油滑和狡诈。
一只脚在海上,一只脚在岸上。
男人永远不会把心思集中在一件事上!
女士们,不要绝望。
忘掉那些男人,听我说几句,
这样快乐就会来到你身边。
请把你所有的烦恼都化为快乐。

只有一颗牙齿嚼不动玉米。
蟑螂是一位出色的律师,他总是穿着律师服;但他永远不会担任首席大法官出现在鸡的法庭上。
山羊拥有世界各地大学的许多学位,但他永远不会在豹子国演讲。
在这个世界上,家庭主妇是最辛苦的职业。一天二十四小时,一周七天,一年五十二周……没有假期,没有加薪,没有养老金。
她多才多艺,既是厨师、护士、洗衣妇、画家和园丁,又是看守员、管家、老师、情人、送信人和司机。
告诉我,到底有什么是家庭主妇不会做的?
尽管如此,就像这个游戏,猴子做了所有工作,而狒狒却吃了所有的食物。
这就是你所知道的生活。
有些人在创造,有些人在毁灭。

这就是你的生活！

有些人在帮助收集存贮，有些人只是为了分散消耗。

这就是你的生活！

在汉斯廷喝酒，一直醉到滑铁卢。

基西的人收获杧果，弗里敦的人则负责销售和享用……

别人的丈夫藏在你的房间里。桌上放着给他吃的柔滑的芙芙和沙丁鱼酱，以此分散他对自己妻子的注意力，迫使他抛弃家庭。

这就是你的生活！

某某先生大腹便便，脖子上挂了几个金项圈。

他对此感到高兴，并称之为"美好生活"。

他不知道自己被迷惑，从而影响自己的理性思考，促使他抛弃了家里的莉莉（一个女人的名字），和"巴朱莫"（一个胖女人）住在外面。

把格拉迪斯留在家里，在外面寻找悲伤。

把埃拉留在家里，在外面寻找"埃莉亚"（麻烦）。

把洛维特留在家里，去外面找"巴塔"（挨打）。

把"阿拉菲娅"（平静的生活）留在家里，去外面寻找"瓦哈拉"（麻烦，困难）。

把欢乐留在家里，在外面找麻烦。

客厅里充满了安慰，他在外面找了"克曼蒂亚"（一个妓女）；

离开忠诚，陷入绝望；

把美女留在家里，寻找外面的野兽；

把南希留在家里，寻找外面的凯希（担心）；

离开老相好玛紫去寻找"仁慈的主"。

你不需要把黑暗锁在家中，因为你必须一直保证陪伴雅拉的时间。

这就是你的生活！

山羊认为很甜的叶子，正是它患上痢疾的罪魁祸首。

将逗号改为句号是很难的，因此，一个人想要证明有文化，应该知道在哪里画句号。

那意味着——

应该避免把勺子伸到所有汤锅里，因为有些汤已经变质发酸了。

This Is the Life That You Live

Ladies, stop sighing;
Stop grumbling and nagging about things.
That will bring you sorrow and leave you broken-hearted.
Men are from the beginning deceitful, slippery and sly.
One foot on the sea, one on the land.
Men never fix their minds on one object!
Ladies, do not despair.
Forget the men and listen to me for a few moments,
So that gladness will come to you.
And transform all your worrying to Hay Nomino.

A one-toothed man cannot chew corn.

Cockroach is a wonderful lawyer. He is always wearing his lawyer's gown; but he will never appear in a court where Fowl is the Chief Justice.

Goat has many degrees from universities over the world; but he will never lecture in Leopard's country.

No "profession" in this world is as difficult as the housewife profession. Twenty-four hours a day, seven days a week, fifty-two weeks a year ... No vacation leave, no increment, no pension.

All in one: she is a cook, nurse, washerwoman, painter, gardener, watchman, steward, teacher, lover, messenger, driver.

Tell me, what is there on earth that a housewife does not do?

In spite of all that, it is a game of Monkey doing all the work, Baboon eating all the food.

This is the life that "you-know-who" lives.

Some are creating, some are destroying.

This is the life that you live!

Some help gather, some are just there to scatter.

This is the life that you live!

Hastings drinks, Waterloo gets drunk.

Kissy harvests its mangoes, Freetown sells and eats them …

Another's husband is hidden in your room. Velvet foofoo and sardine sauce are put on the table for him to eat in order to distract him from his wife, force him to abandon his family.

This is the life that you live!

Mister So-and-so's belly is protruding, several rings are appearing on his neck.

He is happy about it and calls it "Good Living".

Little is known that he had been given a charm to affect his rational thinking, which compels him to forsake Lily (a woman's name) at home, and live with "Bajumor" (a fat woman) out of home.

Leaves Gladys at home, to find Sorrow outside of home.

Leaves Ella at home, to procure "Eleya" (problems) outside.

Leaves Lovet at home, to find "Bata" (beaten up) outside.

Leaves "Alafiya" (peaceful life) at home, to procure "Wahala" (trouble, difficulty) outside.

Leaves Joy at home, to find Trouble outside.

Comfort fills the parlour, he finds "Komandiya" (a commandeering woman) outside.

Leaves Faith, to get stuck to Hopeless;

You leave Beauty at home for Beasty outside;

You leave Nancy at home for "Kasi" (worries) outside;

Leave Mazi for "Lord have Mercy".

You do not clock Blackie because you have to keep "Yala's" (Yellow's) time all the time.

This is the life that you live!

The leaves that taste sweet in a goat's mouth are the leaves that give it dysentery.

It is difficult to change a Comma to a Full Stop; therefore, a man who wants to prove that he is lettered, should know where to put a Full Stop.

That means—

You should avoid putting your spoon into every soup pot, because some soups have gone sour.

蛇、鱼和松鼠

当我再次开始唱《孟德根岱》时,我看到一个男人正沿着小路走着。他走了一小段路就停了下来。我向他走去,紧挨着站在他身边。我们看见一只红松鼠正在爬一根绳子。绳子下面是一片很深的潟湖,这片潟湖虽然很小,但由一条大河为其供水。潟湖里有许多蝌蚪,还有一条大鱼。蝌蚪是那种长着大大的下巴的红色蝌蚪。科帕曼迪人称之为蹦乐,你可以看到它们经常被水流冲上水面,咕嘟咕嘟地喝水吐泡泡,然后又潜入水底。

一只红松鼠看到了蝌蚪,想抓住并吃掉它们。他喜欢吃蝌蚪。他倒挂在绳子上,使身子离湖面足够近,摆好狩猎的姿势,蓄势待发,等待着一次又一次浮上水面的蝌蚪。

与此同时,树上的一条蛇看见了这只松鼠,正悄然爬向他。蛇和松鼠绝不是朋友。蛇开始慢慢地向下移动,把身体盘曲在一起,准备发起一场无声的突袭,就像松鼠蓄势待发,准备捕食蝌蚪一样。

潟湖里的大鱼也看到了红松鼠。松鼠想要吃掉蝌蚪,鱼希望松鼠在捕食蝌蚪时会掉进水里。如果发生这种情况,鱼就能把松鼠一口吞掉;蛇也在向下滑动,他一心只想吃掉松鼠。松鼠进退两难,卡在潟湖里的鱼和绳子上方的蛇之间。蛇继续向下爬;而松鼠的下面,鱼在水里一动不动。二者之间的松鼠也准备捕捉蝌蚪。此刻,情况万分紧急,接下来会发生些什么呢?

蛇滑向松鼠。突然,有只蝌蚪被猛地冲到水面上,松鼠应时而动向下俯冲。大鱼的头紧随蝌蚪一侧伺机而动。看到大鱼,松鼠扭头飞奔而逃,不料却差点冲入蛇的血盆大口,他只好往鱼的方向退去。松鼠发现自己就这样被困在了两个敌人之间,他怒气冲冲地叫道:"咯咯咯,这是什么情况?咯咯咯,怎么搞的?"他喊道:"咯咯咯,来人啊!看看这绝境!咯咯咯,我已经无法形容我的处境了。即使我能再多活几年,我也讲不清。"松鼠以为自己只有死路一条了。

松鼠挂在湖中央的绳子上，离潟湖四周的岸很远。下有鱼上有蛇，他无法动弹。此时此刻，他已经不再想吃蝌蚪了。他东张西望，看向湖岸，蓄积力量，把肌肉拉伸到极限，就像蟒蛇即将攻击时一样。然后他像一支穿云箭一样射了出去，重重地落在岸上，发出一声闷响，在地上翻滚了两圈，然后站了起来，随后紧紧抓住他头顶的另一根绳子。

　　不远处，棕榈树上有一只棕色松鼠。这只棕色松鼠和其他小动物一直紧盯着事态的发展。棕色松鼠问："红红，怎么了？"红松鼠回答说："咯咯咯，我没问题。即使我跌倒翻滚，我也会站起来继续前进。咯咯咯，即使我受伤了，我也会站起来继续前进。"

　　然后，他爬到一棵树上，准备好好休息。他开始检查自己的身体，发现全身青一块紫一块的。他不停地自言自语："咯咯咯，这里也受了重伤！咯咯咯，这是什么样的经历？"休息了很长时间之后，另一只在棕榈树上的松鼠建议他立刻离开。他对红松鼠的妻子说："叫你丈夫赶紧离开，如果它不这么做，那条蛇就会跟踪到这里。现在蛇已经盯上他了，蛇会搜查整个森林，他会的！"

　　这是红松鼠给妻子唱的告别之歌。他的妻子名叫伦德。

{英文对照}

The Snake, the Fish and the Squirrel

As I started singing "Mende Gendei" again, I saw a man walking along the pathway. When he had walked a short distance he stopped. I moved towards him and stood closely by his side. As we stood we both saw a red squirrel climb a rope. The rope was hanging over a deep lagoon which, although small, was fed by a big river. The lagoon contained many tadpoles and there was also a big fish in it. The tadpoles were the red ones with large jaws. The Kpa Mende call them Bonglei. You see them frequently shooting up to the surface and gulping water, and then plunging down again.

The red squirrel had seen the tadpoles and wanted to catch and eat them. It liked eating tadpoles. The rope it had climbed was near enough to the surface of the lagoon. There the red squirrel was poised in readiness to catch the tadpoles as they surfaced now and again.

At the same time, a serpent which was up in the tree saw the squirrel and started sprawling towards it. The serpent and the squirrel are by no means friends. The serpent started moving down slowly. It would gather itself together and then stretch out stealthily, just as when the red squirrel is poised to catch the tadpoles.

The big fish in the lagoon also saw the red squirrel. The squirrel wanted to eat the tadpoles and the fish hoped that the squirrel would fall into the water as it tried to catch them. If this happened, the fish would gulp down the squirrel. The serpent was also moving down. It was bent on eating the squirrel. The squirrel was thus trapped between the fish in the lagoon and the serpent approaching from above. From above the serpent continued to move closer, and just below the fish was poised in the water. Between them was the squirrel also poised to catch the tadpoles. One could expect anything now.

The snake glided down towards the squirrel. Suddenly one of the tadpoles made an upward thrust to the surface of the water. When the squirrel tried to snatch it, the fish pushed its head out next to the tadpole. Seeing the fish the squirrel dashed away only to come face to face with the serpent. It ran back towards the fish. It was trapped between the two enemies. Finding itself thus trapped, the squirrel burst out in anger: "Kokoko, but what is this? Kokoko, but people why this?" There was no going backwards or forwards. It shouted, "Kokoko, my people come and see this dilemma! Kokoko, I can't find the mouth with which to explain this. Even if I should live for many more years, I shan't find the mouth with which to explain this." There was hardly any way out.

The bank was far away on all sides of the lagoon. The squirrel was hanging on a rope over the middle of the lagoon. It could not move down for fear of the fish, nor up because the snake was there. It no longer thought about the tadpoles. It looked at the bank this way and that way. It gathered strength and stretched his muscles to a breaking point, just as the boa would when it is about to strike. Then it shot out like an arrow, landed on the bank with a heavy thud, turned and rolled over twice and got up. It held on to another rope just above its head.

Not far away, there was a brown squirrel in a palm tree. This squirrel and other small animals had been watching the scene. The brown squirrel asked, "Red-Red. What is the matter?" It replied, "Kokoko, there is nothing wrong with me. Even if I should fall and roll over, I would get up and go on. Kokoko, even if I sustained injuries, I would get up and go on."

Then it went to have a good rest in a tree where it began to examine its body. There were bruises all over its body. It kept saying to itself, "Kokoko, so here too was badly bruised! Kokoko, what kind of experience is this?" It rested for quite a long time. Then the other squirrel, still up in the palm tree, advised it to leave at once. It said to the wife of the red squirrel, "Tell your husband to go away in a hurry. If it doesn't do that, the snake is going to trail it here. Now the snake has set eyes on it, the snake will comb the length and breadth of this forest in search of it."

This is the farewell song the red squirrel sang to its wife. Its wife was called Lende.

固执的女孩

（旁白）讲故事的人来了。

（观众）你是自带干粮过来的吗？

从前，有一个村庄因盛产美女而闻名。年底，丰收之后，村民们举办了为期一周的宴会，以纪念他们的祖先。这是一场盛宴，他们邀请了附近所有的村民参加。在这段时间里，人们热情好客，一些没有被正式邀请的人也会来参加。因此，鬼魂、幽灵、魔鬼甚至邪恶的药剂师都来了。

村子里有一个名叫咏宝的固执女孩，她是村里的第一美人，曾拒绝过村里所有的求婚者。在宴会的最后一晚，她突然爱上了一个非常英俊的陌生人：克帕纳。克帕纳长得非常英俊，简直难以用语言来形容。他的头发像年轻的棕榈树一样浓密，牙齿像早晨的沙子那样洁白，皮肤犹如刚孵出的矮种鸡的羽毛一般柔软，声音像织布鸟似的甜美。他的微笑足以给一个饥饿的寡妇带来永恒的幸福；当他从身边经过时，年轻女孩看见了会像着了魔一般地痴迷。但实际上，他是一个精心伪装过的魔鬼。他伪装了全身——头发、牙齿、眼睛、腿，甚至声音，以便在宴会上给年轻女孩留下深刻印象。

在宴会的最后一天，夜幕降临，其他村庄的人们纷纷返回各自的村庄。短暂的浪漫和浮华告一段落。所有有幸遇到意中人的年轻女孩都会陪着自己相中的意中人到村里的小溪边去。这是宴会的高潮部分。从小溪周围的树林里到处传来低沉的哭声、克制的笑声、热烈的喘息和愉快的呻吟，在村子里的每个角落都能听到。这通常会让上了年纪的女人们在宴会结束后，也来到小溪边上沉思，产生一种怀旧的伤感——咏宝和克帕纳也在那里。

按照传统习俗，咏宝和克帕纳交换了礼物和承诺。之后，咏宝表示不愿再回到村庄。"无论你去哪里，我都会跟你一起去。"她固执地说。克帕纳恳求、哀求、用花言巧语哄她，但她态度坚决。于是，克帕纳只好带咏宝一起走了。

他们走进了一片黑暗潮湿的森林,又涉水穿过河流和小溪。这时,克帕纳从口袋里掏出一颗大科拉坚果,把它一分为二,给了咏宝一半。

"这颗科拉坚果是我们之间的定情信物:我一半,你一半。"克帕纳说。

克帕纳进入森林之后,开始释放自我,逐渐露出了原形。他整个人都变了。浓密的头发不见了,取而代之的是又长又脏的卷发,中间还秃了一大块。他的声音变得沉重刺耳。他已经归还了为赴宴而借来的头发。

"嘿嘿,"他说,"我们现在可以走了。"咏宝对这种突然的变化感到害怕和震惊,她说:"我在等我的丈夫。"克帕纳拿出科拉坚果说:"我一半,你一半。"于是,咏宝突然明白了。事已至此,她也只好跟着克帕纳走了。

越往里走,森林逐渐变得黑暗而险恶。克帕纳再次在小路上离开咏宝,一头钻进了森林。当他回来的时候,他有了一颗又长又脏的牙齿,末端还滴着口水。光滑的双腿被可怕的树桩取代,走起路来像雷声一样撼动着整个森林。咏宝觉得非常后悔,坚持要回去,但已经无济于事了,因为克帕纳用患有麻风病的手紧紧握着他们的定情信物——半颗科拉坚果。

他们走啊走,走啊走,来到了森林里的一块小空地上。那里有一座房子和一个谷仓。这是克帕纳的家。

克帕纳是食人族,他的爱好是猎食人肉。每两周,他都会出去打猎,但他保证会带回动物给咏宝吃。

不久,咏宝怀孕了,生下一个男婴。克帕纳非常喜欢这个男孩,给他取名叫冈多。他会在特定的日子和儿子一起唱歌和玩耍。

咏宝的父母十分担心他们的女儿。他们去找巫师占卜算卦,想了解一些关于他们女儿的事情。母亲哭了又哭,哭得伤心欲绝。她的女儿怎么样了?她死了吗?她还能再见到她吗?难道这是对整个家庭的诅咒吗?这些问题一直折磨着咏宝的母亲。一天,她泪眼汪汪地去见孪生占卜师中的一位。占卜师告诉她如何找到女儿以及留住女儿的可怕魔鬼。"她是我唯一的女儿,"女人悲伤地说,"我必须在死之前见到她。"

第二天,这位母亲就大胆地去寻找她的女儿。当她终于来到克帕纳的村庄时,她累得几乎走不动了。幸运的是,这时克帕纳正好外出打猎了。咏宝赶紧把母亲藏在谷仓里,告诉母亲如果她从谷包里下来,克帕纳会吃掉她的。克帕纳晚上回来了。他灵敏的嗅觉很快就发现了陌生人的存在。他对咏宝说:"我闻到一个人的气味。""除了你、我,还有儿子之外,这里没有其他人。"咏宝撒谎道。

两周后，克帕纳又去打猎了，咏宝叫她妈妈下来。她给了她很多东西带回家，包括许多金银财宝和一些衣服。于是母亲高高兴兴地回去了。

回到家里，这位母亲自豪地向全村人炫耀了女婿克帕纳的财富。她把带回来的部分财富分给了一些家庭成员。可是，其中有一些人不高兴了，他们觉得自己得到的还不够多。喜欢嫉妒的姑姑就是其中之一。

"我要自己去看看。我不想听她母亲没完没了地说。毕竟，她是我的亲侄女。"咏宝的姑姑说道。

第二天一大早，姑姑没有征得咏宝母亲的同意就独自去找咏宝了。咏宝一看到她就痛哭起来。"我告诉过妈妈不要再来人找我了，我丈夫会吃人的。我妈妈来的时候，他就差点儿把她吃掉。"

咏宝只好再次把姑姑藏在谷仓里，那是克帕纳的杂物间。他的酒就放在谷仓里。那个酒鬼姑姑喝了谷仓里最烈的酒，醉得一塌糊涂。

这一天，克帕纳正在家里哄他的儿子冈多。

（单人演唱）轻轻地，轻轻地，冈多，别哭了。

（合唱）冈多，快别哭了。

姑姑喝醉了，唱着歌，跳着舞，走下谷仓。

（单人演唱）一个未经岳父、岳母同意就结婚的男人！

一个未经岳父、岳母同意就结婚的男人！

我说，我的岳父、岳母，你们好吗？

（合唱）轻轻地，轻轻地，轻轻地。

克帕纳感到震惊，但同时也很兴奋，因为他期待着这个女人身上的肉很快就能给他带来一顿美味。于是，他也加入一起舞蹈。舞蹈进行到高潮部分时，克帕纳突然魔性大发，将姑姑撕成了碎片，贪婪地舔着血。克帕纳命令咏宝把她姑姑给煮了。咏宝拒绝了，克帕纳一气之下，凶残地把咏宝和儿子冈多也杀了。这就是固执任性的咏宝的下场。

因此，孩子们，你们不应该违抗父母的旨意。你们还应该提防自己将要嫁的男人，特别是遇到一个陌生人的时候，因为我们未必都能遇上良缘。

英文对照

The Stubborn Girl

Narrator: The story-teller is coming.
Audience: Did you come with your own food?

Once upon a time, there was a village known for the beauty of its women. At the end of the year, just after harvest, the villagers observed a week of feasting in memory of their ancestors. It was a feast to which they invited all the neighboring villages. Since it was a period of goodwill, even those who were not formally invited came. As such, ghosts, spirits, devils and even wicked medicine men came.

In this village, there was a stubborn girl called Yombo—the village beauty—who had refused all suitors from the village. On the last night of the feast, she suddenly fell in love with an awfully handsome stranger: Kpana. He was so handsome that it would be impossible to describe him. His hair was as bushy as a young palm tree, his teeth as white as the morning sand, his skin as soft as the feathers on a newly hatched bush fowl, and his voice as sweet as a weaver bird. His smile was enough to bring eternal happiness to a starving widow; and when he walked, he often sent young girls to sleep. But in fact, he was a devil in disguise. He dressed up everything—hair, teeth, eyes, legs, and even his voice to impress young girls in the feast.

On this last night of the feast, people from other villages started leaving for their own villages. The brief period of romance and frivolity was over. All young girls, who had been fortunate enough to win lovers, now had to accompany them as far as the village stream. This was the crowning point in the feast. The muffled cries, suppressed laughter, passionate sigh, and pleasant groan from the woods surrounding the stream would be heard in the village. This normally sends nostalgic ripples through old women as they brood over their days by the stream at the end of the feast. Yombo was also there with Kpana.

After the conventional exchange of gifts and promises, Yombo refused to go back to the village. "I will go with you wherever you are going," she said stubbornly. Kpana begged, pleaded, and coaxed her, but she was adamant. And so, she went with Kpana.

Into the dark, damp forest, they plunged. They waded through rivers and streams. Kpana took a big kolanut from his pocket, split it into two, and gave a half to Yombo.

"This kolanut is a bond between us: my half, your half," said Kpana.

Kpana entered the forest to ease himself. He came back totally altered. The bushy hair was replaced with long dirty curl at the centre of a shining, large head. His voice became heavy and guttural. He returned the hair which he had borrowed for the feast.

"Hee, hee," he said, "we can go now." Afraid and struck by the sudden change, Yombo said, "But I am waiting for my husband." Kpana took out the kolanut and said, "My half, your half", so they went.

The forest became progressively dark and menacing. Kpana left Yombo on the path again and entered the forest. When he came back, he had a long, dirty tooth with water dripping at the end. The smooth legs were replaced with fearful stumps that shook the entire forest like thunder. Yombo felt regretful and determined to go back but was not allowed to because Kpana held his half kolanut in a leprous hand.

They walked and walked and walked, and they came to a small clearing in the forest. There was a house and a barn. This was Kpana's home.

Kpana was a cannibal and hunting for human flesh was his hobby. Every fortnight, he would go hunting, but he made sure that he came back with animals for Yombo.

Soon Yombo got pregnant, and gave birth to a male child. Kpana was so fond of the boy and he called him Gondo. He had special days on which he sang and played with his son.

Yombo's parents were too worried about their daughter. They went to sorcerers and consulted oracles to know something about their daughter. The mother cried and cried and was tired of crying. How was her daughter? Was she dead? Would she ever see her again? Was it a curse on the whole family? These questions had tormented her. One day, with wet eyes, she went to a twin-diviner. The diviner told her about the way to her daughter and the fearful devil that was keeping her daughter. "She is my only daughter," the woman said mournfully. "I must see her before I die."

The following day, the mother boldly went in search of her daughter. She was almost tired of walking when she finally came to Kpana's village. Fortunately, Kpana was away hunting. Her daughter hid her in the barn and told her that if she came down Kpana would eat her. Kpana came back in the evening. His sensitive nose was quick in detecting the presence of a stranger. He told Yombo, "I smell a human being." "There is no other person here except you, your son and me." lied Yombo.

After two weeks, Kpana again went to hunt. Yombo told her mother to come down. She gave her many things to take home: money, gold, silver and clothes. The mother happily returned home.

Back home, the mother proudly told the whole village about Kpana's wealth. She gave part of the wealth she brought back to some members of the family. Some members of the family were not pleased. They felt that they were not given enough. One of these disgruntled family members was Yombo's envious, paternal aunt.

"I shall go and see Yombo myself. I don't need to be told by that talkative mother of hers. After all, she is my niece," she said.

The aunt, without asking the permission of Yombo's mother, went the next morning. As soon as Yombo saw her, she cried bitterly. "I told mother that nobody should come here again. My husband can eat human beings. He almost ate my mother when she came here."

Yombo again hid her in the barn which was also Kpana's general store. Kpana kept his wine in the barn. The aunt who was a drunkard, drank the strongest wine in the barn and got drunk.

On this particular day, Kpana was coaxing his son, Gondo.

Solo: Softly, softly, Gondo, stop crying.

Chorus: Gondo, stop crying.

The aunt, totally drunk, came down the barn, singing and dancing.

Solo: A man who marries without in-laws!

A man who marries without in-laws!

I say, my in-law, how do you do?

Chorus: Softly, softly, softly.

Kpana, shocked, but at the same time excited, at the prospect of the delicacy which the woman's flesh would soon afford him, joined in the dance. At the climax of the dance, Kpana tore the woman to pieces and ravenously licked the blood. He gave the body to Yombo and asked her to cook for him. Yombo refused. Kpana killed her and her son Gondo. That was how the headstrong Yombo ended.

Children, therefore, should not disobey their parents. They should also be careful about the man they marry. A stranger in particular is not always a good match.

死亡是如何进入这个世界的

很久很久以前,在我们的祖先诞生之前,这世界上本没有死亡。当人们衰老到一定程度时,就会像今天的蛇一样蜕皮,然后重获新生。如果不是因为狗的贪食,我们将会继续保持不死之身。

一天,上帝告诉狗和青蛙:

"狗,你将带着生命和永恒的青春来到这个世界。青蛙,你将带着死亡和衰老进入这个世界。"

狗和青蛙要参加一个大赛,从一个村庄跑到另一个村庄——狗带着生命,青蛙带着死亡——获胜者的生命价值将会永远保留。

终于到了大赛之日。上帝是第一个来到比赛起点的人。不久之后,狗和青蛙来了,他们不断吹嘘着自己,挑衅着对方。

"你能做的就是像一个没有经验的邦多舞者一样瞎跳。"狗嘲弄道。

"谢天谢地,我的鼻子并不总是在空气中嗅到人们恶心的后院。我要做的就是给你一根臭骨头,我会赢得比赛的。"青蛙不耐烦地反驳道。

上帝宣布比赛开始,然后返回到天堂去观看他们的比赛。狗和青蛙冲出起点,狗跑得太快了,青蛙落后了几千英里。这只狗确信自己打败了青蛙,就坐下来等。他几乎等了一整天。当狗正要进入终点的村庄时,他看到精疲力竭的青蛙正上气不接下气地痛苦地朝他跳过来。看到青蛙累成这副样子,狗让青蛙走在前面,而自己继续跟在后面嘲弄他。在狗看来,他只要轻轻一跳,就能超越青蛙。

狗悠闲地跟在青蛙后面,嘲笑、羞辱青蛙。这时,一个猎人的女儿把一根肥美的骨头扔到了路旁。一下子,狗就把比赛的事忘到九霄云外了。狗抓起骨头,坐在路边,沾沾自喜地闭上眼睛,把骨头咬成碎片。青蛙走在前面,率先到达了村子,喊道:

"死亡来也!死亡就在这里。"

从那天起,世人便逃不过死亡。是狗的贪食导致了死亡的降临。

{英文对照}

How Death Entered the World

A long, long time ago, before our great, great grandfathers were born, there was no death in the world. People would grow old and old and old until they shed their skins as snakes do today. We would have continued in this way had it not been for his gluttony of Dog.

One day, God told Dog and Frog:

"Dog, you will carry life and everlasting youth into the world. Frog, you will carry death and decay into the world."

Dog and Frog had to run a race from one village to the other—Dog carrying life, and Frog death—the winner would imprint his value on life forever.

The day came for the great race. God was the first to go to the starting point for the race. Shortly afterwards, Dog and Frog came, boasting and challenging each other.

"All you do is to hop like an inexperienced Bondo dancer," taunted Dog.

"Thank God, my nose is not always in the air to smell people's disgusting backyards. What I will do is to give you a stinking bone and I will win the race," impatiently refuted Frog.

God sent them off and returned to heaven to watch them. Off they went. Dog was so fast that Frog trailed thousands of miles behind him. Dog, confident that he had beaten Frog, sat down to wait for him. He waited for almost the whole day. As Dog was about to enter the destined village, he saw Frog, exhausted and gasping for breath, painfully hopping towards him. Seeing that Frog was too exhausted, Dog allowed him to go ahead, while he walked behind him taunting. Dog felt that he only needed a leap and Frog would be left behind.

While Dog was walking at a leisurely pace behind Frog, taunting and insulting Frog at the same time, a hunter's daughter threw a fat bone into the road. Dog forgot about the race. He grabbed the bone, sat by the road, complacently closed his eyes, and tore the bone to bits and pieces. Frog went ahead and entered the village shouting:

"Death has come! Death is here."

From that day, people started dying. Dog's gluttony brought death into the world.

猎 人

有一个猎人,他只射杀大象。他有一个名叫桑科的孩子,他教儿子如何打猎。

任何对这个世界不满的人都会死于贫困。当上天创造世界时,他希望处于任何位置的人都满足于自己所处的位置。如果有谁说他想要超越上天给予他的位置,那么,他便容易陷入为人所不齿的尴尬境地。

这个猎人是个巫师。每当他去打猎之前,他要先念咒语呼唤这些动物。每次打猎时,猎人都会选择一处僻静的地方,坐在那里,嘴里念叨着:

草原上的动物,草原上的动物,草原上的动物。

鹿会来的。猎人说:"我不要你。"灌木丛中的奶牛会来的,灌木丛中的所有其他大型动物也会来。猎人说:"你们,我都不想要。"他再次呼唤:"草原上的动物,草原上的动物。"大象会来的。当一大群大象到来时,他从容地把儿子叫了过来,让他杀死大象。他的魔法的秘密在于咒语:

我说,巴·桑巴,我带着索罗。

我说,巴·桑巴,我带着索罗。

这把枪叫作索罗。子弹上了膛后,猎人就拿着它开始唱:

森林的战士……

(合唱)索亚索亚索。

我带来了索罗。

(合唱)我带来了索罗。

伊尔蒂·提提·伊尔蒂。

(合唱)伊尔蒂·提提·伊尔蒂。

亚班战士。

(合唱)亚班战士。

森林的战士。

（合唱）森林的战士。

我带来问候。

（合唱）我带来问候。

阿伊尔蒂·提提提·提提提提。

（合唱）阿伊尔蒂·提提提·提提提提。

然后，他们杀死了大象。整整一年，父子俩都在屠杀它们。

嫉妒不是好事。有一个叫帕福达的人看到猎人通过打猎变得富有，顿生嫉妒之心。

有一天，猎人的妻子回了娘家。猎人打算出趟远门去把妻子接回来。出发前，他对儿子说："我要出去一趟，你待在家里千万别出门，好好看守住我们辛辛苦苦靠狩猎才建起来的这个家。"儿子桑科说："嗯。""千万不要出去。"父亲警告道。他把儿子带到一个小箱子里锁了起来。被锁住的桑科将待在箱子里很长一段时间。

这天，帕福达打理完农场，回家的路上他顺路去看了看猎人的房子。见猎人家里没有人，他便躺在吊床上，悠闲地舒展着身体。他自言自语道："猎人的富有已经远远超乎我们的想象了。我非得找到他儿子不可，让这个小家伙带我去他父亲经常打猎的地方。"

桑科觉得很饿。小箱子里有蜂蜜，他开始一点一点地舔食。可是，一不小心蜂蜜洒了，漏到箱子外面。帕福达看见有蜂蜜从箱子里漏出来，便用手指蘸着开始舔。他舔着舔着，叫道："桑科。"孩子回答："嗯？""哦，伙计，今天你在这里。出来吧。这里很长时间没有坏人了。现在有人想要吃肉。你父亲把枪留给了我，所以，赶快出来吧。"桑科一听到枪的事，立马就打开箱子钻了出来。

其实，帕福达只不过是拿了一根木瓜秆，把它涂成了黑色，乍一看就像一把枪，他往里面装满了石头，让人拿起来有点分量。桑科问："我们接下来该做什么？"帕福达说："当我们到达那里时，你就开始唱歌。"桑科回答说："好吧。"帕福达本想杀死桑科，但上帝不允许帕福达这样做。

帕福达带着桑科去他们以往经常打猎的地方。帕福达命令桑科："来吧，桑科，念咒语。"桑科于是开始唱道：

草原上的动物，草原上的动物，草原上的动物。

鹿来了，帕福达一见就想逃跑，桑科说："啊！帕福达，你要去哪里？先别走。这些不是我想要召唤的动物。"他们继续走着，桑科又召唤起来：

草原上的动物,草原上的动物;

草原上的动物,草原上的动物。

奶牛来了,帕福达又想跑。然后桑科说:"啊!帕福达,别动。这些不是我所召唤的动物。"帕福达说:"好吧,那我们继续。"

草原上的动物,草原上的动物;

草原上的动物,草原上的动物。

啊!大象成群结队地来了,站在那里。帕福达又想逃跑了。桑科说:"帕福达,别跑,停下,停下。你的枪呢?"帕福达回答说:"我有。"桑科开始唱歌:

我说,巴·坦巴;我说,巴·桑巴,我带来了索罗;

我说,巴·坦巴;我说,巴·桑巴,我带来了索罗。

他继续唱道:

森林的战士。

(合唱)索亚索亚索。

我带来问候。

(合唱)我带来问候。

依宾亚班。

(合唱)依宾亚班。

到了该开枪的时候(这里指的是真枪),帕福达没有开枪,因为他拿的是一根木瓜秆。他敲碎了它之后,仓皇逃走了,把桑科留在那里。大象包围了桑科。一头耳朵被猎人的流弹划伤过的大象走过来说:"小子,你看到我的伤口了吗?这是你父亲的干的好事,如果我能踩到你,我就踩碎你的头。今天就是你的死期。"当大象正要踩他时,另一头大象过来说:"先别踩。小子,你看到我被划伤的臀部了吗?是你父亲的流弹造成的。当你父亲来屠杀我们的时候,你总是这么叫。今天你父亲不在,我感觉离你很近,像在你的耳边呼吸,你以后再也不能帮你父亲打猎了。"一只鹿过来说:"小子,我原本有一条又长又直的尾巴,可是被你父亲剪掉了。你今天怎么又敢来呼唤我们出现?今天,我会让你明白,这个世界属于上帝。你,今天我们就要杀了你。"

桑科很害怕。他说:"好吧。无论发生什么,都冲我来吧!"附近有一棵高高的香料树。桑科说:"不管发生什么,我求求你们。我不是自愿来的。但是如果你们想杀我,请允许我爬上那棵香料树向上帝道别。"有几头大象说:"别放他走,他想逃跑;不能放他走。"桑科说:"我爬的就是面前的这棵树。"另一头大象说:"伙计们,由他去爬吧。我只要轻轻一晃,树就会倒下来。"动物们允许桑科攀爬了上去。

当桑科爬到最顶端的树枝上时,他转向他父亲顺风远行的方向,开始大声呼唤父亲。大象开始催促他说:"孩子,下来。你花了太长时间向上帝道别了。赶紧下来!你以前就是这样唱歌的,然后麻烦就来了。快下来!今天没人理会你的歌声了。无论你唱什么,都不能改变什么!我们要杀了你。赶快下来!"桑科说:"不,我求你了。我请求你们再等一会儿。"他又站了起来,唱得比刚才更大声了。

这时妻子的家人正在给桑科父亲做饭。桑科的父亲听到了歌声,对妻子说:"布拉,麻烦来了。我儿子有麻烦了。我听到了我们每次打猎时唱的那首歌。哎,我必须马上离开。我要去找他!我不吃东西了。"布拉说:"呃,我求求你,别这样,叔叔;请在离开前吃点东西。别饿着去,你会被动物们杀死的。"

猎人答应下午再回来接她。他说:"我会带着食物回来,但我现在不能再等了。"桑科又唱了起来。猎人对妻子说:"等一下,你听。"他再次站起来说:"你听到了吗?我们唯一的儿子有麻烦了。我要走了。"

猎人一出门,就像风一样消失得无影无踪。他循着声音,终于找到了声音的来源。他来到那个地方,看到儿子站在树顶上哭泣。哦,猎人只是往那个地方一站,大象一看到猎人站在那里,瞬间就气馁了。桑科又唱了起来:

我说,巴·坦巴,是的;我说,巴·坦巴,是的;我很快就把索罗带来了。

猎人拿起枪,装上子弹。

森林的战士。

(合唱)索亚索亚索。

我带来了索罗。

(合唱)我带来了索罗。

依宾亚班。

(合唱)依宾亚班。

伊里蒂基·提提提。

(合唱)伊尔蒂基·提提提。

猎人把动物们都杀了。猎人喊道:"我的孩子。""我在这里。"桑科回答道。"桑科!"父亲又叫了一声。"我在这里。"桑科回答。"谁带你来的?"父亲问道。"是帕福达。"桑科回答。"帕福达去了哪里？""他从我身边消失了。"桑科回答。"好吧，我们先回城里吧！"猎人训示道。

一回到城里，猎人就开枪打死了帕福达。

总之，一个有嫉妒心的人不是个好人。如果上天不给你，一定要有耐心。如果上天给予你的同伴，你要支持他。如果你得不到，就照上天要求你的样子去做。

我的故事到此结束。

The Hunter

There was a man who was a hunter. This hunter shot nothing but elephants. He had a child whose name was Sonko, whom he taught how to hunt.

Anyone who is not content with the world will die in poverty. When God created the world, he wanted everybody to be content with whatever position he put him in. If one says he should go beyond the position God puts him in, he will fall into an embarrassing situations despised by otters.

This hunter was a sorcerer. At any time he went to hunt, he would use incantation to call the animals. He would sit in a secluded place, calling.

Animals of the grassland, animals of the grassland, animals of the grassland.

Animals like deer would come. The old man would say, "I don't want you." The cow in the bush would come, and all the other big animals in the bush would come. The old man would say, "I don't want any of you." He would call again, "Animals of the grassland, animals of the grassland." The elephants would come. When they had come in large numbers, he would calmly call his son to kill the animals. The secret of his sorcery depended on this:

I say, Pa Thamba, I bring the soro-o.
I say, Pa Thamba, I bring the soro-o.

The gun was referred to as the soro. The gun loaded itself. After it had loaded itself, the hunter would take it and start to sing:

Forest yibing ...

Chorus: Soya soya so.

I bring the soro.

Chorus: I bring the soro.

Yirti titititi-yirtititi.

Chorus: Yirti titititi-yirtititi.

Yaban yibing.

Chorus: Yaban yibing.

Forest yibing.

Chorus: Forest yibing.

I bring greetings.

Chorus: I bring greetings.

Ayirtititi-tititi-tititi

Chorus: Ayirtititi-tititi-tititi.

They killed the elephants. For one whole year they would be slaughtering them.

Envy is not good. There was a man called Pa Foday. Pa Foday had envious feelings because he saw that this man had become rich through hunting.

One day, this hunter went on a journey because his wife had run away. He went there to get his wife back home. Before he left for his journey, he said to his son, "As I am going away, what you should do is not go out. Stay at this house. You should guard the house which I have built through hunting." The boy said, "Yes." "Don't go out," the father warned. His father took him and put him in a box and locked him in. When he locked him in, he left the child there for a long time.

When Pa Foday returned from brushing his farm, he went to see the hunter's house by the way. Seeing nobody in the house, he lay on the hammock, started swinging himself and said to himself, "This man has become rich beyond our imagination. I have to find his son. I would take this child to the place where his father often hunts."

The child felt very hungry. There was honey in the box which the child started to lick little by little. The honey spilt and started to leak. Pa Foday put his hand under where the honey was leaking and started licking. He licked and licked and called, "Sonko." "Yes," answered the child. "Hm, so you were here today. Get out, fellow; there have been no bad guys for a long time. Someone wants meat, and your father left the gun with me. So, come out." The boy opened the box and got out when he heard about the gun.

Pa Foday took a pawpaw stalk and blackened it to look just like a gun, which he loaded with stones. The boy asked, "What are we to do next?" Pa Foday said, "When we arrive, you will do the calling." The boy answered, "All right." Pa Foday intended to kill Sonko, but God did not allow that.

This man brought Sonko to the hunting spot where they often hunted and commanded the boy, "Come on, Sonko, call." Then the boy started calling:

Animals of the grassland, animals of the grassland, animals of the grassland.

The deer came and the man wanted to run away, and the child said, "Ah; Pa Foday, where are you going? Don't go yet. These are not the animals that I want to call." As they went, the boy called again:

Animals of the grassland, animals of the grassland;
Animals of the grassland, animals of the grassland.

The cow came and the man wanted to run again. Then the boy said, "Ah, Pa Foday, stop. These are not the animals that I am calling." And Pa Foday said, "All right; let's continue."

Animals of the grassland, animals of the grassland;
Animals of the grassland, animals of the grassland.

Ah! The elephants came in a large number and stood. Then Pa Foday wanted to run again. The boy said, "Pa Foday, don't run, stop, stop. Where is your gun?" Pa Foday replied, "I have it." The boy started to sing:

I say, Pa Thamba; I say, Pa Thamba, I bring the soro;
I say, Pa Thamba; I say, Pa Thamba, I bring the soro.

He continued to sing:

Forest yibing.

Chorus: Soya soya so.

I bring greetings.

Chorus: I bring greetings.

Yibing yaban.

Chorus: Yibing yaban.

When it was time to shoot "Yiritititi" (that's the sound of the real gun), there was no shooting because Pa Foday took the pawpaw stalk, broke it and fled. He left the hunter's child, and the elephants surrounded him. An elephant whose ears had been cut by his father's stray bullets came and said, "My boy, do you see this cut? It was the work of your father. If I can just tread on you, I'll cut your head off. Today your life is finished here." As he was about to tread on him, another elephant came and said, "Don't tread on him yet. My boy, you see my cut hip? It was your father's stray bullets that made it this way. That was the same call you always give when your father comes to destroy us. Today your father is away. I feel just like breathing on you so you will never do it again." A deer came and said, "My boy, I once had a long and straight tail; you father cut it and now you have come and stood here to call us again? Well, today you will believe that God owns the world. You, we shall finish you today."

The boy was afraid. He said, "All right. Whatever will happen to me." There was a tall spice tree standing nearby. The boy said, "For what has happened, I beg you. I did not come here of my own accord. But if you intend to kill me, please allow me to climb up that spice tree to say goodbye to God." Some of the elephants said, "Don't let him go; he wants to run away; don't let him go." The boy said, "It is this one standing here that I will climb." One other elephant said, "Fellows, leave him to climb. I will just toss the tree and it will fall down." They allowed him to climb, and he did.

When the boy climbed up, he turned to the direction where his father had gone. His father travelled by the wind. The boy climbed to the topmost of the branches and started calling his father. The elephants started urging him and said, "Boy, come down. You have taken too long a time saying goodbye. Come down. This was how he used to sing, then trouble would come. Come down; today your singing has no effect. Whatever you sing, nothing will happen until we kill you. Be quick; come down." The boy said, "Pa, I beg. I beg all of you to wait for me." He stood again and sang louder than before.

At this time the wife's family were cooking food for his father. His father heard the song and said to his wife, "Burah, trouble has come. My son is in trouble. The song which we used to sing during shooting is what I am hearing. Well, I must leave you. There'll be no more eating." Burah said, "Eh; I beg, don't do it, Uncle; please eat before you leave. Don't go with hunger and the animals will kill you."

So the hunter promised to pick her up in the afternoon. He however said, "I will come back with the food, but I shall not wait any longer." The boy sang again. The hunter said to his wife, "Wait a while; listen!" He stood up again and said, "Do you hear? My only son is in trouble. I am going."

He went out and the wind took him off, following where the voice was coming from, until he arrived. He came to the place and saw his son standing on top of the tree and crying. Oh! He just came and stood. As soon as the elephants saw the man standing, they were discouraged. The boy sang again:

I say Pa Thamba yea; I say, Pa Thamba yea; I bring the soro quickly.

The hunter took his bullet and loaded the gun.

Forest yibing.

Chorus: Soya, soya so.

I bring the soro.

Chorus: I bring the soro.

Yibing yaban.

Chorus: Yibing yaban.

Yiritiki-titititi.

Chorus: Yiritiki-titititi.

He killed them all. The hunter said, "My boy." The boy answered, "Yes." "Sonko," the father called again. "Yes," the boy answered. "Who brought you here?" asked the father. "Pa Foday," the boy answered. "Where has Pa Foday gone?" "He disappeared from me," the boy answered. "Well, let us go to the town," the hunter instructed.

As soon as they arrived, the hunter shot Pa Foday.

Therefore, a person with envy is not a good person. If God does not give to you, be patient. If God gives to your companion, support him. If you are not able to get, stay as you are as God made you.

That's the end of my story.

服务两位主人的方式

请大家仔细听,以免误解我的故事和歌曲。

听好了!我要给你们讲的是关于鹿和蝙蝠的故事。鹿和蝙蝠住在比昆都。他们都非常努力工作,每年都会建造大型农场。在那些日子里,每当工人们在农场工作时,总有一位赞美歌手唱起赞歌,赞美他们,让他们开心。在比昆都,只有一位赞美歌手,他就是兔子。

有一年,鹿和蝙蝠分别建立了大型稻田农场。农场彼此相邻,但鹿和蝙蝠都不知道对方在干什么。他们的农场被一条小河隔开。他们把农场粉刷了一遍,烧了一些草木灰作肥料,下一步就准备犁地了。犁地可不是一件容易的事,所以他们都各自雇了一群年轻人来帮忙。剩下的就是让兔子——这位赞美歌手来搞搞气氛,鼓励年轻的雇工在农场上努力干活。

鹿找到了兔子,付了费用后,得到了某日唱赞歌的服务。蝙蝠也去找了兔子,他也给了兔子相应的费用。兔子决定在他去鹿的农场的同一天也去蝙蝠的农场里工作。兔子的妻子对丈夫说:"兔子,你这样做很糟糕,很危险。你从鹿和蝙蝠那里都得到了钱,承诺在同一时间为他们各自的农场鼓励和赞美工人们。你知道你是这个镇上唯一的赞美歌手。你不觉得这是在给自己找麻烦吗?"兔子回答说:"别担心,我知道怎么做。"

第二天早上,鹿和蝙蝠的农场都挤满了雇工。每个农场都分配好了工作,雇工们做着自己分配到的工作,所有雇工都听着兔子的音乐准备开始工作。鹿看见兔子在附近,告诉他,自己的雇工们准备好开始干活了。蝙蝠也对兔子说了类似的话。

兔子只是坐在两个农场中间的小溪边敲打他的鼓,边敲边唱道:

鹿,鹿,鹿来犁地吧。

蝙蝠,蝙蝠,蝙蝠来犁地吧。

鹿，鹿，鹿来犁地吧。
蝙蝠，蝙蝠，蝙蝠来犁地吧。

鹿，鹿，鹿来犁地吧。
蝙蝠，蝙蝠，蝙蝠来犁地吧。

鹿，鹿，鹿来犁地吧。
蝙蝠，蝙蝠，蝙蝠来犁地吧。

鹿，鹿，鹿来犁地吧。
蝙蝠，蝙蝠，蝙蝠来犁地吧。

鹿，鹿，鹿来犁地吧。
蝙蝠，蝙蝠，蝙蝠来犁地吧。

英文对照

A Way of Serving Two Masters

Everyone, please listen carefully so that you will not misinterpret my story and song.

The story I am going to tell you is about Deer and Bat. Deer and Bat lived in Bikundu. Both of them were very hard-working and built large farms every year. During those days, there was always a praise-singer who would entertain and praise workers whilst they worked in farms. At Bikundu there was only one praise-singer, Rabbit.

One year Deer and Bat built large rice farms respectively. The farms were adjacent to each other, but neither Deer nor Bat knew what the other was doing. Their farms were divided by a small stream. They had brushed their farms, burnt plant ash as fertilizer and the next was to plough the field. Ploughing was not an easy job, so each of them hired a group of young men to help them with their ploughing. All that was left was to get Rabbit, the praise-singer to entertain and encourage them to work hard on the farm.

Deer went to Rabbit and got his services for a certain date after paying him his fee. Bat went to Rabbit too. He gave Rabbit his required fee and Rabbit decided to play in Bat's farm on the same day he had agreed to be in Deer's farm. Rabbit's wife said to her husband, "Rabbit, what you are doing is very bad and dangerous. You have received money from both Deer and Bat and you have promised to entertain and praise workers for both of them at the same time in their different farms. You know that you are the one and only praise-singer in this town. Don't you think you are putting yourself in trouble?" Rabbit answered, "Don't worry. I know how to go about it."

The following morning, Deer's farm was full of workers and Bat's farm was also full of workers. On each of the farms, work was divided among the participants and all the participants of both farms were set to start work in accordance with Rabbit's music. Deer saw Rabbit around and told him that his workers were ready to plough. Bat also told Rabbit that his workers were all set to work.

All Rabbit did was to sit in the middle of the stream that divided the two farms and beat his drums, singing:

Deer, deer, deer has come to plough.
Bat, bat, bat has come to plough.

Deer, deer, deer has come to plough.
Bat, bat, bat has come to plough.

Deer, deer, deer has come to plough.
Bat, bat, bat has come to plough.

Deer, deer, deer has come to plough.
Bat, bat, bat has come to plough.

Deer, deer, deer has come to plough.
Bat, bat, bat has come to plough.

Deer, deer, deer has come to plough.
Bat, bat, bat has come to plough.

忧他人之忧

在一个小村庄，有个小混混。他太喜欢惹是生非了，几乎听不进任何人的话。他一贯为所欲为。小村庄非常偏僻，只有一条小路可以进出。这条路一直通往村民们的农田。

一天早上，小混混走进一个灌木丛，砍下几根藤条和树枝，把它们带回到村子里，走到那条唯一的小路上，开始横跨小路设置陷阱。一些路过的老人看到了正在干坏事的他，愤怒地责骂道：

"以你废物老爹的名义起誓，你说说你到底在干什么。在这条唯一的道路上设置陷阱。这会给你的先辈们无处归依的灵魂带去诅咒的！你这废物就不能消失在灌木丛中吗？"

"你们这些老头，不饿吗？不去找点东西吃，闲得慌在这里给我说教？！你们说的我都懂，即使是三岁小孩，也知道这个陷阱是给动物准备的，而不是给爱管闲事的人准备的。"男孩无礼地回答。于是老人们悻悻继续各自赶路。

当陷阱设得差不多的时候，有只猫跳了出来，问道：

"你在这条唯一的小路上干了什么，这个陷阱是为了捕猎，还是为了害人？"

"你这蠢货，滚开！你看不出这是捕猎用的吗？"他咒骂道。猫耐心跟他解释了陷阱对村民和整个村子的影响，但男孩不听。猫只好去村里找人来阻止小混混的危险举动。

首先，猫跑去找村长：

"村长，一件危险的事就要发生了。那个小混混，正在唯一的小路上设置陷阱。我知道你有能力阻止他。赶快去阻止他吧，不然到时候就晚了。"

"他告诉过你那是用来害人的吗？"村长问道。

"不，他说是用来捕猎的。"猫回答。

"嗯，陷阱不会伤害到我和我的家人，随他吧。"

"我知道陷阱不是针对你和你的家人的，但会影响到你。"猫警告说。

之后，猫找到村里最大的公鸡，告诉他：

"一个小混混正在小路上设置陷阱。快去阻止他。你知道这确实不会直接影响到你，但也可能会对你造成间接影响的。"

"做你自己的事吧，这个陷阱不是针对村里的家禽的。"公鸡把猫赶走了。

猫去找羊。羊也不理睬他："你那是愚蠢的推理，应该允许小男孩打发时间的无聊之举。"而奶牛则把猫往外驱逐，他深感冒犯地朝猫咆哮道："你看不出我有多强大吗？一个小混混的陷阱和我这强大的肉体有什么关系？"

"时间会证明一切的，到时候你们就知道谁会被这个陷阱伤害了。"猫叹了口气说。

小混混已经设好了陷阱。村民们还是如往常一样做着自己的生计。但陷阱就在路上，强大而危险。人们来来往往，无论天气好坏，但陷阱仍在那里。

有一天，一条有毒的大眼镜蛇溜进了陷阱，它的尾巴被夹住了，它在不断挣扎中渐渐丧失了体力，感到极度饥饿。眼镜蛇心想："如果我将死于这个陷阱，我也要拉一个垫背的。"

它藏在陷阱旁边的茂密的灌木丛中，等待第一个倒霉蛋的出现。

到了晚上，村民们在农场里吃了一顿丰盛的大餐，然后高高兴兴地往村子里走。第一个走近陷阱的是村长的漂亮妻子。眼镜蛇一听到她轻快的脚步声，就把毒牙里的毒液准备好，耐心地等着她。女人毫无戒备地走过来，饥饿的眼镜蛇抬起沉甸甸的头，猛咬了她一口，绝望地把所有的毒液全部注入女人体内。女人很快死了。

人们把她的尸体抬回村子，为她沐浴更衣，准备下葬。猫走到村长跟前，在他耳边低声说："我告诉过你陷阱的事，如果你听我的，这事就不会发生了。"

村长叫来了一些掘墓人，指示他们为他的妻子挖一座坟墓。村里的妇女们被通知前往为掘墓人准备食物。因为天已经黑了，没有肉可供做汤。村长命令把那只最大的公鸡宰了。人们把公鸡抓起来，绑到树上。猫走到树前提醒他：

"你现在怎么看那个陷阱？我希望你别忘记我曾警告过你！"公鸡很快就被宰掉吃了。

下葬七天后，村里为死者举行"过河仪式"。需要宰一只羊，把羊血洒在坟墓上祭祀。

羊被抓起来绑在柱子上。当它站在阳光下悲伤地"咩咩"叫时，猫提醒羊说："我的劝告不是凭空的威胁。因为你不听我的，他们很快就会杀了你。"当天羊就被宰了。

四十天后，人们为死者举行了最盛大的仪式。仪式要求献祭一头母牛。村里最大的奶牛成为首选。猫走了过去，讽刺地提醒他：

"现在，让我们看看，你强大的肉体是否能拯救你。"不久后，奶牛就被宰了。

所以说，小混混设下的陷阱最终影响了整个村子——从村长到最小的动物。因此，我们应该忧邻居之忧。某个人的麻烦事就是每个人的麻烦事。

英文对照

Somebody's Business Is Everybody's Business

There was a little rascal in a small village. He was so mischievous that he hardly listened to what people told him. He did whatever came into his head. The village in which he lived was so isolated that only a small path led into and out of the village; and this path led to the village communal farming area.

One morning, the little rascal went into the bush, cut a few ropes and sticks, brought these to the village, went to the only path, and started setting a trap right across the path. Some elders met him at work and furiously scolded him:

"What in the name of your useless father do you think you are doing? Setting a trap right across this only path. Can't you take your useless self into the bush rather than bring a curse for your wandering ancestors?"

"I think starving old people should mind their own business rather than tell me what to do. Even a baby ought to know that this trap is for animals and not for busybodies," the boy replied impudently. The people went about their way.

When the trap was nearly finished, Cat came and asked the little rascal:

"What are you doing on this only path? Is it a trap for men or animals?"

"Get away, you stupid thing. Can't you see that this trap is for animals," he scolded. Cat explained the effect the trap would have on the villagers and the entire village, but the boy wouldn't listen. Cat went to the village to get somebody to stop the little rascal's dangerous move.

First, Cat ran to the village chief:

"Chief, a dangerous thing is about to happen. The little rascal is setting a trap right across the only path. I know that you have the power to stop him. Stop him quickly before it is too late."

"Did he tell you that his trap was for human beings?" the chief asked.

"No. He said his trap was for animals," the cat replied.

"Well, the trap is not for me or my family; let him go ahead."

"I know that the trap is not for you or your family but it will affect you," Cat warned.

Next, Cat went to the biggest cock in the village and told him:

"A little boy is setting a trap right across the path. Go and stop him. I know this actually does not concern you directly, but it may affect you indirectly."

"Go about your own business, his trap is not for the fowls in this village," Cock dismissed Cat.

Cat went to Sheep. Sheep also dismissed him: "That's stupid reasoning. The little boy should be allowed to indulge in a past time." Cow, on the other hand, expelled Cat, offendedly roaring: "Can't you see how mighty I am. What has a little rascal's trap got to do with this formidable flesh?"

"Time will tell who shall be affected by this trap," Cat sighed.

The boy set his trap. The villagers went about their daily affairs. But the trap was on the path, strong and menacing. People came and went, in bad and good weather, but the trap was still there.

One day, a big poisonous cobra entered the trap. The cobra was caught by the tail. It fought and fought and lost energy, feeling extremely hungry. "Well, if this trap is going to kill me, I won't die alone," reasoned the cobra.

It hid in the thick bush by the trap, waiting for the first human being to show up.

In the evening, after a good meal in their farms, the villagers happily started their long trek back to the village. The first human being who came close to the trap was the chief's most beautiful wife. As soon as the cobra heard her light footsteps, it sent all the poison into its mouth, patiently waiting for her. When the unsuspecting woman approached, the hungry cobra raised its heavy head and gave her a desperate and poisonous bite—draining all the poison into her body. She died immediately.

The woman was taken to the village, they washed her, ready for burial. The cat went to the chief and whispered in his ears, "I told you about the trap. Had you listened to me, this would not have happened."

The chief sent for the grave-diggers, and instructed them to dig a grave for his wife. The women were told to prepare food for the grave-diggers. Since it was already dark, there was no meat for the soup. The chief ordered that the biggest cock be killed. The cock was caught and tied to a tree. Cat went to the tree and reminded him.

"What do you feel about the trap? I hope you won't say that you were not warned!" The cock was soon killed for the grave-diggers.

Seven days after the burial came the "cross-the-river ceremony" for the dead woman. A sheep was to be killed and the blood was to be scattered on the grave.

Sheep was caught and tied to a post. As it stood bleating sorrowfully in the sun, Cat reminded him, "My advice was not an empty threat. They will soon kill you because you did not listen to me." Later that day Sheep was killed.

The biggest ceremony for the dead woman came forty days later. The ceremony demanded the sacrifice of a cow. The obvious choice was the biggest cow in the village. Cat went and sarcastically reminded him:

"Now let's see if your formidable flesh will save you." Cow was killed shortly afterwards.

Thus the trap set by the little rascal affected the whole village—from the chief to the smallest animal. Therefore, our neighbor's concern should also be our concern: somebody's business is everybody's business.

哈贝，狡猾之王

嘿，兄弟姐妹们，且听我说。

所有的动物都聚集在一起，决定从他们中间推选一个能够划船摆渡他们过河的人。"谁能成为我们的摆渡人？"大家都想知道。"我不能，因为我不知从什么时候起一直患有麻风病。"鹿以头痛为借口。

人们常说，如果你不想帮助别人，就不要说任何带有冒犯他人的事。狡猾的兔子说，如果他做摆渡人，大家一定会嘲笑他的，因为大家都知道，他在过去几年身体一直不适。"你们瞧瞧我，就我这孱弱的身体状况，我怎么能完成用独木舟载人渡河的大任呢？"他建议取消自己的资格。"看看，看看我的四肢有多虚弱。你们怎么能指望一个病号用独木舟穿越这条凶险的河流？"他狡黠地大声抗议道。

兔子那狡黠的话语激怒了豹子。于是，豹子自告奋勇道："如果所有的动物都拒绝承担这个责任，那就让我来吧。"

豹子开始担任摆渡人的角色后的第二天，鹿要去河对岸。每个动物都需要过河，因为他们要去河对岸觅食。"豹子？""是的！""请过来，用独木舟载我过去。"鹿恳求道。"你是谁？""是我，鹿。""哦，你们这些动物，谁都不愿意干这份苦差事，可是你们都要过河。"豹子想到能一个接一个地吃掉他们，心里暗自高兴。"在他们过河时，你去生火。"豹子对他的妻子说。

鹿勇敢地登上了船。他的前脚刚离开河岸，豹子就贪婪地咬住了他的喉咙。"谁，谁！"鹿一阵挣扎。随后鹿被扔到船上，很快就死了。豹子重复着这些举动，动物的数量随之大幅减少。

有一天，哈贝（狡猾的兔子）对自己说："我要穿过那条河，不再忍饥挨饿，一天比一天瘦。我们要去河对岸找吃的。我们没有其他办法可以得到食物。从前渡河的动物全都一去不复返了，我会想出一个办法来解决这个问题。"第二天一大早，天气很冷，兔子去见狮子说："我来找你了！我的好哥哥。""为什么来找我?"狮子问。"豹子在河边成了暴君,现在我们几乎无法到对岸寻找食物。正如你所见,我已经饿得皮包骨头了,都快饿死了。"兔子解释道。"你亲眼见过豹子吗?"狮子问。"他就在河边做摆渡人。"哈贝确认道。"上帝保佑!"狮子喊道,他想知道怎么才能在不把豹子吓跑的情况下到达对岸。兔子说:"我有办法。"他摊开一张垫子,让狮子躺在上面。他又去了见老虎,说豹子和狮子禁止所有动物过河,他们无法获得食物。"你在哪里看到狮子的?"老虎问道。"河岸那边。"他解释说,"其他所有动物都被禁止在河边寻找食物。""愿主保佑,你所说的话是真的。我一直渴望见到狮子,如果你能帮我接近他的话就更好了。"老虎告诉兔子。

他把老虎裹在垫子里,卷起垫子带到河边,还带了一把开裂的特制扫帚,这是休谟秘密社团的首领用的。然后,兔子开始叫豹子。"豹子?"兔子挥舞着扫帚,"请过来,把我摆渡到对岸,我非常饿!"豹子立刻跳上了独木舟:"感谢上帝,所有动物中最狡猾的兔子都来了,这些天一定是他阻止了其他动物过来。你可以直接去起锅烧热水了。"豹子指示他的妻子。当独木舟即将抛锚时,豹子开始向哈贝露出了獠牙。"啊,豹子!"哈贝说:"我一直把你当成我的侄子,我的孩子们现在生病了,你不应该有任何吃掉我的想法,我把他们带到你这里来,举行休谟仪式,帮助他们康复。"

"愿上帝保佑你的体贴。"豹子祈祷道,因为如果等兔子到岸后再攻击的话捕猎是容易失败的。兔子在上船之前,事先把狮子放在离豹子最近的船头,旁边还放着老虎。他坐在船尾,让豹子开始划独木舟。在渡河途中,狮子对豹子的仇恨开始慢慢加剧。可是,豹子毫不知情,他还边划船边唱歌:

(合唱)巴沃勒·马萨·巴沃勒

巴沃勒·马萨·巴沃勒……

哈贝说过他不会很快渡河。

豹子以为哈贝不会很快渡河。

(合唱)巴沃勒·马萨·巴沃勒

巴沃勒·马萨·巴沃勒……

等我们渡过河,我要把你吃掉。

感谢上帝给我这个机会。

(合唱)巴沃勒·马萨·巴沃勒

巴沃勒·马萨·巴沃勒……

如果你吃掉我,狮子会吃掉你,

然后老虎会把狮子吃掉。

（合唱）巴沃勒·马萨·巴沃勒

巴沃勒·马萨·巴沃勒。

在他们互相暗示之后，豹子才突然意识到垫子里藏着的是什么。豹子还没来得及转过身去看看发生了什么事，危险降临了。狮子咬住了豹子的喉咙，而老虎又咬住了狮子的喉咙。豹子想乘机跳进河里逃跑，但当他把一条腿伸进河里时，被鳄鱼狠狠地咬了一大口。他立刻把腿缩回来，拿起桨，唱着歌又开始划独木舟。

（合唱）曼波·维奥，曼波·维奥

我觉得好冷。

曼波·维奥，曼波·维奥

我被休谟的扫帚冻住了。

请保持安静！在内心深处！狮子把豹子的头浸入河里，老虎则紧紧地咬住狮子的喉咙，哈贝被船上发生的事情吓了一跳，跳到河里一条鳄鱼的头上。"什么时候天亮？"哈贝害怕地问鳄鱼。"你不应该问我这个问题，因为你才是来自陆地的。"鳄鱼回答。

就是在那个时候，哈贝对我唱道：

（合唱）他们过去常说的词，

女人，她们常说的话，

我们又开始跳舞了。

女士们，我向你们致敬。

帮我打败基利，

妈妈为我打败了基利，为我跳舞。

他们常说的话，

女人，她们常说的话，

格邦巴又开始跳舞了，

女士们，我向你们致敬。

姐妹们，请安静！我的头又开始痛了。

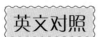

Hagbe, the King of Craftiness

Heh, my brothers and sisters, listen now.

All the animals came together and decided to choose from amongst them a cross-over, someone to canoe them across the river. "Who can be our cross-over?" they all wondered. "I cannot become the cross-over because I have been suffering from leprosy since God knows when," Deer excused himself. Deer gave a headache as an excuse.

It is usually said that if you don't want to help somebody, don't tell him anything offensive. Cunning Rabbit said that they would be laughing at him if they asked him to become the cross-over, since they knew he had been suffering from a malaise for the past couple of years. "Look at me! In my condition, how can I canoe people across the river?" he disqualified himself. "Look, look, how frail my limbs are! How do you expect me to canoe across such a rough river?" he cunningly protested.

It was Cunning Rabbit's cunning words that angered Leopard when he suggested he become the cross-over for all the animals. "If all the animals refuse to take up this responsibility, then let me shoulder it," he volunteered.

The day following Leopard's assumption of the role as a cross-over, Deer came to cross the river. Every animal would need to go across the river because all the food they needed was on the other side of it. "Leopard?" "Yes!" "Please come and canoe me across," Deer pleaded. "Who are you?" "It is me, Deer." "Oho, you animals were reluctant to do this job, but you shall all have to cross the river here." Thinking of eating all of them up one after the other, he rejoiced inwardly. "Make the fire whilst they cross the river," Leopard said to his wife.

Boldly, Deer stepped into the boat. He had hardly left the riverbank when Leopard grabbed him by the throat greedily. "Who, Who!" Dear fought back. He was flung against the boat, and died instantly. Leopard did this until the animals were considerably reduced in number.

One day, Hagbe (Cunning Rabbit) said to himself, "I am going to cross that river to stop growing thinner and thinner every day. All the food we need is on the other side of the river. There is no other way we can get food, and each time any animal goes he does not return. I will try to devise a means of solving this problem." Early the following morning, it was quite a cold morning. Hagbe went to Lion and said, "I have come to you, my elder brother." "Why?" Lion asked. "Leopard has become a tyrant at the river side. Now we can hardly come to the other side in search of food. As you can see, I am almost starved to death," Hagbe explained. "Have you seen him with your own eyes?" Lion asked. "He is right there acting as a cross-over," Hagbe confirmed. "God bless!" Lion exclaimed, but wondered how he could get to the other side of the river without Leopard being frightened away by the sight of him. "There is a way," Hagbe said. He spread out a mat and asked Lion to lie on it. He went also to Tiger and said that Leopard and Lion had forbidden all animals from crossing the river, and that there was no way they could get food to eat. "Where did you see Lion?" Tiger enquired. "By the riverbank. He and Leopard have prevented all other animals from crossing to the other side of the river in search of food," Hagbe explained. "May the Lord bless you for what you have said. I have been longing to see Lion. If you can only help me to get at him, so much the better," Tiger told Hagbe.

He wrapped Tiger in the mat, rolled up the mat, took it to the riverbank, took a Wulie, a special broom used by the head of the Humui secret society, and began to call Leopard. "Leopard?" shaking the Wulie, "Please come here and canoe me to the other side of the river. I am extremely hungry!" Leopard jumped into the canoe immediately. "Thank God, the craftiest of all the animals is coming. He must have stopped the others animals from crossing all these days. You can go right ahead and set a pot on the fire," he instructed his wife. As the canoe was about to anchor, Leopard started to show his teeth to Hagbe. "Ay, Leopard! You whom I regard as my nephew, should not have any desire to eat me at this moment when my children are sick, and I am bringing them to you to conduct the Humui rituals for their recovery," Hagbe said.

"May the Lord bless you for your thoughtfulness," Leopard prayed, because he did not want to attack Hagbe on the bank, lest he missed him. Hagbe, before getting into the boat, put Lion close to Leopard, and Tiger next to Lion. He sat at the extreme end and asked Leopard to start canoeing. As they were sailing, Lion's hatred for Leopard began to intensify. Unaware of what was going on, Leopard began to sing as he canoed the boat:

Chorus: Gbawule Masa Gbawule
Gbawule Masa Gbawule ...
Hagbe had said that he would not cross the river soon.
Leopard had thought that
Hagbe would not cross the river soon.

Chorus: Gbawule Masa Gbawule
Gbawule Masa Gbawule ...
When we cross I'll eat you up
Thank God for the opportunity.
Chorus: Gbawule Masa Gbawule
Gbawule Masa Gbawule ...
If you eat me up, Lion will eat you up.
And then Tiger will eat him up.

Chorus: Gbawule Masa Gbawule
Gbawule Masa Gbawule.

It was after they had made such hints at each other that Leopard realized what was lurking in the mat for him. Before he could turn round to see what was happening, it was too late. Lion was already reaching out for his throat, whilst Tiger was also reaching out for Lion's. Leopard wanted to jump into the river and swim away, but as soon as he put one of his legs into the river, Crocodile cut a large slice off it. He put it back into the canoe immediately, took the paddle and began to canoe again, singing.

Chorus: Mbombo Wiyo, Mbombo Wiyo

I am chilled.

Mbombo Wiyo, Mbombo Wiyo

I am chilled by your Humui.

Please be silent! Deep down! Lion dipped Leopard's head into the river. As Lion was doing this, Tiger caught him by the throat tightly, and Hagbe, frightened by what was going on in the boat, sprang and landed on the head of a crocodile in the river. "When did the day break?" Hagbe asked Crocodile in fear. "You should not ask me this question, since you are coming from the land." Crocodile answered.

It was at that time that Hagbe sang to me:

Chorus: The word they used to say,

Women, the word they used to say,

We have commenced a dance again.

Women, I salute you.

Beat the Kilie for me,

Momoh beat the Kilie for me to dance.

The word they used to say,

Women, the word they used to say,

Gbomba has commenced a dance again.

Women, I salute you …

My sisters, please be silent! My head hurts again.

碾 米

像这样,像那样。
那边那几英亩地
上面没有种稻子。
(合唱)卡玛·沃利,卡玛·沃利耶。卡玛·沃利,卡玛·沃利耶。

像这样,像那样。
那边那几英亩地
上面没有种稻子。
(合唱)卡玛·沃利,卡玛·沃利耶。卡玛·沃利,卡玛·沃利耶。

一个成年人,即使他喝了棕榈酒,醉了,
也该知道不责备年迈的爸爸。
哦,是的。

不要让任何人不尊重长者。
苏达,去给我表演,
谢谢,谢谢。
骂我,苏达,帮帮我吧,
哟哟。
哟哟。

英文对照

Rice Thrashing

Like this, like that.
Those acres of land over there
There is no rice on them.
Chorus: Kama Woli, Kama Woli yes.
Kama Woli, Kama Woli yes.

Like this, like that.
Those acres of land over there
There is no rice on them.
Chorus: Kama Woli, Kama Woli yes.
Kama Woli, Kama Woli yes.

A grown-up man, even if he is drunk with palm wine,
is sensible enough not to abuse an elder papa.
oh yes.

Let nobody disrespect an elder.
Ah Soda, go and perform it for me.
Thank you, thank you.
Abuse me oh, Soda, go and do it for me,
Yo yo.
Yo yo.

军蚁与人类

啊!这个世界!这个世界很大,但它在人类的控制之下。先生们,这个故事发生在很多年以前。

上帝创造万物,悲悯他们:鱼、人类、苍蝇、虱子、蚂蚁、军蚁①。每一个会呼吸的生物,只要有骨头、血液、水、血脉、空气,上帝都爱他们。

但是军蚁对人类在这个世界上的生活方式感到不满。有一天,他们来到上帝面前抱怨。他们通常把人称作"两条腿"。他们说:"万能的造物主,我们不是来抱怨的,但我们担心你创造这个世界的方式。"

"你们担心什么?"万能的上帝问他们。他们说:"'两条腿'与我们一起生活在这个世界上。我们中的一些有四条腿、六条腿或更多。我们有很多条腿,还有尖尖的嘴可以用来叮咬,我们真的在忍受他们造成的痛苦。我们不敢进入他们的家。如果我们这样做,他们就会用点燃的柴火来杀死我们。"

"就这些吗?你们想让我怎么办?"上帝问道。"我们要求你教会我们如何变得足够强大,能够抵御他们。"军蚁们回答。

上帝对他们说:"你们知道吗?我创造了这些人。他们想要的是被温柔对待。他们想要温柔。他们是非常聪明的人。如果你们对他们使用暴力,他们大脑的一小部分比你们的嘴要锋利十万倍。他们会报复你们的。所以,你们应该对他们温柔一点。""我们明白了。"他们说,"我们将尽最大努力。""听着。无论何时你们想去他们那里,都要安静地去。不应该咬伤他们。人类不

---

① 军蚁(driver ant):蚂蚁的一种,以凶狠而闻名,有"微型杀手"的别称。军蚁集体捕食,它们出发时排成密集的纵队,而有些军蚁采取广阔的横队形前进。它们一离开宿营地,就分支再分支,包抄围困攻捕食对象。它们将猎物撕咬成碎片,以便携带,然后再以行军的队形前进。前进时,前卫线上和两翼是长着巨颚的兵蚁,中间是工蚁。它们如汹涌的潮水,所到之处,庄稼没有了,甚至荒草、树皮也没有了,几乎所有遇到的大小动物都无一幸免。这种蚂蚁有巨大的颚,活像一把锋利的剪刀,就是大蟒蛇和羊,也会在几个小时内被军蚁群吃得只剩下一堆骨架。它们小小的身躯竟有如此的威力,不得不让人感到惊奇。

喜欢看到自己的血洒出来。如果他们看到自己的血,他们就会生你们的气。你们必须轻轻地接近他们。""我们知道了。"军蚁们说。从上帝那里回来之后,他们召开了一次会议,向所有的亲朋好友致辞:"你们都听说上帝对我们说的话了。谁都不应该再用暴力攻击'两条腿',你们听到了吗?"大家都说:"我们知道了。"

一天晚上,当人类都上床睡觉时,一伙军蚁入侵了人类的家园。当他们找到第一个人时,他们在他的床两侧排成了队。他在两队之间翻身睡觉。其中有一只军蚁非常固执。他无视上帝的建议,不顾人类需要温柔对待的需求,狠狠地咬了那个人一口。那人立刻喊道:"唔!"然后把手移到身边。他站起来点灯,发现到处都是军蚁!他对邻居喊道:"哦,成千上万的军蚁来啦!"莫莫说:"什么!我们现在该怎么办?"

我们赶紧去吧,每个人都为了自己。

我们赶紧去吧,每个人都为了自己。

我们冲向那里;这里每个人都是为了自己;冲吧。

呃,这是它们开始的一些宫殿;不要睡觉。

我们冲向那里;每个人都为自己;冲吧。

啊,我们的敌人来了;不要睡觉。

我们冲向那里;每个人都为自己;不要睡觉。

哎哟,我们现在该怎么办?

周围有这么多敌人,不管是谁,这个镇上的每个人都别睡了。

我们赶紧去吧;每个人都是为了自己。

这首歌表达了他们要做某事的决心。人类唱着这首歌,要求大家冲出去杀死军蚁。任何人都不应该待在室内。每个人都应该带上一根点燃的柴火棍。他们一边唱歌,一边消灭了所有的军蚁。

Driver Ants and Human Beings

Ah, this world! This world is wide, but man is in control of it. Gentlemen, something happened many years ago.

God made all creatures, and He loves them all: fish, human beings, flies, lice, ants, driver ants. Every creature that takes air in and out; that has bones, blood, water, veins, air … God loves them all.

But the driver ants were unhappy about the way human beings carried on in this world. One day, they went to God and made a complaint. They usually referred to man as "Two-legged". They said, "Almighty God, we do not complain, but we are worried about the way you created this world."

"And what is worrying you?" the Almighty God asked them. They said, "These Two-legged live with us in this world. Some of us have four, six or more legs. We have many legs and sharp mouths that bite with a sting. We are really suffering at their hands. We dare not enter their homes. If we do, they will kill us with lighted firewood."

"Is that all? And what do you want me to do about that?" God asked. "We ask you to show us how we can become strong enough to withstand them," they replied.

God said to them, "You know what? I created these people. What they want is gentle treatment. They want gentleness. They are very clever people. If you use violence against them, a small fragment of their brains is a hundred thousand times sharper than your mouth. They will take revenge on you. So, you should be gentle with them." "We have heard you," they said. "We shall do our best." "Listen. Whenever you want to go to them, go quietly. You should never bite and wound them. Human beings do not like to see their blood spilt. If they see their blood they will become mad at you. You must approach them gently." "We have heard," they said. And they returned. They called a meeting and addressed all their kith and kin: "You have all heard what God has said to us. No one should ever again attack those 'Two-legged' with violence, do you hear?" They all said, "We have heard."

One night, when everybody had gone to bed, the ants invaded the homes of human beings. When they got to the first man, they formed lines on both sides of his bed. He lay between them. There was one ant among them who was very stubborn. Ignoring the advice given by God that human beings needed gentle treatment, it bit the man sharply. Immediately, the man shouted, "Kpoo!" and moved his hand to his side. When he got up and lit the lamp, there were ants everywhere! He yelled. He called out to his neighbor, "Ngo Momoh, driver ants have come in their thousands!" Momoh said, "What! And what are we going to do now?"

Let's rush there, everyone for himself.
Let's rush there, everyone for himself.
Let's rush there; here is everyone for himself; let's go.
Eh, it's some palace they have started; let's not sleep.
Let's rush there; everyone for himself; let's go.
Ah, our enemies have come; don't sleep at all.
Let's rush there; everyone for himself; don't sleep at all.
O ya yo, what can we do now?
With so many enemies around, whoever may be in this town doesn't sleep.
Let's rush there; everyone for himself.

Their determination to do something is expressed in this song. The human beings sang the song. They asked everyone to rush out and kill the ants. No one should stay indoors. Each should bring along a lighted piece of firewood. As they sang they destroyed all the ants.

曼迪族谚语

不想被践踏的山上种植不了食用菌。
当一只秃鹫爱上一只灌木丛中的鸟时，它将死于枪杀。
友谊有很多种：牛粪友谊表面上很坚固，而底部却是一摊臭水。
不管你长得多高，你永远都不会比你的头发高。
割草的人不会无缘无故吹嘘自己睡在象鼻草里。
大洞是一点一点地被挖出来的。
大象从来不会觉得自己的象鼻笨重。
一棵有前途的车前草生长在主植物旁边。
说到割草，新的牧场最招人喜欢。
在稻田割草从来都不是新鲜事。
变色龙留下美丽的脚印，但尾巴会把那些脚印抹去。
你白天认识的那棵树，就是你晚上剥掉树皮的那棵树。
你只能试着去摘你手能够得到的叶子。
提问能使人找到正确的答案。
人不能把一个饥饿的人送到食品店。
猎杀凶猛动物的猎人应该得到镇长的现金补偿。

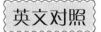

Mende Proverbs

A hill that doesn't wish to be trodden on must not grow edible mushrooms.

When a vulture falls in love with a bush fowl, she dies in gunfire.

There are different kinds of friendship: A cow dung friendship has cement on the surface, while the bottom holds a pool of smelly water.

However tall you grow, you will never be taller than the hair on your head.

The mower doesn't boast of sleeping in the elephant's grass for nothing.

It is bit by bit that the great big hole is dug out.

An elephant doesn't get tired of carrying his trunk.

A promising young plantain grows by the main plant.

As for cutting-grass, man likes new grazing land.

Cutting-grass is never a stranger on a rice field.

The chameleon leaves beautiful footprints, but the tail wipes them off.

The tree you know by day is the one whose bark you remove at night.

You should only attempt to pick leaves which your hand can reach.

Asking questions will enable one to find the right answer.

One cannot send a hungry man to the food store.

A hunter who kills a fierce animal should get cash compensation from the town chief.

竞争之果

很久以前，花生只有一种——白色花生，覆盖着红色的果皮。马穆德以种植花生为生。他有七英亩花生地。

马穆德有两个妻子。玛丽是他的第二任妻子，他们结婚还不满一年。玛丽从来没有种过花生，因为在她的家乡，人们更多的是种植水稻。马穆德的第一任妻子法图对种植花生了如指掌。她种植花生已有二十多年了。马穆德给他的妻子每人一英亩地，让她们自己种花生。法图不喜欢玛丽。她嫉妒玛丽，因为玛丽比她年轻漂亮。从玛丽第一天到她家成为马穆德的第二任妻子起，法图就不喜欢她。尽管她们一起吃饭，一起做了很多事情，法图还是希望玛丽不要妨碍她，这样她就不必和另一个女人分享她的丈夫。

玛丽请法图教她如何种植花生。"玛丽，你从没种过花生吗？"法图问道。"我这辈子从来没有。"玛丽回答。"我的家乡都种植水稻。"她补充道。

"这很简单，"法图说，"剥花生壳。然后把果仁放进锅里，在炉火上烤。"玛丽没有理解法图的意思，不过她还是照着做了，然后把烤花生种在了土里。法图原以为这些花生会在土壤中腐烂，但令她惊讶的是，这些花生长得异常地好。

法图不敢相信自己的眼睛。

"你真的按我说的做了吗？"法图问道。"是的。"玛丽回答。

法图的花生也长得很好。到了除草的时候，她们给花生地除草。丈夫帮助她们在农场周围种植棕榈树，以防啮齿动物进来偷吃花生。第一批黄色的花开了，不久就凋谢了。当花生第二次开花，绿叶开始枯萎时，他们知道花生已经成熟了。

法图和玛丽都收获了自己的花生。她们摘下花生，清洗干净外壳上的泥土，玛丽剥开花生壳，想看看它们是否好吃。这些花生有漂亮的白皮，每个人都对玛丽种出的花生新品种表示羡慕。他们以前从未见过如此好的花生。

有人问玛丽是如何得到这种味道如此甜美、不同寻常的花生的。她告诉人们是法图让她在播种前先烤好种子的。

法图感到非常羞愧。她本打算毁掉玛丽的植物，但坏事变成了好事。

每个人都称赞玛丽种出的花生。他们把它们命名为"竞争之果"——对手的嫉妒心创造了一种新型花生。

英文对照

The Rival's Groundnuts

Long ago, there was only one type of groundnut—the groundnut with the red skin covering the white nut. Mamoud planted groundnuts for his living. He had seven acres of land on which he planted groundnuts.

Mamoud had two wives. Marie is the second wife. They were married less than a year before. She had never planted groundnuts because people grew more rice where she came from. Fatu, Mamoud's first wife, knew all about groundnuts for over twenty years. Mamoud gave an acre each to his wives to grow their own groundnuts. Fatu secretly nursed some ill feelings for Marie. She was jealous of Marie because Marie was younger and more beautiful than her. From the first day Marie came to her home to be Mamoud's second wife, Fatu disliked her. Although they ate together and did many things together, she wanted Marie out of the way so that she would not have to share her husband with another woman.

Marie asked Fatu to show her how to grow groundnuts. "Have you never planted groundnuts, Marie?" asked Fatu.

"Never in my life," replied Marie. "We grow rice where I come from," she added.

"It is simple," said Fatu. "Shell the groundnuts. Then put the nuts into a pot and roast them over the fire," continued Fatu. Marie had no cause to disbelieve Fatu. She carried out Fatu's instructions and then planted the roasted nuts. Fatu expected the nuts to rot in the soil, but to her greatest amazement, the groundnuts grew well.

Fatu could not believe her eyes.

"Did you really do what I told you to do?" asked Fatu. "Yes," replied Marie.

Fatu's groundnuts also grew well. When it was time for weeding, the women weeded their groundnut field. Their husband helped them to put palm trees around the farm to keep away rodents. The first yellow flowers showed and died soon after. When the groundnuts flowered a second time and the green leaves began to wither, they knew that the groundnuts were ready to harvest.

Fatu and Marie both harvested their own groundnuts. They plucked the groundnuts from their roots and washed the soil from the groundnuts. Marie shelled some of the groundnuts to see if they were good. The seeds had nice white skins and everybody admired them. They had never seen such beautiful seeds before.

Marie was asked how she managed to get such unusual seeds that tasted so sweet. She explained how Fatu had told her to roast the seeds before planting them.

Fatu felt very ashamed. She had meant to destroy Marie's plants but the evil she had intended for Marie had turned to be good.

Everybody praised Marie's groundnuts. They named them "the rival's groundnuts". The jealousy of a rival introduced a new type of groundnut.

西非民间口头文学作品欣赏（塞拉利昂篇）

三个文盲

　　三个文盲被要求去学习如何识字。这些人只去了三天，就回来了，因为他们都自认为已经学会了。酋长想找三个人帮他看守大门。这三个被认为是会识字的男人担任了这一职务。有一天，一个叫帕凯的人收集了很多好东西，要送给酋长。当帕凯到达第一扇大门时，看门的人让他停下来，并要求帕凯保证他从酋长那里得到的任何东西都会与他分享，不然他就不放帕凯进去。帕凯同意了，答应给看门人"二十"。这看门人从来没有问过这个"二十"究竟是什么意思，只是用张纸，签了自己的名字，算作协议，拿给帕凯，让他通过了第一扇大门。同样的事情也发生在另外两扇大门，帕凯继续承诺将会送给另外两个看门人"二十"。

　　酋长见到帕凯时，非常高兴，决定给他很多金子、钻石和钱。但帕凯拒绝接受任何奖励，而是要求被杖责一百下。酋长对此感到非常惊讶，但帕凯坚持他的要求。于是，酋长叫他的信使把拐杖拿来，并让帕凯躺在地板上。在他被打了四十下后，帕凯让信使停下来。然后，他请酋长邀请第一个看门人过来。当酋长问为什么时，帕凯解释说他们之间有协议。

　　酋长叫来了看门人，帕凯叫信使打看门人二十下。看门人想拒绝，但是帕凯拿出协议给他看。酋长于是命令信使杖责看门人，赏给他二十大板。第二个和第三个看门人也依次被叫来，他们也受到了同样的惩罚。在整个惩罚结束之后，三个人决定去学点真本领。

　　这个短故事背后的寓意是，不懂装懂是很危险的。

The Three Illiterate Men

Three illiterate men were asked to go and learn how to read. The men only stayed there for three days and returned, assuming that they had become literate. The chief then asked for three men to guard his gates. The three men who were assumed to be literate took up the post. One day, a man called Pa Kay gathered many good things to send to the chief. When Pa Kay reached the first gate, the man at the gate asked him to stop and promise that whatever he got from the chief would be shared with him before he would be allowed to pass through. Pa Kay agreed and promised to give the gatekeeper twenty. The man at the gate never asked what twenty meant, but allowed Pa Kay to pass with his signature on a piece of paper. The same thing happened at the other two gates, and Pa Kay continued to promise to give twenty to the other two gatekeepers.

When the chief saw Pa Kay, he was so pleased that he decided to give him plenty of gold, diamonds and money. Pa Kay refused to take any reward but asked that he should be given a hundred lashes of the cane. The chief was very much surprised at this, but Pa Kay insisted on getting the lashes. The chief then called his messenger to bring the cane and asked Pa Kay to lie on the floor. After he was given forty lashes, Pa Kay asked the man with the cane to stop. He then asked the chief to invite his first gatekeeper. When the chief asked why, Pa Kay explained that he had an agreement with him.

The chief called for the gatekeeper. When he came, Pa Kay ordered the cane-man to give him twenty lashes. The gatekeeper wanted to refuse, but

Pa Kay took out the agreement paper and showed it to him. The chief then ordered the cane-man to thrash the keeper giving him twenty lashes of the cane. The second and third gatekeepers were called and the same punishment was given to them. After the whole punishment, the three men decided to go and do actual learning.

The moral behind this short story is that to pretend to know what one doesn't know is dangerous.

我只是来问问

我只是来问问;
我只是来问问;
老人家,我只是来问问。
(合唱)会发生吗?
这真的会发生吗?
我只是来问问;
我只是来问问;
老人家,我只是来问问。
(合唱)会发生吗?
这真的会发生。

英文对照

I've Only Come to Ask

I've only come to ask;
I've only come to ask;
Old man, I've only come to ask.
Chorus: Will it take place?
Will it really take place?
I've only come to ask;
I've only come to ask;
Old man, I've only come to ask.
Chorus: Will it take place?
It will really take place.

烦 恼

哎！烦啊！
（合唱）他们很烦恼。
青春已逝。
（合唱）他们很烦恼。
他们很烦恼。
（合唱）他们很烦恼。
青春已逝。
（合唱）他们很烦恼。
他们走了，离开了我们。
（合唱）他们很烦恼。

英文对照

Worries

Oh! Worries!
Chorus: They are worried.
The youth has gone.
Chorus: They are worried.
They are worried.
Chorus: They are worried.
The youth has gone.
Chorus: They are worried.
They've gone and left us.
Chorus: They are worried.

再见了,妈妈

再见了,妈妈!
妈妈们,年轻人要走了哦!
再见了,妈妈!
(合唱)桑巴马尼哦!妈妈们,哦!
再见了,妈妈!
妈妈们,年轻人要走了哦!
再见了,妈妈!
(合唱)孔可娜尼哦!妈妈们!
大家,再见哦!
所有的年轻人都要走了!
再见了!
(合唱)孔可娜尼哦!妈妈们!
大家,再见哦!
(合唱)啊!妈妈们,年轻人要走了,
不说再见。
孔可娜尼哦!妈妈们!

西非民间口头文学作品欣赏（塞拉利昂篇）

英文对照

Mothers, Goodbye

Mothers, goodbye oh!
Oh! Mothers, the youths are going oh!
Mothers, goodbye oh!
Chorus: Sangbamani oh! Mothers, oh!
Mothers, goodbye oh!
Mothers, the youths are going oh!
Mothers, goodbye oh!
Chorus: Konkonani oh! Mothers oh!
All of you, goodbye oh!
All of you, the youths are going oh!
Goodbye oh!
Chorus: Konkonani oh! Mothers oh!
All of you, goodbye oh!
Chorus: Ah! Mothers, the youths are going oh!
Without saying goodbye.
Konkonani oh! Mothers oh!

被鹿拖走的陷阱设置者

很多年前,塞布韦马有一个叫法旺德的人。他非常喜欢吃肉。这个故事会告诉你,法旺德这个名字是怎么来的。

真有趣!真有趣!鹿是如何把法旺德拖走的故事只能由目击者来讲述。这件事发生在贾卢阿洪和塞布韦马之间。

内珀是塞布韦马的建立者,是一名陷阱设置者。这个叫塞布韦马的部落从没有现在这般闻名于贾卢阿洪酋长的领地。它以前叫邦迪沃,是一个只有两栋房子和一个谷仓的小村庄。我们今天所知道的这个城镇是由其他人建立的。

有一次外出捕鱼时,我在各地转悠,来到了一个名叫邦迪沃的村庄。当我走近村民时,他们问我:"你要去多远的地方?"我告诉他们,我是个渔夫,哪里有鱼就去哪里。他们说:"可是,这一带没有很深的河流。"

"好吧,请带我进去,让我做你们的客人。我在外游荡太久了。"我对他们说。

他们给了我一个房间睡觉。那天晚上,当我们躺在床上时,听到有人不停地敲门。当门打开时,门口站着一个强壮的老年男子和一个女人。

"老人家,你叫什么名字?"我问那个年长的人。

他说:"我叫内珀,来自班达朱马·科尔维格布阿马。我是个陷阱设置者。"

"你的妻子尊姓大名?"

"她叫塔鲁瓦。"

村民们给了他们一个房间住下。第二天醒来时,村民们问他:"你接下来打算做什么?"

"我打算在这个村子里待一段时间。"他告诉他们。

"我们不反对,我们从不拒绝来村子里的陌生人。但有件事需要提醒你。

在邦迪沃和达鲁之间有一座山叫雅各山。火车每每行驶到那里总是会抛锚。那是一座圣山。你不是说你是个陷阱设置者吗？千万不要在那里设陷阱，听到了吗？"

"好的，我知道了。"他答道，没在那里设下过任何陷阱。

起床之后，老人立即动身去寻找设置陷阱的绳索。那时候，人们没有电线，只能使用酒椰子树的纤维做的绳子来设置陷阱，绳子被系在匍匐茎上，鹿一旦踏入，必死无疑。找到匍匐茎并不容易，老人到处找都找不到。最后，他去了圣山，在那里他发现了一段匍匐茎，他把匍匐茎砍下带走。他清理出一片空地，在那里设置了陷阱，并将那里命名为达米耶马（长着大量匍匐茎的地方）。这个地方就是塞布韦马酋长领地的行政法庭现在所在的位置。欲知详情，可向当地的居民去询问。

当内珀彻底清理好这片区域后，他决定在那里定居下来。他说："对于一个陌生人来说，这是一个多么美好的住处啊！这里干燥而不积水。"不久，其他一些人也搬到那里定居。他们说："这是一个美丽的定居点。"

旱季结束前，内珀向村里请求耕种土地。他得到了足够的土地。他说："这是一个我以前从未干过的工作。"那一年，这片土地上发生了严重的饥荒。

在他完成基本的农田耕种之后，他的妻子怀孕了。农场烧过了草肥，稻种也播好了，地也耙完了。播完种子后，杂草也被拔除得干干净净。在稻花飘香的时节，他妻子生了一个活蹦乱跳的男孩。丈夫给孩子取名："我的孩子叫塞。"

"塞什么？"人们问道。

"塞·达姆比耶马，"他回答，"塞就是塞布韦马，这个地名开头的第一个字。"

当时正是饥荒最严重的时候，内珀准备收割水稻。全世界的人都来到了这个农场。达玛人来了。来自高拉、尼加鲁阿洪、农戈瓦和班巴拉酋长领地的人也来了。他们都来收割稻子。

啊，我的兄弟！只需对他的儿子塞说一句赞美的话，人们就可以获得免费的稻谷。塞常常赤身裸体地躺在干草里，让所有人都看到他。

"嘿！老内珀，这孩子很帅。哦，你的孩子多有前途啊！他长大后会成为一个有权势的首领。老家伙，好好照顾这个孩子，我以后要嫁给他。"

老人会对他们说："好吧，去收割一些稻子吧。"他想让他们有点东西吃，因为他们已经把整个国家土地上的野生山药和食用作物吃得一干二净了。后来，大家都养成了去内珀那蹭吃的习惯。他们会说："让我去看看塞。"于是这个地方被称为塞布韦马（"去看看塞"的意思）。随着西方文明的到来，这里逐渐扩展成了一个名叫塞格布韦马的大城镇。

哦，我亲爱的兄弟们！你常常会听到人们说："让我去看看塞。也许我能拿到点吃的。"

每个师傅都会有徒弟，亲爱的。内珀有一个名叫法旺德的学徒。他住在班达朱马·科尔维格布阿马。有一天，他说："我要去找我的师傅，他已经离开家乡太久了。"

当他找到内珀时，内珀很高兴地接待了他。内珀说："哦，我的同胞们，这是我的徒弟，他来看望我"。

"年轻人，你叫什么名字？"他们问道。

"我叫法旺德。"

"你是做什么的？"

"我是个陷阱设置的学徒。"

"不要在圣山周围设陷阱，它位于达鲁和这个叫邦迪沃的村庄之间。"

"我听说了。"

但法旺德是个非常贪吃的人。他无肉不欢，每当他和别人握手时，他都会舔自己的手。如果有人吐口水，法旺德就会迅速转过身来，看一看，因为他太贪吃了。哦，法旺德！哦，仁慈的上帝！哦，法旺德！

第二天，法旺德出去砍了许多匍匐茎，用以设置陷阱。很快，到处都是陷阱了。他从圣山出发——就是人们警告过不能在那里设置陷阱的地方，一路设置陷阱，师傅内帕和镇上的人浑然不觉。法旺德太喜欢吃肉了！

他的陷阱从塞布韦马一直延坤到塞法杜以及其他地方，甚至是到了法国（几内亚）的领土！他一边走一边把陷阱设置好。在另一个方向，他布设的陷阱从塞格布韦马开始，穿过马莱河，一直延伸到坎波依山及更远的地方。陷阱到达了布拉玛和列夫马·坎杜。到处都有他的陷阱。怎么会有这种人！

每当他遇到动物的脚印时，他甚至会把它们踏过的尘土舔一遍。设置陷阱的当月，法旺德已经迫不及待，逐个去检查这些陷阱有没有逮到动物。

他首先去圣山检查。那就是鹿把他拖走的地方。当他到达那里时，他发现一只鹿被困在一个陷阱里。他立刻爬上一棵树，砍下一根树枝，然后立刻用棍子打那只鹿；他很残忍地一边抽打一边喊着：格博博乔，格邦巴贾，格邦巴贾，格邦巴贾。他每次击打完都会舔舔棍子。当鹿完全没有反应后，他便跑回镇上。啊，法旺德！多么喜欢吃肉啊！

进城后，他开始做一根结实的绳子，把它紧紧地系在腰上。当他这样做的时候，他自言自语道："这只鹿今晚将不会睡在那里了。"他回到山上，把绳子的另一端系在鹿身上。然后他拉着鹿，和它说话："你从来没有停止过四处游荡。今晚，你不会睡在这里。"他使劲拉绳子。他一边拉，一边继续狠狠地抽打那只鹿：卡班、卡班、科邦、科邦、格博博乔、格博巴贾、科邦、格博博乔。突然，鹿从陷阱里蹿了出来！

法旺德绝望地喊道："哦，天啊，我要死了！"他真是个懒惰的人，而那只鹿又那么大！他试图抓住他能摸到的任何东西，但鹿把所有东西都连根拔起来了，包括篱笆和树木。法旺德浑身是血，他又喊又哭，声音如此之大，以至于森林里回荡着他的声音，周围的人都听到了他的声音。他喊道："请在我和鹿之间筑起一道路障。"

（合唱）请在鹿和我之间设一道路障，

哦，仁慈的上帝！

快点来吧，鹿要把我拖走了。

各位，如果你们不快点的话，鹿会把我拖走的。

快点来吧，动物正把我带进它的巢穴。

动物正把我带到山上，家人们，我可能再也不会回来了。

呃，现在能做什么？

呃，动物把我拖走了。

乡亲们啊，这只鹿多强壮啊！

这片森林里没有人来帮我吗？

亲爱的朋友们，难道这片森林里就没有人设置陷阱吗？

请砍下一棵树来阻止我们的前进。

请快醒过来吧，难道这个镇子上的人都睡着了吗？

啊，我要完蛋了。

噢，我正经受着一种怎样的经历啊！

噢，它正在拖着我离去。

人们警告过我，可我却没当回事。

呃，我倒霉透了，这只动物太强壮了。

呃，我忘了我的砍刀放在哪里了。

每一棵我紧紧抓住的树都被这动物拖倒了。

你们建造的这个弱不禁风的棚子，也被推倒了。

主啊，主啊，主啊，

主啊，我完蛋了。

我走了，我走了，这动物把我拖走了。

卡普，我可能永远不会回来了。

呃，等一下，我可以吟唱我的死亡之歌了：

请在我们前面设一道路障，在鹿和我之间。

请在我们前面设一道路障，在鹿和我之间。

请在我们前面设一道路障，在鹿和我之间。

棘手的是，事实上每个人都有适合自己的东西，

所以，有的人会因为贪吃而迎接他的死亡！

呃，仁慈的主啊！

呃，这真是个灾难！

请在我们前面设一道路障，在鹿和我之间。

这就是为什么一个人永远不应该做过分的事情的原因，尤其是那些可能导致毁灭的事情。鹿把法旺德带走了，从此再也没有人看见过他了。

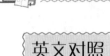

The Trap-Setter Who Was Carried Away by the Deer

There was a certain man called Fawunde in Segbwema many years ago. He was a great lover of meat. I am going to tell you the story of how he came to be called Fawunde.

Oh how funny it was! Oh how funny! The story of how the deer carried Fawunde away can only be told by a witness. It happened between Njaluahun and Segbwema.

The founder of Segbwema was called Nepor and he was a trap-setter. The settlement that is now called Segbwema was never known as such throughout Njaluahun Chiefdom. It used to be called Gbandiwo. It was a hamlet comprising only two houses and a barn. The town, as we know it today, was founded by somebody else.

As I wandered around on a fishing expedition, I arrived in a village called Gbandiwo. When I approached the people, they asked me, "How far are you travelling?" When I told them I was a fisherman, they said, "But there are no deep rivers around here."

"Well," I said to them, "take me in and let me be your guest. I have wandered about for too long."

They offered me a room to sleep in. As we lay in bed that night we heard someone knocking at the door repeatedly and when the door was opened there was a strong, aged man and a woman at the entrance.

"Old one, what is your name?" I asked him.

"My name is Nepor," he said. "I come from Bandajuma Korvegbuama. I am a trap-setter."

"And your wife, what is she called?" I asked again.

"My wife is called Taluva," he replied.

The villagers offered him a room to sleep in. When they woke up the next day they asked him, "And what do you intend to do next?"

"I intend to stay with you in this village for a little while," he told them.

"We do not object," they said. "We never reject strangers in our village. But there is something here you need to be warned against. Between this village, Gbandiwo, and Daru there is a hill called Yargueh. That is where the train used to frequently break down. It is a sacred hill. Didn't you say you are a trap-setter? Do not set traps there, do you hear?"

"Yes, I have heard," he said. And he never set any traps there.

He immediately set about to prepare twines for setting traps. In those days, there were no wires, so raffia twines were used. These were tied to creeping stems to form death traps for the deer. It was not easy to locate creeping stems, and the old man looked everywhere in vain. Eventually, he went to the sacred hill and found a creeping stem there which he cut and carried away. He cleared an area of land, set his traps there and named the area Damiyiema (where creeping stems were abound). That is the place where the Chiefdom Administration Court in Segbwema now stands. You may ask any of the local citizens about this.

When Nepor had cleared the area thoroughly, he decided to settle there. He said, "What a nice settlement for a stranger! Here no water can settle." Soon, others moved there to settle as well. They said, "This is a beautiful settlement."

Before the end of the dry season, Nepor asked for land to cultivate and he was given enough land. He said, "This is a mission I never fully prepared myself for." That year, famine broke out in the land.

The old man's wife became pregnant just about the time he had finished cultivating his farm land. The farm was burnt and the seed was sown. After the farm had been seed-harrowed the weeds were removed. When the rice was in the tillering stage, the wife gave birth to a bouncing baby boy. And the husband named the child. "This child of mine is called Sei, " he said.

"Sei what? " the people asked.

"Sei Dambiyiema, " he replied. "That was the beginning of the name Segbwema. "

It was at the height of famine that Nepor was ready to harvest rice. The whole world descended on the farm. The people of Dama came. Those from Gaurah, Njaluahun, Nongowa and Bambara Chiefdoms came too. They all came to harvest the rice.

Ah, my brother! Anyone who wanted to harvest some rice only needed to say a word of praise about the child, Sei. He would be laid haked in the hay for all to see.

"Old one, Nepor, this child is very handsome. Oh, what a promising child you have got there! He will grow up to be a powerful chief. Old one, take good care of this child. This child is my husband. "

And the old man would say to them, "Well, go and harvest some rice. " He wanted them to have something to eat, because they had exhausted the land of all the wild yams and edible crops. Later they all formed the habit of visiting Nepor, just to have something to eat. They would say, "Let me go and take a look at Sei. " And so the place came to be called Seigbema (taking a look at Sei). With the advent of Western civilization, the settlement expanded into a large town which came to be called Segbwema.

Oh, my dear brothers! You would often hear everyone saying, "Let me go and have a look at Sei. Maybe I will get something to eat. "

But every expert has an apprentice, my dear. Old man Nepor had an apprentice named Fawunde. He lived at Bandajuma Korvegbuama. One day, he said, "I am going to look for my master. He has been away for too long. "

When he found his master the latter was very glad to receive him. Nepor said, "Oh, my people, this is my apprentice who has come to visit me. "

"Young man, what is your name?" they asked.

"My name is Fawunde," he said.

"What work do you do?" they asked again.

"I am an apprentice trap-setter," he replied.

"Well," they said, "do not set traps around the sacred hill. It lies between Daru and this village, Gbandiwo."

"I have heard," he said.

But Fawunde was a glutton. He loved meat so much that whenever he shook hands with someone else he would lick his hands. If one spat around, Fawunde would swiftly turn and look, out of gluttony. Oh, Fawunde! Oh, Gracious Lord! Oh, Fawunde!

The next day, Fawunde went out and cut a lot of creeping stems to set traps with. Soon there were traps all over the place. He started from the very sacred hill where he had been warned not to set any traps, and set traps all the way. His master did not know a thing about it and nor did the town people. He loved meat so much!

His traps spread from Segbwema to Sefadu and beyond, as far as the French territory. He just set them as he went along. In another direction, the traps started from Segbwema and crossed the River Maleh to go on to the Kamboi Hills and beyond. The traps reached Blama and Levuma Kandu. He just set them everywhere. What a man!

Whenever he came across the footprints of animals, he would take the soil and suck it. The month he set the traps had not ended and Fawunde was already out on an inspection tour of them!

The first place he visited was the sacred hill. And that was where the deer carried him away. When he arrived there he found a deer caught in one of the traps, and he at once climbed a tree and cut off a branch. He immediately fell to hitting the animal with the stick; and he did so ferociously: gbogbojo, gbangbaja, gbangbaja, gbangbaja. Each time he struck he licked the stick. When it seemed to him that striking the animal with the stick was not producing any results he rushed to the town. Ah, Fawunde! What a great lover of meat!

Once in town, he set about making a strong rope which he tied around his waist very tightly. As he did so he said to himself, "This deer won't sleep here tonight." He went back to the hill and tied the other end of the rope around the deer. Then he started pulling and talking to the deer, "You never stop wandering about. Tonight, you won't sleep here." And he pulled hard at the rope. As he pulled he continued to hit the animal viciously: Kaban, kaban, kobon, kobon, gbogbojo, gbangbaja, kobon, gbongbojo. And then the animal escaped from the trap!

Fawunde shouted in desperation: "Oh, my people, I am gone!" He was such a lazy man, and the deer was so big! He tried to hold on to whatever he could touch, but the deer rooted everything out. Fences and trees fell. There was blood all over Fawunde's body and he shouted and cried so loudly that the forest echoed his voice and everyone around heard him. He cried: "Please form a barricade before us, the deer and me."

Chorus: Please form a barricade before us, the deer and me.
Oh, Gracious Lord!
Oh, come, the deer has carried me away.
People, if you don't hurry up, the animal is dragging me away.
Come, oh, the animal is carrying me into its den.
The animal is carrying me into the hill, my people, I may never come back.
Eh, what can I do now?
Eh, the animal is carrying me away.
My people, what a strong deer this one is!
Is there no one in this forest to come to my aid?
Is there no trap-setter in this forest, dear friends?
Cut down a tree and block our progress, please.
Are you all asleep in this town? Please wake up.
Eh, I am gone,
Oh, what an experience I am going through!
Oh, it is carrying me away.
They warned me to no avail.
Eh, unfortunate me; this animal is very strong.
Eh, I no longer know where my machete is.

Every big tree that I hold on to is felled by this animal.

You, who built this weak barn, we have pulled it down.

Oh Lord, Oh Lord, Oh Lord,

Oh Lord, I am gone.

I am gone, oh I am gone, the animal has carried me away.

Kpoo, I may never return from this journey.

Eh, wait a minute, so I may sing my death song:

Please form a barricade before us, the deer and I.

Please form a barricade before us, the deer and I.

Please form a barricade before us, the deer and I.

Tricky one, it is true that everyone has something that fits him.

So, a man can meet his death through gluttony!

Eh, Gracious Lord!

Eh, what a mishap!

Please form a barricade before us, the deer and I.

This is why one should never over-do anything, especially that which is likely to cause one's destruction. The deer carried Fawunde away and no one ever set eyes on him again.

巴·桑吉·班古拉酒店

巴·桑吉·班古拉酒店,你离开我们的地方,
如果还不够的话。
巴·桑吉·班古拉酒店,你离开我们的地方,
如果还不够的话。
(合唱)巴·桑吉·班古拉酒店,你把我们丢在哪里了?
哦,是的!你把我们丢在哪里了?
回来玩吧,你这个波罗会①的会长。

注释 ① 波罗会(Poro):一种特有组织。在万贾玛人、科曼迪人和蒂姆内人中都有;科帕曼迪人(Kpa Mende)中的文迪(Wende)协会、林巴斯人中的邦巴尼协会等与此类似。波罗会是专门为男性而设的。福迪·贾洛(Foday Jalloh)指出,在曼迪人中,波罗会是一种强大而重要的社会管理工具。即使是最高酋长也依赖波罗会来让人们遵守风俗习惯、法律法规和日常行为规范。波罗会可以作为一个社区的执行委员会或法庭,做出仲裁,并作为终审法院。

当男孩们长大成人之后,进入波罗会的秘密丛林开始训练。会员们在丛林里学习传统音乐和舞蹈、历史、狩猎、农业,学习如何利用自然条件进行治疗,如何在成年后使用弓箭、弹射器、吊索等传统武器进行防御,以及怎样设置丛林陷阱和鱼类陷阱等。他们学习如何制作自己的工具。铁匠培训非常重要,这些技能在社区中受到高度重视。所有这些技能都是通过实践操作或模仿来学习的。波罗会的毕业学员会在脖子、背部和胸部留下疤痕,以确定他们的身份和等级,区分他们的原籍村庄。这些组织也保留着一些陈规陋习。

西非民间口头文学作品欣赏（塞拉利昂篇）

英文对照

Pa Santigie Bangura

Pa Santigie Bangura, where you've left us,
It's not enough.
Pa Santigie Bangura, where you've left us,
It's not enough.
Chorus: Yeah! Pa Santigie Bangura, where have you left us?
Oh, yeah! Where have you left us?
Come back to play, you Chief of the Poro society.

忘恩负义的代价

从前，有一对夫妇，坦巴和芬达。他们很穷，生活很艰难，过着食不果腹的日子。一天，芬达的妹妹邦杜来看她，为她带来了一只母鸡。虽然很穷，芬达还是热情地欢迎邦杜。芬达说："我们不吃这种家禽。我要把它养大。"芬达饲养家禽。没人知道家禽是他们的财富来源。上帝总是通过其他人向接受者施以怜悯、爱和仁慈。

没过多久，这只母鸡下了很多蛋，这些蛋孵出了很多很多小鸡。这些小鸡长成了又好又漂亮的母鸡和公鸡。坦巴和芬达惊叹于上帝创造的奇迹。他们卖掉了一些公鸡。他们用这笔钱买了一群绵羊和山羊。绵羊和山羊大量繁殖。他们卖掉了一些山羊和绵羊。他们赚了很多钱，成了全世界最富有的人。人们羡慕他们的生活。他们幸福地生活了很多很多年。

一天，芬达准备为丈夫迎娶一位少女。她说："我正在变老，我需要有人帮我分担家务，陪伴我丈夫。"她为丈夫找到了一位美丽的少女。婚后，少女很快成了坦巴家族的焦点。坦巴家的房产和人口可以比得上色法都及其周边地区。坦巴一家的生活是甜蜜的，而坦巴是最最幸福的。他拥有一切。他的房子里挤满了漂亮的年轻女人，他很快就淡忘了他的第一任妻子芬达。他没有时间陪伴芬达。芬达是他的幸福源泉，现在却被抛之脑后。芬达没日没夜地哭。坦巴从来不想看芬达一眼。甚至连她看他一眼都会让坦巴感到极度不快。

芬达说："哦，这是多么可怕的情况啊！我从来不知道我会被这样对待。我尽我所能让我的丈夫开心，却没意识到他会抛弃我。"她每天以泪洗面。

一天晚上，她做了一个梦。在梦中，她死去的母亲出现在她面前，对她说："我一直在听你诉苦。我受够了你丈夫这样对待你。明天，我会帮你解决所有的问题。"

亲爱的听众们，让我提醒你们，上帝从不偏心。他爱我们所有人，他会为我们做必要的准备。你所要做的就是相信他。男人不应该利用女人，不管男人们为女人们付出了多少嫁妆。女人是我们不可或缺的一部分。他们对我们的成功贡献很大。每个成功男人的背后都有一个伟大的女人。因此，亲爱的人们，女性应在社会中享有应有的地位。

芬达的母亲继续在梦中和她说话。"你明天去农场时，不要跟随你的同伴去收割稻谷。拿走谷仓里的一点点谷粒。把它们弄干，在你丈夫回家的路上敲打它们。"第二天，芬达照做了。那天，坦巴去了农场。除了芬达，他向所有人打招呼。他刚吃了一个漂亮的年轻女人为他做的饭。在他回城的路上，他看到芬达在他面前敲打着一些稻谷。他轻蔑地吐了一口唾沫，然后恶狠狠地瞪了她一眼，走另一条路继续赶路进城。芬达一边敲打稻谷一边唱道：

坦巴，为了爱，我嫁给了你。

坦巴，为了爱，我忍受了苦难。

坦巴，为了爱，我卖掉了我的鸡。

坦巴，为了爱，我卖掉了我的山羊。

坦巴，为了爱，我卖掉了我的绵羊。

坦巴，为了爱，我才给你找了这么多女人。

坦巴，为了爱，我练就了耐心。

坦巴，为了爱，但事实证明你是个狡猾的人。

坦巴，为了爱，你现在为什么连老天爷都骗？

当芬达敲打完稻谷时，坦巴所有的财富，包括金钱、房子、家禽、绵羊、山羊、女人，都消失了。这就是忘恩负义的下场。

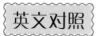

The Wages of Ingratitude

Once upon a time, there lived a couple, Tamba and Finda. They were as poor as a church mouse. Life was extremely hard for them. Even food to eat was difficult to come by. One day, Finda's younger sister, Bondu, visited her. She brought a fowl for her sister. Finda happily welcomed Bondu amidst their poverty. The former said, "We are not going to eat this fowl. I am going to rear it." She reared the fowl. No one knew that the fowl would be the source of their wealth. God always extends his mercy, love and kindness through some other persons to the receiver.

Within a very short period, the fowl laid many eggs which hatched into many, many chickens. The chickens grew to be nice and pretty hens and cocks. Tamba and Finda marvelled at God's wonders. They sold some of the cocks. They used the money to buy a flock of sheep and goats. They also reared the goats and the sheep. The sheep and the goats multiplied in millions. They sold some of these goats and sheep. They got so much money that they became the richest people in the whole world. People admired their life. They lived happily for many, many years.

One day Finda decided to marry a young lady to her husband. "I am growing old," she said. "I need someone to help me with the domestic work and keep my husband company." Finda got a beautiful lady for her husband. The girl became the center of attraction of the Tamba family; and Tamba's household was as large and populated as Sefadu and its environs. Life was sweet for the Tamba family; but more particularly for Tamba. He had enough of everything. His house was so full of beautiful young ladies that he soon forgot about his first wife, Finda. He had no time for Finda. Finda who was the source of his happiness was pushed to the background of everything. She cried day in and day out. Tamba never wanted to have a look at Finda. Her sight caused unhappiness and severe pain to him.

"Oh, what a horrible situation it is! I have never thought I would be treated in this way. I did all I could to make my husband happy, little realizing that he would turn his back on me," Finda said. She would cry and cry every day.

One night she dreamt a dream. In the dream her dead mother appeared to her and said, "I have been hearing all your woes. I am fed-up with the treatment your husband is giving you. Tomorrow, I will solve all your problems for you."

Let me remind you, my dear audience, that God is not partial. He loves us all; and he will make the necessary provisions for us. All you should do is to believe and trust in him. Men should not take advantage of women, irrespective of any heavy dowry they have paid for them. Women are part and parcel of us. They contribute a lot to our success. Behind every successful man there is a great woman. Thus, my dear people, women should be given their rightful place in society.

Finda's mother continued to speak to her in the dream. "When you go to the farm tomorrow, don't follow your companions to harvest rice. Take the little bit of rice grain you have in the barn. Dry it and beat it along the road your husband would walk to go back home." The following day, Finda did exactly what her mother told her. During that day, Tamba went to the farm. He greeted everybody except Finda. He ate a meal cooked by one of his beautiful young ladies. As he was on his way back to town, he saw Finda pounding some rice right in front of him. He spat contemptuously. He gave a nasty look to the woman; took another course, and continued his journey to town. Finda sang as she pounded the rice:

Tamba, it was for love that I married to you.
Tamba, it was for love that I endured hardship.

Tamba, it was for love that I sold my fowls.

Tamba, it was for love that I sold my goats.

Tamba, it was for love that I sold my sheep.

Tamba, it was for love that I got all these women for you.

Tamba, it was for love that I exercised patience.

Tamba, it was for love, but you have proved to be a slippery customer.

Tamba, it was for love, why do you now deceive even nature?

By the time Finda had finished beating the rice, all Tamba's wealth, including money, houses, fowls, sheep, goats, women vanished. That is all the more reason why ingratitude is not nice.

西非民间口头文学作品欣赏（塞拉利昂篇）

男孩和他的姐姐

男人正在专心地砍树，砍着砍着，一片木屑突然溅了出来，慢慢飘落到地面，顷刻间化作一位年轻丰满的姑娘，姑娘从地上站了起来。这位年轻美丽的姑娘生活在这个世界，拒绝了所有男人的求婚。她说不想找一个有任何瑕疵的男人。

直到有一天，一个魔鬼打扮得整整齐齐地走了过来。当他走近时，女孩说："哦！妈妈，我的如意郎君来了。"她母亲问："你想要嫁的人出现了吗？"她回答："是。"她母亲说："这是件好事。既然有了合适的人选，我希望你现在就结婚。"但是，她们不知道，这是一个会吃人的魔鬼。

为了欢迎男人的到来，她们抓了一只鸡煮给他吃。她们把食物送到他房间。男人挖了一个很深的洞，把一部分食物放进洞里，收拾好剩下的，让她们以为他吃了。夜幕降临之前，他们就住在一起了。晚上，他们共度良宵。

当这个女人准备要搬到她夫家的婚房去住时，她那有先知天赋的弟弟说："妈妈，我要陪我姐姐去她丈夫家。"但姐姐说："我不会带你去的。"男孩接着说："姐姐，让我跟你去吧。""我不会带你一起去的。"姐姐回答。她头顶着篮子和她丈夫一起出发了。

男孩看着他们离开。他们走的时候，男孩把自己变成了一枚漂亮的金戒指，躺在路上。姐姐走着走着，发现了戒指，说："亲爱的，我找到了一枚戒指。"他回答说："好吧，把它放进你的篮子里。"她把它放进篮子里。他们继续前行，走着走着，男孩说："姐姐，快把我放下来。你把我顶在头上已经有一段时间了。"她把他放下来，用鞭子打了他好几下，把他留在原地。

男孩又再次把自己变成一把精致的梳子，躺在路上。他们一到那儿，她就说："亲爱的，我捡到了一把梳子。"他说："好吧，把它放进去。"她把它放进篮子，然后他们继续赶路。男孩说："姐姐，快放我下来。今天你已经把我顶在头上很久了。"她又打了弟弟一顿。后来，那男人建议道："别管他。

如果你弟弟硬是坚持要和你一起走,那一定是有原因的。我们一起走吧。"

他在前面带路,他们继续前进,终于来到了魔鬼的家。在这个魔鬼的家里,有许多骷髅头在里面,挨挨挤挤的。魔鬼检查了他的房子。男孩打开门,对姐姐说:"姐姐,你看到了吗?愿上帝保佑,我得把你留在这里了。"姐姐吓得瘫倒在地上,乞求弟弟帮帮她。

晚上,要睡觉了,弟弟被安顿在房间的一个角落休息。男孩说:"你们睡哪里我就睡哪里!"于是,他们在床的一侧为弟弟另外准备了一个地方。魔鬼和他的妻子也要睡了。魔鬼给姐姐下了药,姐姐很快便睡得很沉。

魔鬼有一把斧子,磨快后可以砍任何东西;如果竖立着,它就会变得不那么锋利。男孩没有睡觉,他在暗中保护他的姐姐。趁姐姐睡着后,魔鬼悄悄地从床上爬了起来,拿起斧头在石头上磨锋利。

当他举起斧头要砍男孩的姐姐时,男孩说:

别睡了,天哪,别睡了。

(合唱)肯肯亚萨,别睡了;

那把沉重的斧头正在威胁我们的生命;

肯肯亚萨……

魔鬼只好走开了,把斧头放回原处。他问男孩:"你要做什么?"男孩回答说:"我不习惯在地上睡觉,只习惯睡在床上。"魔鬼急忙为男孩铺床。男孩躺下了。姐姐还在打鼾。过了很长时间,魔鬼站起来看着男孩。男孩假装闭上眼睛。魔鬼又举起了斧头。

就在他准备用尽全力剁向姐姐时,男孩再次说道:

别睡了,天哪,别睡了。

(合唱)肯肯亚萨,别睡了;

那把沉重的斧头来了。

肯肯亚萨。别睡了。

魔鬼只好又走开了,把斧头放回原处。他又问男孩:"又怎么了?"男孩回答说:"我好渴,但我只想喝网里的水,要用我们家乡的篮子去装。"于是,魔鬼拿着网和篮子去取水。去小溪的路很远,比去玛雅村还要远。魔鬼去取水了。男孩留下来叫醒他的姐姐:"醒醒,我整晚都在守护着你。你亲爱的丈夫想杀了你。"码头上有一艘船,那是魔鬼的船。男孩上了船,开始和姐姐一起划船,他们逃走了。当魔鬼试图用网把水捞上来时,水漏了出来,怎么也盛不满篮子。天快亮了。魔鬼回来了,听到了划船声:

哗哗哗

（合唱）哗哗哗

当魔鬼回到家寻找他们时，发现床上放着一个别的什么东西，突然应声倒地。

哗哗哗

（合唱）哗哗哗

在他们临走时，男孩拿着杵和研钵，把它们放在床上并盖上一块布，假装这是熟睡中的他们。魔鬼来了，说了声"帕扬"和"博克罗"，便转身出去了。

他脑子里快速地闪出了一些念头。他发现他们已经在海中央了。在他们即将到达陆地时，他甩出一个钩子。船的一端被钩住了。他开始把船拉近，然后开始唱歌：

凯克尔，来吧；凯克尔，过来哦。

（合唱）耶耶凯克尔，来吧；凯克尔，来吧；

耶耶……

女孩开始大哭起来，直到她弟弟把钩子割断。他们继续往前走，魔鬼甩出了他所有的钩子，都被弟弟一一砍断了。弟弟把船划到了岸边，和姐姐一起逃走了。

在他们计划逃跑时，男孩随身携带了一种果冻状液体、木炭和一块石头。这些东西都是他们逃跑途中用得上的东西。魔鬼不知道该怎么办。在追赶的途中，他撞上了一棵非常高大的木棉树，树倒了下来。魔鬼把它打造成一艘船。船造好后，他登上船，用手当桨。他的手发出了这样的声音："巴斯蒂亚·卡波纳。"他在海的另一边也登岸了。他紧紧跟着他们。那男孩继续和姐姐一起逃命。他们跑的时候，男孩把木炭扔了出去，霎时间，到处一片漆黑，魔鬼再也看不见路了。姐姐和他继续逃跑，在他们逃跑的方向有阳光。魔鬼在黑暗中四处游荡，后来他说："全能的上帝，你是创造奇迹的人；如果你是的话，请把这黑暗驱散，让我能看见我的妻子。"于是光出现了。魔鬼快追上他们的时候，男孩说："你丈夫来了。他离我们更近了。"姐姐说："弟弟，该怎么办？"弟弟回答说："亲爱的姐姐，不久前你还用鞭子抽打了我，不让我跟来。"姐姐恳求道："好弟弟，求你救救我，求你救救我。"魔鬼离他们越来越近了，他们扔下了石头。在他们身后，突然裂开了一道峡谷，魔鬼无法越过它。魔鬼只好沿着这条峡谷的一侧走，他拿起一根棍子，挖了一个洞，穿了过去。男孩说:"姐姐,你丈夫来了。他还在追赶我们。他现在离我们更近了。"姐姐说:"我们快走吧。"他们边走边把果冻状的液体倒在了路上。魔鬼一踩到那些东西,脚下一滑就滑倒了。在跌倒的一刹那,魔鬼发现自己躺在自己家的床上。男孩和他的姐姐终于回到了他们城里的家。

　　我的故事到此结束。

The Boy and His Sister

There was this tree that the man was cutting, cutting and cutting. A piece of it came out and fell down slowly. A very young lady with full breasts emerged from it and stood up. This beautiful young lady lived in this world. She refused to marry all the man who wanted to marry her. She would say she didn't want any man with a flaw.

This problem continued until one day a devil dressed himself up neatly and came. As he approached, the girl said, "Oh! Mother, my husband has come." Her mother asked, "Has your husband come?" She answered, "Yes." Her mother said, "It's a fine thing. As you have said your husband has come, I want you to be married now." This devil would eat nothing other than human beings. But they did not know this.

To welcome the man, they caught a fowl. A very mighty cock was cooked for the stranger. They took the food into the room. The man dug a deep hole, and put some of the food into the hole. He took the remaining food and arranged it so they would think he had eaten. Before nightfall they were lodged together. At night he entered the room with the lady and slept.

When the lady was getting ready to go to her married home, her younger brother who had the gift of second sight, said, "Oh, Mother, I will accompany my sister to her husband's home." But his sister said, "I will not take you along." The boy then said, "Sister, I will go." "I will not take you along," replied the sister. She took her calabash and went with her husband.

The boy was watching them as they left. As they were going, the boy changed himself into a nice gold ring and lay down on the road. As soon as the lady reached the place, she saw the ring and said, "Dear, I have found a ring." He replied, "Well, take it and put it in your basket." She took it and put it in her basket. They continued on the journey. As they were going, the boy said, "Sister, put me down. You have carried me on your head for a long time now." She got him down, flogged and flogged and flogged the boy, and left him on the road.

The boy continued again and changed himself into a very fine comb and lay down on the road. As soon as they reached there, she said, "Dear, I have found a comb." He said, "Well, take it and put it in." She took it and put it in and they continued to go. The boy said, "Sister, put me down. You have carried me on your head for a long time today." She gave him another beating, but later the man advised, "Leave him alone. If a child insists on travelling with you, there must be a cause. Let us go."

He led the way and they continued their journey, and arrived at the house of the devil. At the house of this devil there were many human heads packed in a room. The devil examined his house. The boy opened the door and called his sister and said, "Sister, do you see? But by God's grace, I will leave you here." The lady fell down on the ground begging her brother.

At night they went to sleep. A place was prepared for the boy in a corner. The boy said, "Where you sleep is where I should sleep." They prepared a place for him on one side, and the devil slept with his wife. He drugged the lady into a very deep sleep.

He had an axe which, when sharpened, would be able to cut anything; if left standing it would remain blunt. The boy did not sleep. He was guarding his sister. The lady was sound asleep. The devil got up carefully, took the axe and sharpened it on a stone.

As soon as he raised the axe to chop the lady, the boy remarked:

No time to sleep; oh me; no time to sleep;
Chorus: Kenke yasa; no time to sleep oh;
The heavy axe is disturbing us;

Kenke yasa …

The devil had to go away and put the axe back. He asked the boy, "What do you want?" He replied, "I'm not used to sleeping on the ground. I'm only used to sleeping on beds." The devil hastily prepared and spread a bed for the boy. The boy lay down. The young lady was still snoring. After a long time, the devil got up and watched the boy. The boy pretended to close his eyes. The devil took up his axe again.

As he was about to use his full strength to chop the young lady, again the boy remarked:

No time to sleep; oh me; no time to sleep;

Chorus: Kenke yasa; no time to sleep oh;

The heavy axe is coming;

Kenke yasa; no time to sleep.

The devil had to go away and put the axe back again. He asked the boy again, "What is the matter?" The boy replied, "I am feeling thirsty; but I only want to drink water that is fetched in a net and put into a local basket." The devil took the instruments and went. It was a long way to the stream. To travel there is farther then travelling to Mayombo Village. The devil went away to get the water. The boy remained to wake up his sister. "Wake up; I have been guarding you throughout the night. Your beloved husband wanted to kill you," said the boy. There was a boat at the wharf; it was the devil's boat. The boy got in the boat and started to row along with his sister, and they went. As the devil was trying to get the water with the net, it leaked out. It was almost daybreak. The devil returned and heard the rowing:

Gbafthi kalafthi

Chorus: Gbafthi kayifog

When he looked for them where he had left hem, there were other things there, which fell down with a sound.

Gbathi kalafthi

Chorus: Gbafthi kayifog

When they were about to go, the boy had taken the pestles and the mortars and placed them on the bed and covered them with a cloth. When the devil came, he said "Paryan" and then "Gbokro". He turned his back and went out.

He had some tricks in mind. He found them already in the middle of the sea. As they were about to reach the land, he stood and swung one of his hooks. The boat was drawn to one end. He started to draw the boat nearer, then he began to sing:

Kegkle, come on; makese kegkle, come on.

Chorus: Yeye kegkle, come on; makese kegkle, come on.

Yeye ...

The young lady started to cry loudly until her brother cut the hook. They continued to go and the devil used up all his hooks. All were cut by the boy. The boy rowed the boat to the land and he ran away with his sister.

When they were about to escape, he had taken with him a jelly-like liquid, charcoal and a stone. He had these things for the journey. The devil did not know what to do. When he came, he struck a very mighty cotton tree and it fell. He carried it hastily and made it into a boat. After he had made the boat, he boarded it and used his hands as paddles. It was his hands that sounded: "Basthiaya Kabona." He landed on the other side of the sea. He followed them. The boy continued to escape with his sister. As they went along, he dropped the charcoal and the place became dark. The devil could not see his way any longer. But there was daylight in the area where they were going. Both his sister and himself were escaping. The devil was just moving around in this darkness and he later said, "Almighty God, be it that you were the creator of miracles; and if you were, let this darkness be cleared off so that I can see my wife." The light appeared. As he was about to reach them, the boy said, "Sister, your husband is coming. He is nearer to us now." She said, "Brother, what's to be done?" He replied, "My dear, not long ago you flogged me so that I would not follow you." She pleaded, "Brother, I beg you to save me. Please save me." They were going, and the devil was getting nearer to them. They dropped the stone. They went and a hilly pavement sprang up. The devil could not cross it. He followed the side of this hilly pavement, took a stick and made a hole and went through it.

The boy said, "Sister, your husband is coming. He is still following us. He is nearer to us now." She said, "Let us go." As they were going, they dropped the jelly-like liquid on the road. When the devil reached the place, as he stepped on the road, he slipped and fell. As he fell, he saw himself lying on his bed in his house. The boy and his sister finally returned to their town.

This is the end of my story.

三兄弟

从前有对夫妻。女人做事非常敏捷麻利,她的丈夫非常钦佩她。他们在一起幸福地生活了很长一段时间,可惜的是,他们没有孩子。

后来,丈夫去世了。在他去世之前,他把妻子叫到身边对她说:"亲爱的,我们已经结婚很长时间了,但我们没能生下一儿半女。现在,我祈祷在我死后,上帝会给你一个比你更敏捷的孩子。"

丈夫去世三个月后,她嫁给了另一个男人。她很幸运地为这个男人生了三个孩子,都是男孩。第一个名叫布里马,第二个名叫阿卜杜拉,最小的名叫阿马杜。

孩子们长大后,母亲总是把他们叫到一起,问他们当中谁的速度最快、谁最敏捷。每个孩子都想向母亲证明自己速度最快。

老大是第一个证明自己的人。他家的房子后面有一棵苹果树,所以他决定从树上摘一些已经成熟了的苹果。他爬上了树。他没有一个一个地摘,而是摇了摇树枝,让苹果掉落下来。许多苹果掉了下来,就在苹果即将落地的一瞬间,他飞速地从树上下来,把衣服脱下来并摊开,让所有的苹果都落到了他的衣服上,没有一个掉落在地上。

老二说自己速度更快。于是老大向他提出挑战。正当他们争论的时候,一只老鹰正在他家的母鸡上空盘旋,母鸡刚孵出小鸡,正在外面找吃的。在老鹰俯冲下来抓到小鸡的一刹那,老二快速跑进房子,拿起一个篮子,不到一秒钟就把所有的鸡都捡起来放进了篮子里,并盖上了盖子。

最小的那个说:"我肯定比你们两个快。"两个哥哥向他挑战。一天,他和父亲一起去打猎,这时突然变天,眼看就要下雨了。他们在一片开阔地上,周围无处避雨。小儿子对父亲说:"等一分钟。我来试试做些什么。"他飞快地走进附近的灌木丛,用他的小斧头,砍了些木头。回来后,他找到了一片空地将木头放在那里。小儿子迅速行动起来,在雨点刚要落下来之前,就盖好了一间小屋。

在这三个男孩中,你认为谁的速度最快、谁最敏捷?

西非民间口头文学作品欣赏（塞拉利昂篇）

英文对照

The Three Brothers

Once there lived a woman and her husband. The woman was very fast and agile and her husband admired her very much for her agility. They lived happily together for a very long time, without having any children.

Some time later the husband died. But before he died, he called his wife and said, "My dear, we have been married for quite a long time now but we have not been blessed with any children. Now, I am praying that when I die the Lord will give you a child who will be more agile than you."

Three months after her husband's death, she married another man. She was lucky to have three children for this man, all boys. The first was named Brima, the second Abdulai and the youngest Amadu.

When they grew up, their mother would always call them together and ask them who was the fastest and most agile among them. Each one wanted to prove to their mother that he was the fastest.

The eldest was the first to try. There was an apple tree behind their house, so he decided to pick some ripe apples from it. He climbed the tree. Instead of picking them one by one, he just shook the branches and the apples fell down. Many apples fell, but before they fell on the ground, he had climbed down, removed his clothes and spread them out so that all the apples fell right onto his clothes. None fell on the ground.

The younger one said he was faster. So the eldest challenged him. While they were arguing an eagle was hovering over their hen which had just hatched its chickens who were out finding something to eat. Before the eagle came down to snatch one of the chickens away, he had run into the house, collected a basket, and within a second had collected all the chickens, put them into the basket and closed it.

The youngest one said, "I am sure I am faster than you two." So they challenged him. One day he went hunting with his father. While they were going, the weather suddenly changed. It was going to rain. They were in an open field and there was nowhere where they could take shelter. He said to his father, "Wait a minute. Let me try and do something." He hurriedly went into a nearby bush, took out his cutlass and cut some wood. He came back, cleared an area, and in no time built a hut for them before it began to rain.

Among these three boys, who do you think was the fastest and most agile?

谁会为我的死哀悼

（合唱）耶伦得，耶耶伦得，耶耶伦得耶耶
我丈夫坎约洛
坎约洛离开了我
我丈夫坎约洛
坎约洛离开了我
（观众）这是什么意思？
（故事讲述者）就是这个意思。

啊，那时候的财富！那时的财富意义重大，影响很大。

有一个叫坎约洛的人，非常富有。他有许多妻子和仆人。"如果我骗你，那我会说他有50个老婆，但我不是骗子，所以实话实说，他有200个妻子。"

除了妻子和仆人之外，还有许多其他人仰慕他。整个地区的一切都需要仰仗这位富豪。

有一天，坎约洛对自己说："我有这么多妻子要照顾。我想测试一下她们的真心，看看我死后谁会真正为我哀悼，谁是真正爱我的。"

富豪召集了村子里所有的长者，尤其是他信任的长者，并透露了他的意图。他告诉他们，他有一个计划，想测试出哪个妻子最爱他。他告诉长者们，如果哪天听说他死了，不用担心。于是，长者们各自回了家。第二天早上，有人来探望坎约洛时，发现他死了。那时，他所有的妻子都在各自的农场。仆人被派往周围所有的村庄给他的妻子们报信。按照习俗，他的每个妻子都哭着来了："孩子爸爸离开了我，孩子爸爸离开了我。"但她们没哭喊多久就走了。每个人都回到了自己的农场。其他人来参加同样的仪式，他们每个人都会说："让我去吃斋饭吧。我要吃我那份饭。"

她们中最年轻的一个在丈夫"去世"前本来请了假，去照顾生病的母亲，当她得知丈夫去世的消息时，她前来哀悼。她双手放在头上，开始哭泣："邦果邦果，要在婚姻中找到一个好丈夫并不容易——希亚邦果，我丈夫离开了我。"

耶伦得，耶耶伦得，耶耶伦得耶耶

我丈夫坎约洛，

坎约洛离开了我。

我丈夫坎约洛，

坎约洛离开了我。

她把丈夫抱起来，把他转来转去，伤心地哭着。

坎约洛离开了我。

我丈夫离开了我。

她叫道："坎约洛啊坎约洛！要在婚姻中找到一个好丈夫并不容易。坎约洛！我亲爱的丈夫，我亲爱的丈夫！"

我丈夫坎约洛离开了我。

我丈夫离开了我。

她把丈夫抱在胸前，继续唱道：

我丈夫坎约洛离开了我。

我丈夫已是一片枯叶。

牛儿来背走我丈夫，

来给我丈夫穿衣服。

她哭得死去活来，直到丈夫被感动。他开始发抖，几秒钟后坐了起来。富豪宣布："我复活了，我已经复活了，上帝要求我回到世上。"他召集了整个村子里的人，包括所有的妻子。他问所有在场的人："你们想知道我为什么这样做吗？"

他们都回答说："不知道。"

"我这样做是为了知道，哪个妻子爱我，在我死后会真心为我哀悼。"

坎约洛命令他的长辈们杀死一头最肥的母牛，为他们准备食物。这是一种祭奠，也是为了向其他人表明，最小的妻子目前是他唯一想要的妻子。富豪与其他所有妻子都离了婚，并要求她们立即返回到各自的家中。

坎约洛说，只要她们每个人遇到难处，他都会给她们奶牛、衣服等，给她们钱花，只希望在他死后，她们会为他哀悼。坎约洛还道出了他装死期间妻子们所说的话。他特别注意到她们中的一些人说："我要吃我的那份饭。"甚至有的妻子说："我要吃我留下的米饭，以后再来。"

因此,坎约洛责令那些人立刻离开他的家,最小的妻子除外。

我想问问各位听众:离婚是谁的错?是富豪,还是他的妻子们?

(听众)是妻子们。

英文对照

Who Will Mourn When I Die

Chorus: Yelen—nde, nde—yele—le nden, nden yelen nden nden

Kanjolo my husband

Kanjolo has left me

Kanjolo my husband

Kanjolo has left me

Audience: What does that mean?

Narrator: That means that.

Aa, riches in those days! Riches in those days meant much. They had great influence.

There was a man called Kanjolo who became very rich. He had many wives and many servants. "If I were a liar there would be fifty, but since I am not a liar, there were two hundred."

He had many other people who looked up to him apart from the wives and servants. The whole region depended upon this rich man for all its needs.

One day, Kanjolo said to himself, "I have such a large number of wives to care for. I want to test them to see who will really mourn for me when I die or who really loves me."

The rich man summoned all the elders, especially the ones he trusted, and revealed his intentions. He told them he had a plan and wanted to find out which wife loved him most. He told them not to worry if they heard he was dead. The elders left for their own homes. The following morning when

Kanjolo was visited, he was found dead. During this time all his wives were away on their own farms. Servants were dispatched to announce his death in all the surrounding villages as well as to his wives. According to custom, each of his wives came crying: "Father has left me. Father has left me." But this was only for a short while. Each returned to her own farm. Others came to perform the same ceremony and each of them would leave saying, "Let me go and eat my rice flour." Others would say, "Let me go and eat my rice."

The youngest of them all, who had taken leave of the husband before his "death" to attend her mother's illness came when she was told about her husband's death. With both hands on her head she started weeping, "I Bango, I Bango, it is not easy to get a good husband in marriage—Sia Bango, my husband has left me."

Yelen—nde, nde—yele—le nden, nden yelen nden nden

Kanjolo my husband,

Kanjolo has left me.

Kanjolo my husband,

Kanjolo has left me.

She lifted up the husband turning him here and there crying pitifully.

Kanjolo has left me,

My husband has left me.

She called, "Kanjolo—ee Kanjolo—ee aa! It is not easy to get a very good husband in marriage. My husband, my husband."

Kanjolo my husband has left me.

My husband has left me.

She raised the husband up to her chest and continued the singing:

Kanjolo my husband has left me.

Cold leaf my husband.

Cow my husband.

Clothes my husband.

She wept and wept till the husband was moved. The husband started shaking and a few seconds later, he sat up. The rich man declared, "I have been raised up. I have been raised up. God asked me to return to earth." He summoned the whole compound including all the wives. He asked all those present, "Do you know my motive for playing a trick like this?"

All of them answered, "No."

"I did it to test my wives, to know which of them loves me and would mourn for me when I die."

Kanjolo ordered his elders to kill one of the fattest cows to prepare food for them to eat. This was to serve as a sacrifice and to declare to the rest of the people that the youngest wife was now the only wife he wanted. He divorced all the others and asked for their immediate return to their own homes.

Kanjolo remarked that he had spent his money, given cows, clothes, etc. whenever each of them had a problem with the hope that, when he should die, they would mourn for him. Kanjolo revealed to them all the comments they had made during the time he pretended to be dead. He had noted especially that some of them had said, "I am going to eat my rice." Others said, "I am going to eat my rice which I left behind and will come later."

Kanjolo therefore ordered all of them to leave his house with the exception of the youngest wife.

The question now is: "The rich man or the wives, who was responsible for the divorce?"

Audience: It was the wives who were responsible for the divorce.

山　洞

"那啥，阿卡丽夏。都说你当观众的时候很认真，所以咱们才会在这表演，但瞧瞧你现在的表现！别的先不说，虽然你当观众的时候挺认真，但这儿为什么这么吵？这么吵让人来表演可不合适，今天咱们得定个规矩。如果有观众打断我说话，我们就不在这表演了，我们会到其他的地方去，这样的话，你们就谁也看不成了。"

真主创造了这一天。在柯兰科语里，我们将狮子称为"亚热"。有一天，突然乌云密布，狂风呼啸，乌云里积攒着瓢泼大雨，时刻准备倾泻而下，整个世界都仿佛笼罩在黑暗中，让人感到心惊胆战。

当大地上正在发生这一切的时候，狮子正在旷野里游荡。狮子想："行吧，去那山洞里边吧，就那个大山洞，我进里边躺一躺。"狮子一颠一颠地径直钻进了那个山洞。

狮子慢条斯理地躺下。他自语道："等风停雨歇了，我就走。"

正当狮子要躺下的时候，同样也住在旷野里的鬣狗也进来了。他想着："这样的风可真是少见啊，真担心大风把一棵树刮断，然后砸到我身上，把我这条小命带走。"

鬣狗一颠一颠地径直钻进了那个山洞。此时，洞里同时有狮子和鬣狗两只动物了。

该蟒蛇登场了。在曼丁哥，蟒蛇又被叫作"萨"，而在柯兰科语中被叫作"吞夫巴"，有些柯兰科方言里叫作"琦"。那条蟒蛇摩挲着爬行，和前两位一样径直爬进了那个山洞。

蟒蛇也感叹："真是少见的风！"他想："我的小命可别栽在这风手上。要是哪棵树被刮断了，那指不定就会砸到我身上，老天！我可不想白白丢了性命。风停雨歇之后我就出去，总能找到吃的。"

当这三位躺在洞里的时候，一只在柯兰科被叫作"克然"的小松鼠也悉悉索索地进来了。

小松鼠想："这风太少见了，周围都没有我以前挖过的洞，现在又来不及新挖一个，连树洞都没有见着一个。等会儿！我就进去那个大山洞里吧。"松鼠也径直钻进了那个山洞。

狮子说："瞧瞧，咱们四个都聚在这山洞里了，咱们属于不同的种群。今天，咱们就来聊聊别人做什么最冒犯自己吧，咱们可别互相冒犯。"

鬣狗、蝰蛇和松鼠都觉得狮子的提议不错。

他们对狮子说："你先进洞的，那就你先来说说什么事最冒犯你吧。"

"从现在起到雨停，但凡你们其中有一个敢盯着我看的，我就会被激怒。只要有一个敢跟我目光对视，你们就完蛋了。"

"嚯！"鬣狗说，"要想把头一直低着可不好办啊。如果连对方的脸都不能仔细看的话，那你和对方怎么能生活在同一屋檐下呢？"

"伙计，"其余动物对鬣狗说，"给咱们说说怎么才算冒犯你吧。"

鬣狗说："世上没人能冒犯我，除非这样。瞧好了，我浑身布满斑点，这是我的红斑点，这是黑的，倘若你们谁敢把泥点子溅到我这些斑点上的话，那就是在挑衅我，那样的话，啥事都有可能发生，那样做的人必须承担后果。把泥点子溅到我的斑点上就是冒犯我，谁都不许把泥点子溅到这些斑点上，谁都不许！"

"伙计，"其余动物对蝰蛇说，"跟咱们说说怎么会冒犯你吧。"

蝰蛇说："你们别看我现在躺在这里心平气和的，如果有人来来回回踩到我，我都不会生气，但哪个敢踩我的尾巴，就会惹火我！对不起，后果自负，我会缠在他身上勒死他。"蝰蛇宣告完毕。

其余动物对小松鼠说："说说怎么才算冒犯你吧。"

小松鼠说："这世上没人能冒犯我，看看我，跟你们比起来多么矮小。'把我当作最弱的对手，无视我的存在'就是对我的冒犯。"

狮子说："你们个个可真是刀子嘴啊。"

其他动物对狮子说："因为是你先进来洞里的，你先躺下吧。"

狮子躺到洞口处，面朝洞外，背对着洞里的其他动物，就像一扇门一样，把其他动物隔在洞里。

动物们对鬣狗说："你有地方躺了。"鬣狗躺到洞穴的中间，和狮子背朝背，像是中间的一道屏障。

他们又对蝰蛇说："躺下吧。"

蟒蛇伸长身子，头挨着洞穴的最里面，尾巴一直伸到外面的灌木丛里。"我宁可尾巴被淋湿也不愿意别人踩在上面。"就这样，蟒蛇也躺好了。

他们问小松鼠："你想躺哪里？"

小松鼠回答道："我去洞穴的最深处，也是最黑暗的地方，我就躺那里。"

早上，雨又开始下了，一直下了一整天，到下午的祷告时间过了也没停。风和雨也丝毫没有要减弱的样子。动物们陷入了窘境。

小松鼠说："真主伟大！这场雨今天是停不了了。"他们都在僵持和对他人的恐惧之中筋疲力尽了。

小松鼠说："天呐，我来挖个洞吧，也不知道情况会怎么样。"

小松鼠开始挖起洞来，稀里哗啦，一直挖到了大路上。他设计了一条能通向外面，能看到阴沉沉的天空的逃跑路线。

当小松鼠挖完洞后，他就有了一条地下通道。他从地下回到洞里，地道建好了。他看了看其他动物，又看向鬣狗，见鬣狗正在睡觉。他又返回他的地道里继续拱土。他看向狮子，见狮子也在睡觉。

山洞里流淌着滴进洞底的水，湿漉漉的，那就是松鼠要去拱土的地方。他用爪子和嘴拱着泥水，离鬣狗的头越来越近，抬起的后腿不小心朝鬣狗的头上溅了点泥点。

鬣狗的头上于是被泥点溅到了。

"主啊！我跟你说过，这是在惹我发火！除了你这只小松鼠以外，没人敢这样惹我。天呐，万能的真主，"鬣狗说着，"我今天非得把你这只小松鼠撕个粉碎不可！"

鬣狗在洞里搜捕小松鼠，他搜来搜去但就是找不到在哪。

松鼠早就偷偷地溜进了地道并把后头的入口堵住了，他也只能那样做了。松鼠进地道时会挖出自己的路线，并把泥土推到后面堵住身后的路，把地道堵得死死的。

鬣狗还在黑漆漆的洞里搜寻，但他找不到松鼠，他敲开一块又一块石头，而地道把松鼠藏得严严实实的，鬣狗根本看不见。

鬣狗愤怒地号叫着，他报复的欲望被打击了，他叫道："那只该死的小松鼠跑出去了吗？"

他过去狮子那边问，狮子说没看见。

他又去问蟒蛇，蟒蛇也说没看见。

他说："该死的小玩意！"

他走到洞外,在岩石上来回踱步,眼睛在旷野里搜寻着松鼠的踪迹。

此时狂风呼啸,雨倾盆而下。他找不到小松鼠,于是,又只好回到了洞里。

就在这时,他和狮子相对而视了。狮子说:"喂!喂!喂!我说过的,这是在惹火我!谁都不许看我的脸!等等,你根本不是在找松鼠,而是想要激怒我!"

狮子弓起背扑向鬣狗,把他撞向地面。鬣狗命殒当场,尸首被狮子留在原地。

狮子回到洞里的时候,一颠一颠地一不小心踩到了蝰蛇的尾巴,把蝰蛇的尾巴压进了泥里面。狮子经过那里想躺回他原先躺的地方,自信地面对着旷野,那是狮子的天性使然。

蝰蛇将身体蜷成一团,摩挲着,蓄势待发,说:"伟大的真主啊!我的创造者,我的主!我告诉过他们怎么会冒犯我,难道我没告诉过你谁也不准踩在我尾巴上吗?不论谁踩在我尾巴上都是在冒犯我。等等,这狮子根本不是在找鬣狗,而是在惹我,这狮子有意要惹我,你们都看见了,是他冒犯了我!"

蝰蛇舞动身体,将空气灌进体内,他越来越快地舞动着身体,然后把自己压缩成一个手肘的长度。他挺起头直盯着狮子的眼睛,又站立起来,整个身体鼓了起来,极其愤怒。他的头变得比身体其余部位还大,猛扑到狮子面前,咬了狮子一口。他把毒液注射进狮子的鼻孔里,随后掉落在狮子的爪子下。

狮子睁开眼。"谁咬我?"狮子叫道,"是你蝰蛇咬了我?"狮子张开口,咬住蝰蛇的背将其撕成三段。天呐!蝰蛇的尾巴还悬在他一侧嘴角,他吐掉残留在口中的那段。"哼!蝰蛇死了!"

下午祷告的时间前,黄昏时分,蝰蛇毒液侵入了并且完全损毁了狮子的肺。狮子一阵踉跄后也死了。天呐!狮子、鬣狗和蝰蛇都死了。

小松鼠掀开地道侦察情况,造成一切冲突的松鼠这才发现,蝰蛇、狮子和鬣狗都死了。

小松鼠说,"伟大的真主,我早说了,别小瞧矮个子!"

说完,松鼠便扬长而去。

亚当的子孙们,如果有人问你哪些因素会导致人的失败,告诉他——一个人可能败于他最弱的对手,因为你是那么容易地失去最可靠的盟友。

愿真主保佑亚当的子孙们,免于遭受不起眼的对手的算计。

英文对照

The Cave

"Oh, Alikaliya. It was said that we would come to stage the performance here because you are a good audience, but look at how you are behaving! Nevertheless, undoubtedly you are a good audience, but why this uproar? Such an uproar is not suitable for the task those people came to do. Today we will make a rule. We will not perform here today if these people recording are interrupted. Instead we will perform where they are lodging. Then no one will witness it."

This is what Allah did one day. In the Koranko language, we call the lion Yare. One day rain clouds gathered. A violent wind was blowing. The black clouds were heavy with rain. The world was clothed in darkness. Everyone was frightened.

While this was happening on earth, Lion was wandering in the wilderness. Lion thought, "Ah, ah, let me go to the cave, to that big cave. Let me lay myself down in the cave." The lion came daki, daki, daki and forced his way into the cave.

Lion laid himself down carefully. He said, "After the wind and rain have ceased, I will leave the cave."

While Lion was lying in the cave, Hyena came. Hyena also lived in the wilderness. He also thought, "Today's wind is exceptional. Let not the wind break a tree. Let not the tree fall on me. Let not the tree destroy my life."

Hyena came. Hyena came daki daki and forced his way into the cave. Living things in the cave numbered two.

Huge viper got ready. In Mandingo it is called Saa, and in Koranko it is called Tunfuba. Other Koranko dialects say Kee. That one also came crawling, mosososo, and forced his way into the cave with them.

That one also said, "The wind is exceptional. Let not the wind destroy my life. If the wind should break a tree, if the tree should fall on me. Let me not die in vain! When wind and rain have ceased, I will go out into the open. I will then find my food."

While those three were lying in the cave, a wee squirrel we call in Koranko Keran came yema, yema.

That one also said, "The wind is exceptional. Not one of my old holes is nearby, and I cannot dig a new hole now. There is no tree hollow nearby. Wait! Let me go to this big hole, this cave." That one also went and forced his way into the cave.

Lion said, "Ah, look, the four of us have found ourselves in one cave. We are not of the same species. Let us tell each other the greatest offence one can do against us. Let us not offend each other."

Hyena said, "Well spoken."

Viper said, "Well spoken."

Squirrel said, "Well spoken."

They all said, "Lion has spoken well."

They said to lion, "You first tell us what most offends you because you first entered this cave."

Lion said, "From now until the rain ceases, I will be offended if anyone, if anyone at all, looks me in the face. If any of your eyes meet mine today, you will be destroyed."

"Po! Eh!" said Hyena. "It is no easy task to always keep one's head low. How can you live in the same house with someone, if you cannot even see each other's faces?"

"Namu," they said to Hyena, "tell us your own offence."

Hyena said, "No one in the world can offend me except in this way. Look! I am spotted all over my body. I am spotted. My red spots are here and black spots are here. If any of you splashes mud on these spots, you will offend me. Then anything can happen. You must suffer the consequences. This is my offence. No person should splash mud on these spots. No one should dirty these spots."

"Namu," they said to the viper, "tell us the greatest offence against you."

Viper said, "Look at me, lying here peaceful and easy-going. Even if one repeatedly steps on me, I will not be offended. But if you step on my tail, you will offend me. In that event, you must suffer the consequences. I will fasten myself to your back." He finished his speech.

They said to the wee squirrel, "Tell us the greatest offence against you."

Wee squirrel also said, "Eh, no one in the world can offend me. But, look at me, so small among you." He said, "My offence is 'Do not underestimate your weakest opponent'. This is my offence."

Lion said, "Lie down, you sharp-tongued thing."

They said to the lion, "Because you first entered the cave, you first lie down."

Bin! He lay by the cave's entrance, similar to the door of this barrier. The other animals remained inside. Eh! He turned to face the wilderness with his back to the others who remained in the cave.

They said to Hyena, "You find a place to lie down."

Hyena laid himself down in the middle of the cave, similar to the middle of this barrier. He laid down with his back to the lion.

They said to Viper, "Lie down."

Viper stretched himself all the way to the corner of the cave with his tail out in the bush. "Even if rain falls on my tail, it doesn't matter as long as no one steps on my tail." So he also lay down.

They asked the wee squirrel, "Where will you lie down today?"

He answered, "I will go to the deepest part of this cave where the cave and the earth meet, in the dark there in the cave. There will I go to lay myself low."

It began to rain in the morning. It rained continuously the whole day until the time for afternoon prayers had passed. It kept raining. The wind and the rain never let up. This was their predicament.

Wee squirrel said, "Allah is great. This rain will certainly not end today." They were all completely exhausted from the strain. Lion was exhausted. Hyena was exhausted. The big viper was completely exhausted. Eh, my friends, they lived in fear of each other.

Wee squirrel said, "Eh, let me dig a hole. I do not know what the outcome will be."

Wee squirrel began digging, korote, korote, korote. He dug as far as from this barrier to the road. He made an escape route from which he could see the cloudy sky outside.

When he finished, he had a tunnel under the earth. Melete, melete, he slowly entered the cave from below. His tunnel was completed. He looked at the others. He looked towards the hyena and saw that he was sleeping. He went back into his tunnel to mix mud. He looked towards the lion and saw that he was sleeping too.

The rain water which was draining in under the cave was flowing in wuda, wuda, wuda. That is where he went to mix mud. He rolled and rolled the mud with his paws and mouth closer and closer to the hyena's head. He kicked up his hind legs splashing mud onto the hyena's head.

The hyena's head was spattered with mud.

"Allah is great! Did I not tell you that this is what offends me! No other person has offended me except this wee squirrel. Eh, Allah, the Almighty," he said. "I will crush this wee squirrel today!"

Hyena searched inside the cave for Wee squirrel. He searched and searched but he was not able to find him anywhere.

Wee squirrel had stealthily entered his tunnel and blocked off the back entrance. This was what he had done. When a squirrel enters a tunnel, he will dig his way through sending the mud back to block the path behind him. He closed off the tunnel completely.

Hyena kept searching inside the dark cave, but he did not see him. He knocked over stone after stone, covering completely the tunnel in which the squirrel was hiding so that he never saw him.

He cried. The hyena's desire for revenge had been frustrated. He said, "Has this wee squirrel gone out?"

He approached the lion to ask him. The lion said, "I did not see him."

He asked the big viper. He said, "I did not see him."

He said, "He is so small. So very small."

He went out into the light. He paced back and forth on the rock. He searched the wilderness.

All this time the rain was falling and the wind was blowing. He did not find the wee squirrel. He returned to reenter the cave.

Just at that moment, his glance caught the eyes of the lion. Lion said, "Ah! Ah! Ah! Did I not tell you that this is what offends me! That no one should study my face! Behold, you were not looking for the squirrel at all. You were trying to offend me!"

Lion tensed himself and pounced on the hyena dashing him against the ground. The lion killed the hyena. The lion left the hyena dead.

Approaching the cave; daki, daki, he stepped on the viper's, the big viper's tail, pressing it into the mud. He passed by to lie down in his place. That is what the lion did. He faced the wilderness. He was completely confident.

The viper coiled itself in readiness to spring, moin, moin. The big viper said, "Allah is great! Ah my Creator, my Lord. All have stated what offends me. Did I not tell you that no person should step on my tail! Whoever steps on my tail offends me. Behold, this lion was not looking for the hyena at all. He was trying to offend me. The lion intentionally offended me. Don't you see that he offended me?"

Ah, the viper puffed himself up. He inflated himself with air. He puffed himself up more and more. He shortened himself to an armspan in length. He raised his head up to look the lion into the eye. He drew himself up. He raised his head again to look at the lion in the eye. He drew himself up again. He swelled up, furiously angry. His head became bigger than the rest of his body. He struck directly in the lion's face. Ah! Eh! He bit the lion in the face. He injected his poison into the nose of the lion. He fell under the lion's feet.

The lion opened his eyes, "Who has struck me?" the lion said. "Is it the big viper that has struck me?" The lion opened his mouth. He snapped at the back of the viper, cutting it into three pieces. Gbado! The tail of the viper hung from one side of his mouth. He spat out the piece that remained in his mouth. "Eh! The viper died. Eh! Ah!"

Before the time for afternoon prayers, at about dusk, the viper's poison had reached the lion's lungs and destroyed them completely. The lion trembled. The lion also died. Eh, the lion also died! The viper was dead. The hyena was dead.

The wee squirrel opened his tunnel to observe what had happened. He who was the cause of all that commotion, found the corpses of the viper, the lion and the hyena.

The wee squirrel said, "Allah is great! Did I not say that you should not underestimate your weakest opponent!"

He went far away.

That is why, children of Adam, if they ask you what will cause your downfall, children of Adam, a person's downfall can be caused by his weakest opponent. Your weakest opponent can cause you to lose your good friends just that easily.

May Allah save the children of Adam from that disaster, from that action of their weakest opponent! Ah!

陷　阱

　　我们把我们所处的世界称为现代世界,一个被白人操控的世界。现今"陷阱"这个词是有不同种类和含义的,有时是针对"低等"动物的简单装置,但其含义也多种多样。我要给你讲述的这个故事发生在非常遥远的过去,一个你在白人的著作里的任何一页都找不到的过去。

　　很久很久以前,离镇子几英里的一幢农舍里住着一个老妇人,名叫娅耶诺。她住得有些偏僻,只有奶牛、山羊和公鸡与她做伴。在她房子不远处,有一个她经常照料的菜园子,她常从菜园子里采摘水果和蔬菜。在菜园子旁的灌木丛里,住着一只作恶多端的老鼠,他常常偷偷潜入娅耶诺的菜园子里糟蹋作物。娅耶诺为此很烦恼,她尝试了很多办法想要找出糟蹋庄稼的罪魁祸首,但每次都无功而返。娅耶诺对此束手无策,因为她实在找不出到底是谁在这样针对她。

　　一天,老妇人下决心用强硬手段来根除后患。她在菜园子里的土豆栅栏边设置了一个陷阱,希望能抓住肇事者,她想这样的话一定能抓住肇事者。老鼠看到陷阱后,认为那东西对他的生存是个威胁。他冷静下来,在脑海里不断思索要采取的对策,最终他得出结论,应该先找到奶牛、山羊和公鸡,和他们一起商讨办法。第二天一大早,老鼠就去找奶牛,对她说:"奶牛小姐,我得跟你讲个非常严重的事,跟咱俩都关系重大。有个陷阱被隐藏在菜园子里,正威胁着你、我和大家的安全呢!虽然说,我住在灌木丛里,但咱俩关系好,我看要不咱俩一起去跟老太太求求情,让她把陷阱给撤了吧。"

　　奶牛回答道:"老伙计,陷阱能奈我何?你看看我这脖子,啥样的陷阱在它面前都像笑话似的,我一点儿都不关心那儿有没有陷阱,我就不去跟老太太讲了,再见!"老鼠很失望,他鼓起勇气决定再去跟山羊谈谈这个问题。于是,他就跑到山羊面前说:"今天晚上咱来聊聊关乎你我的事,老太太在菜园子里设了一个陷阱,咱都有可能被它害了,咱俩一起去跟老太太求求情,让她把陷阱给撤了吧,你看咋样?"

山羊笑了笑,跟老鼠说:

"伙计,你在开玩笑吧?你觉得我会放着那些肥美的草料不吃,而去跟老太太要求撤掉这个陷阱吗?不管怎么样,那陷阱都不是我该担心的,那是你该担心的事,所以你就别指望我了。"老鼠的信念动摇了,一切于他都像是白费力气。但他还是没有放弃,决定再去跟公鸡谈谈这事。他找到公鸡,把跟奶牛和山羊讲过的话又跟公鸡重复了一遍。

公鸡吃惊地看着老鼠说:"我不懂你在说什么,难道你不知道那菜园子跟我八竿子打不着吗?我不用到那儿去找吃的,只要娅耶诺还吃饭,就有我吃的,你说的陷阱只是你头疼的问题,自个儿解决去吧。"

老鼠对三只禽畜的劝诱相继失败,他非常受挫,于是只能远离菜园子一段日子,试图找到绕过陷阱的办法。

一个阳光明媚的下午,眼镜蛇想去老妇人的菜园子里散步,享受一下那里的阴凉。在菜园子里,眼镜蛇想靠在土豆田里休息,不料触发了陷阱。他挣扎着想摆脱但无济于事。他突发奇想,退缩成一团,看似人畜无害,假装死了。整个下午他就躺在那里。正午时分,老妇人走进园子想摘点土豆叶当午餐,可怜的老妇人丝毫没有察觉到等待着她的是什么。她径直走向土豆田开始摘叶子。还没等她摘到一把土豆叶子,眼镜蛇的毒牙就咬到了老妇人的脚上。毒蛇的毒液飞快地侵入了她的身体,不到两分钟老妇人就一命呜呼了。

老妇人死亡的消息像野火一般迅速传遍了附近的村庄,不到一小时农舍里就聚集了几百人。老妇人是个德高望重的女士,养活了十双儿女,但都住在远乡。人们派人去给他们报信,孩子们和他们的家眷都赶回来见老妇人最后一面。根据习俗,必须为来吊唁的宾客准备丰盛的食物。于是,老大就向其他兄弟姐妹建议把奶牛给宰了。十兄弟身强力壮,很胜任这项工作。奶牛拼命挣扎反抗,但前后腿都被绑了起来,最后还是被宰了。其间,老鼠躲在离奶牛躺着等待被屠宰的地方不远处的角落里。老鼠朝奶牛叫道:

"奶牛小姐,现在你知道为什么我说那个陷阱也威胁到你了吧?你今天就等着被宰吧。没错,就是那个陷阱困住了咬死老太太的蛇;也正是老太太的葬礼导致了你被宰,要是你之前不那么自私的话,你现在的处境是完全可以避免的。"

奶牛很后悔没有听老鼠的话,但为时已晚,她被宰了。

接下来便是葬礼的第四十天,这天对死者来说最为重要,人们要向死者作最后的告别，所以老妇人的孩子们、朋友们和其他亲戚都参加了葬礼，又要准备食物了，这次轮到山羊了。山羊先被放倒，然后被宰了。在山羊被宰之前，老鼠跑到他跟前，说了他跟奶牛也说过的话。山羊很后悔没把老鼠的话当回事。

有一个老妇人的亲家是从很远的地方赶回来，所以到得很晚，当他赶到的时候，所有东西都被吃光了。家里人这时想起还有只公鸡，于是，就轮到公鸡被宰了。人们抓住公鸡，当公鸡被宰之前老鼠跑来跟他说：

"老伙计，现在你知道为什么要撤掉那个陷阱了吧，那个陷阱把你们都害了。你们都不知道事情会发展到这一步，自私可不是好事，这就是代价。"老鼠溜走了，然后公鸡就被宰了。

这就是为什么要听别人的话，因为你不知道你会掉进怎样的一个陷阱里，所以，做人啊，千万不能自私！

The Trap

We would like to call our world a modern world. A world in which we play with the white man's tools. Well, there are different kinds of traps today with their diverse implications. Times there were when traps were simple mechanisms aimed at "lower" animals, but the implications were also diverse. The story I am going to tell you happened in the very distant past, a past which you cannot find in any page of the white man's books.

A long, long time ago, an old woman lived in a farm house which was miles away from the town. She lived in a kind of seclusion. Her only company was her cow, goat, and cock. This woman kept a garden near her farm house. She used to get fruits and vegetables from this garden. Ya Yenoh was the name of this woman. She would tend her garden regularly. In the nearby bush lived a troublesome rat. This rat often quietly crawled into Ya Yenoh's garden and destroyed the crops. The woman could not understand how this happened. She tried different methods to find out who was destroying her crops but failed. Ya Yenoh became frustrated as she had no idea who was doing this to her.

One day the old woman decided to take desperate steps to put a stop to this wicked act. She set up the culprit by putting a trap on one of the potato beds. By doing this, she thought, the culprit would be caught. The rat saw the trap and knew it was a threat to his existence. He calmed down and debated in his mind what measures to take. He came to the conclusion that he should meet Miss Cow, Mr. Goat, and Mr. Cock to discuss this matter with them. The next morning the rat went to the cow and said, "Miss Cow, I have come to discuss a serious problem with you. This concerns us all. There is a trap in the garden and it is disguised. This is a threat to you and me and everybody else. Although I live in that bush, I am your friend. I want us to meet the old woman and plead with her to disconnect the trap."

The cow replied, "My friend, traps are not my business. Don't you see my neck? It is not meant for those funny things you call trap. It is not my concern and I don't care whether it is there or not, and I talk to no old woman about it: Bye Bye!" The rat was disappointed. He summed up courage and decided to discuss this issue with the goat. So he went to Mr. Goat and said, "I have come to you this evening to discuss something that concerns you and me here. There is a trap in the old woman's garden. Anyone of us can fall a victim to this trap. I want us to meet Ya Yenoh and plead with her to disconnect this trap. What do you think?"

Mr. Goat smiled and said to the rat:

"My friend, you certainly are not serious. Do you mean I will leave my rich grass here to go to talk to the old woman to disconnect a trap? In any case the trap is not my worry. It is your worry. So leave me alone." The rat's belief started dwindling. The whole thing seemed to him a fruitless endeavor. But he decided still to raise the issue with Mr. Cock. He met Mr. Cock and explained the situation to him as he did for Miss Cow and Mr. Goat.

The cock looked at the rat with amazement: "I don't understand what you are talking about. Don't you see that the garden is not my problem? I don't need to go there to get my food. As long as Ya Yenoh continues to eat rice, I will always eat. Your trap story is your own headache. Go to solve it yourself."

The rat failed to convince any of these three. He became frustrated. He decided to keep off the garden for quite some time, trying to see how he could circumvent the trap.

One sunny afternoon, Mr. Cobra decided to take a stroll in the old woman's garden to enjoy its cool atmosphere. In the garden, he was going to rest on the potato-bed when he got himself trapped. He struggled and struggled to release himself but to no avail. He stumbled upon an idea. He would recoil into a seemingly harmless mass and feign death. He was lying there that afternoon when the old woman came to the garden to get some potato leaves to prepare her lunch. Little did this poor old woman know what was in store for her. She went straight to the potato-bed and started picking the leaves. Before she could get a handful, Mr. Cobra drove his poisonous teeth into the woman's foot. The snake's poison ran into the old woman's body quickly. In less than two minutes the old woman was dead.

News of her death spread to the surrounding villages like wild fire. In less than an hour hundreds of people gathered in the farm house. She was a well-known woman, and raised ten sons and ten daughters, all of whom lived in distant places. They were sent for. The children and the in-laws all came to pay their last respects to the old woman. As was the custom, plenty of food had to be provided for the sympathizers, relatives and friends. So the eldest of the children suggested that the cow should be slaughtered. Ten able-bodied men were assigned the task of slaughtering the cow. The cow was confronted, knocked down and had her fore and hind legs tied. During this time the rat was hiding at a corner near where the cow was laid waiting for the butcher's knife. Mr. Rat called Miss Cow and said to her:

"Miss Cow, do you now see how the trap I told you about was your worry too? Today you are here waiting to be slaughtered. Well, it was the trap that caught the snake which killed the old woman; and it is the old woman's funeral which has occasioned your death. If you had not been selfish, your present situation could have been averted."

The cow regretted having ignored the rat's suggestion, but it was too late. She was slaughtered.

Then came the fortieth-day ceremony. This was the most important occasion for the dead. It was the time people were going to pay their very last respects to the dead in that manner. So the children, friends, other relatives all came to the ceremony. Again it was time for plenty of food. This time it was the goat's turn. He was also knocked down and slaughtered. But before he was slaughtered, the rat came to him and said to him the same thing he had said to the cow. The goat also regretted that he failed to take the rat seriously.

There was one in-law who came from afar and so could not come in time. By the time he arrived, all the food had been eaten up. The people then remembered that there was a cock. Then came the cock's turn. He was caught, but before he was killed, the rat came to him and said:

"My good friend, do you now see why it was necessary to get the trap disconnected? This trap has trapped all of you. You did not know it was going to happen this way. It is not good to be selfish. This is the reward for it." The rat went away and the cock was killed.

This is why it is good to listen to others, to be less selfish for you never know how you can come into a trap.

巴兰基乐手

很久以前，巴福迪亚的酋长邀请世界上所有的巴兰基乐手为他演奏。那些乐手齐聚到酋长的围场列成两队，一队在左，一队在右。

其中一个乐手迟到了，他走到一个可以俯瞰整个巴福迪亚的隐秘丛林里，在那开始演奏，等着被人听见。演奏的时候，他嘴里还哼着小曲：

舍瓦里，舍瓦里，你在哪儿？

货真价实的唐巴卡乐师来了。

听到丛林里传来的悠扬乐声后，人们感到很好奇，都认真地听着。这时，他又拿出他那把巴兰基，开始唱起来：

舍瓦里，舍瓦里，你在哪儿？

货真价实的唐巴卡乐师来了。

经过两次"心灵交流"后，他决定加入围场的另一队乐手。他一出现，酋长就对众人说："大家静一静！你们听到这篇迟来的乐章了吗？你们看到这大师级别的演奏了吗？"

人们纷纷找位置坐下，把舞台让给了他。他一登台就开始演奏起了巴兰基，并唱着：

舍瓦里，舍瓦里，你在哪儿？

舍瓦里，舍瓦里，你在哪儿？

这是真的，我的孩子们。

这是真的，我的孩子们。

我从唐巴卡被邀请

到此演奏。

他在吟唱时，其余巴兰基乐手也随着一起和声唱道：

静静听，静静听，孩子们。

静静听，静静听，孩子们。

此时此地，舞台属于他一个人。他低吟浅唱，众乐手和声而歌：
舍瓦里，舍瓦里，你在哪儿？
货真价实的唐巴卡乐师来了。
后来者居上，迟到者最终成了全场的焦点，并被酋长授予了最高的奖赏。

英文对照

The Balangi Players

Once upon a time, balangi players all over the world were invited by the chief of Bafodea to play for him. They assembled at the chief's compound and took their positions at two ends, one set on the left and the other on the right.

One of the balangi players arrived late. When he got to the secret forest that overlooked Bafodea, he started to play, waiting to be received. He accompanied his music with a small song:

Where has Sewali been?

Where has Sewali been?

The real musician from Tambaka has come.

Upon hearing his music, the crowd became curious and listened attentively. He struck his balangi again and started to sing:

Where has Sewali been?

Where has Sewali been?

The real musician from Tambaka has come.

After the second "communication" he decided to join the other musicians at the chief's compound. When he finally appeared, the chief said to the assembly, "Silence! Can you all hear the music of this late arrival? Can you see how expertly he plays?"

People took their seats, and he was soon made to take the floor. No sooner did he appear on the stage than he started to play his balangi and to sing:

Where has Sewali been?
Where has Sewali been?
My children, it is true.
My children, it is true.
I've been invited from Tambaka
To come and play.

While he was singing the other balangi players joined in the singing with him:

Children be quiet, quiet, quiet.
Children be quiet, quiet, quiet.

The stage became solely his, and he sang on and on with the other musicians reechoing him:

Where has Sewali been?
Where has Sewali been?
The real musician from Tambaka has come.

Though he came in last, he stole the show and was given the first prize.

嫉 妒

很久以前,一个人教导他的儿子说外面的世界很险恶,但是他儿子偏偏坚持要去外面的世界看看。

男孩是他的独生子,他对儿子说:"孩子,你知道,我就你这么一个儿子,就别出远门闯荡了。"

男孩央求道:"爸爸,行万里路胜过读万卷书,您就让我去吧。"在儿子的百般央求下,老父亲最终还是应允了。

老父亲说:"好吧,你打算什么时候动身?"

男孩回答:"起码要三天之后吧。"

老父亲说:"好吧,你走的时候告诉我一声,我还得教你点外出闯荡的智慧。"

男孩动身的那天对老父亲说:"爸爸,我今天就要走了。"

老父亲问:"今天就走吗?"

男孩回答:"是。"

老父亲说:"行吧,你在路上的时候,遇到跟你搭讪的,他们的要求你都别拒绝。"

男孩问:"您说的'跟我搭讪的'是指什么?"

"任何生物,不管是一只蚂蚁、蜜蜂也好,大象也罢,只要跟人一样能喘气的都算。记住我跟你说的,跟你搭讪的东西,即使再吓人你都别怕。"

"我记住了。"说完男孩就出门了。

他走了一整天,最后走进了一片小树林,地面上堆积满了枯叶,覆盖了整个地面。他刚踏上落叶堆的时候,一队白蚁突然探出头来。

男孩问道:"你们是谁啊?"

那队白蚁回答:"我们就是我们,我们打算跟着你了。"

男孩又问:"你们埋在枯叶下面怎么能跟着我呢?"

那队白蚁回答:"先把你背着的行囊放下吧。"

男孩刚把行囊放下,那队白蚁就趁他不注意涌入其中。他捡起行囊继续赶路。走着走着,碰上了一段倒下的树干,横亘在路上,边上有条大蛇,乌黑的大蛇慢悠悠地晃着脑袋。正当男孩要越过树干的时候,看见了那条大蛇,他大叫起来:"好大的蛇啊!"

蛇对他说:"蛇有什么好奇怪的,我现在要跟着你了。"

男孩说:"你长得这么可怕,怎么能跟着我呢?"

蛇说:"我不会靠近你的,你把行囊放下。"

男孩立即回想起父亲的教诲,于是把行囊放下,那条蛇哧溜一声就钻进去了。男孩见此,不敢将行囊捡起来了。蛇察觉到后,就对男孩说:"你把行囊捡起来吧,你感觉不到我在里面的,但是我又确实跟你一起赶路,你甩不掉我的,你怕的时候就颠一颠行囊,你会发现就跟我没在里面一样。"

男孩捡起行囊,发现里面的确跟什么都没有似的,他就带着这条身轻如羽的蛇一起赶路了。

他走着走着,又碰上一个蚁巢,里面住着成千上万只蚂蚁。正当男孩感叹"好壮观的蚁巢啊!"时,那些蚂蚁回答:"蚁巢有什么好感叹的,我们现在要跟着你了,你把行囊放下来。"

男孩不可置信地问:"你们全部都要进去吗?"

蚂蚁们回答:"对啊,把行囊放下来吧。"

他放下行囊,男孩看不出蚂蚁们有什么动静。男孩问道:"怎么样了?我可以走了吗?"

蚂蚁们说:"我们进来了,走吧。"

男孩继续赶路,一直走,最后到了一座城里。他去拜访了那座城里信奉异教的一位酋长,作为客人,男孩慢慢地得到了那位酋长的赏识。酋长让男孩自报家门,男孩回答过后,把自己的理想和未来抱负也一并告诉酋长。

酋长有一个传令官,叫迦巴涅。酋长非常重视传令官的谏议,丝毫不敢轻视,以至于传令官似乎可以左右他的命运和地位。但是,酋长太欣赏男孩了,男孩一旦不在场,他就连饭都吃不下。

每次酋长吃饭的时候都会传唤男孩一起陪同就餐。通常去传唤男孩的就是传令官迦巴涅。可是,迦巴涅看男孩不顺眼,在男孩来之前他还能从酋长的残羹剩饭里捞点好处,但现在自己什么都捞不着了,因此,他对男孩心生嫉恨。每次去传唤男孩的时候,迦巴涅都要发发牢骚:"这算啥事儿啊?这年头，人没饿着就烧高香了！可那小孩儿就跟酋长娶的小老婆似的。"

他见到男孩就说："小伙计，老头儿又叫你去陪着一起吃饭了，你去不去？其实你不饿吧？你现在该去睡了。"

男孩会回答："不不不，老伙计，我会去。"他不仅会去赴宴，还每次都胡吃海喝。就这样，男孩成了迦巴涅的眼中钉。迦巴涅开始暗自盘算要怎么除掉男孩。

有一天大清早，迦巴涅跑去酋长那儿敲门说："老爷，您得做点取舍，否则就大难临头了。小的我刚听到神谕，说要您叫身边的外人把城里的那棵木棉树移走，一片叶子都别留，这样您既能升官发财，又能在位子上坐得稳。"

那棵木棉树大得四个大人合抱都围拢不过来！酋长急得焦头烂额，他对迦巴涅说："你呀！你的谏议我又不能不听，否则我的脑袋和官位都难保！你说祖先们要咱们找个外人把木棉树移走？但你说说，除了那个来做客的小伙子，我还有啥'外人'在？"

"您让他试过了吗？他也没说不行啊。"迦巴涅说道，"老爷，如果您觉得这事儿无关紧要的话，那您就当我没说。"

酋长立即说："既然你这样说的话，那我真得试试了。"

酋长把男孩叫过来并对他说："城里有棵木棉树……咱们要举办一场庆典，你又是刚来的外人，外人来了就必须把那棵木棉树移出城，做不到的话就得处死。"

男孩叫了起来："什么！这可事关重大，我得好好想想。"

男孩回到住所，在房间里神情恍惚地站着。白蚁们看到他魂不守舍的样子，就对他说："我们早就知道会发生这事，所以我们才会跟你过来。去告诉他们，你办得到。告诉酋长你答应了，破晓前你还找得到那棵木棉树的话，就当我们白跟着你了。"

男孩于是回到酋长跟前说："老爷，您要我办的事，我答应了。"

迦巴涅神情兴奋，他挽起长袍的袖子，拿着一把他用来赶身上苍蝇的小拍子，跟酋长说："老爷，我告诉过您，咱所有人都觉得那个小伙子能把木棉树连根拔起，从来就没怀疑过他！"

男孩回到房里，当天晚上白蚁们就把消息传到了马可尼、蒙罗维亚、加纳和世界的每个角落，把所有的白蚁都召集到了城里。他们爬到木棉树上把枝叶都啃光了，钻到根部又啃了一遍，每次把肚子填满了就跑去林子里去排泄掉再回去接着啃。整棵木棉树三下五除二就被白蚁们啃食光了。

不久后,迦巴涅又有了新的坏点子。他对酋长说:"老爷,您要举办庆典,但我很担心您的安全,神谕说有六桶芝麻被撒在城里,要您的外人小伙子一粒一粒捡起来,放到庆典的宴会上。"

男孩又被叫去了,并被告知:"小伙子,这就是我们这次给你的任务。"

"我想想吧。"男孩说。

在回住所的路上,他连逃跑的打算都有了,但蚂蚁们告诉他:"别想着逃,既然我们跟着你,就不会让你出洋相,你先安心睡吧。"

设宴台被里里外外打扫了一遍。

"明天早上的时候,芝麻粒必须都堆在这里。"城里的长老们说。

迦巴涅很确信芝麻被撒在了各个角落——垃圾堆里、稻谷壳里,到处都有。整整六桶啊,迦巴涅已经迫不及待想将男孩置于死地了!

伟大的主啊,蚂蚁们不知道从什么地方冒出来了,出现在城里的各个角落。每只蚂蚁只带两粒芝麻就把六桶芝麻都放到了举办宴会的地方。

蚂蚁们跑去跟男孩道别。"我们之所以会跟着你就是因为这件事,现在我们该走了。"

"你们已经帮我完成任务了吗?"

"是的。"蚂蚁们回答道,然后就走了。

第二天,迦巴涅又对酋长说:"让您的女儿加入邦多会吧。"那是酋长最疼爱的女儿,邦多会接纳了她。邦多会的新人通常会在毕业典礼结束时被带到宴会上。现在轮到蝰蛇登场了,它将为男孩在城里赢得了极大的尊重。

蝰蛇趁着夜色行动,藏在设宴台的步梯下,待会儿新人会聚在设宴台上。新人不一会儿就要到了。除了酋长的女儿外,所有人都平安无事。正当酋长的女儿迈出脚要登台阶的时候,蝰蛇咬了她,她重重地从台上摔了下来,当场就香消玉殒了。蝰蛇当即就消失得无影无踪,溜回了男孩的房里。

太可怕了!迦巴涅当即就提议,或许只有男孩能让酋长的女儿起死回生。酋长大怒:"什么!这只有万能的上帝才能做到。"

"如果您真这样认为,那我也没办法了。"迦巴涅一边说着,一边用手里的布条赶着苍蝇。

酋长说:"去把那个小伙子叫来,要是他做不到的话,我就杀了他!"

当男孩到了那里,众人告诉他:"酋长的女儿被蛇咬伤离世了,而你这个外人必须做到我们神谕里所要求的一切。为了人与人之间的和平相处,我们需要你帮帮我们。你要是没帮到的话,我们就只好杀了你。我们也不愿意看到那样,你就尽力吧,小伙子。"

"我可不是神,"男孩告诉众人,"请给我点时间,我马上就回来。"

他一回到房间打开门,蟒蛇就说:"我早就告诉过你了,回去告诉他们,你能办得到。你要征求他们的同意,把女孩的尸体带到这儿来。"

男孩回去说:"我能帮你们,但是一定要把尸体放在我房间里。"

迦巴涅在前面豪横地开道,领着后面抬着尸体的一队人到了男孩的房间。蟒蛇在房间里和女孩的尸体待了一整夜。拂晓时分,蟒蛇对着尸体不停地吹气,酋长女儿慢慢苏醒过来了。男孩一直坐在旁边看着她。

酋长得知情况后,就把他所有的臣民都召集到城里。他叫人把三张吊床挂在宴会的正中央,分别是为男孩、酋长的女儿和他自己准备的。酋长认为,是时候把女儿从男孩房间里迎到宴会上了,他将在那里召开臣民大会。当酋长女儿从房里出来的时候,现场顿时爆发出了雷鸣般的掌声,那掌声的回声至今依然在世界各个角落里回荡着。

城里有几个克里奥尔人,他们有时会带着善意插手别人的事,他们目睹并记录了城里发生的一切,他们用克里奥语写了一首歌。他们说:"小人的阴谋让男孩儿差点颜面扫地,但终究未能得逞。那奸诈小人已经成了个笑话,最后的赢家还是那个男孩。"

他们用克里奥语唱道:

奸人输矣良人胜,罔罪害人未能成。

奸人输矣良人胜,罔罪害人未能成。

英文对照

Jealousy

Once upon a time, a man gave some wisdom to his son. The boy insisted on going out into the world.

He was the only child the man had and his father said to him, "Son, you know that you are my only child. Please, do not go away." And he boy replied, "Dad, if one does not go out into the world one cannot gain wisdom. So, please let me go." The boy pleaded with his father who eventually agreed.

"Well," said the father, "When would you like to leave?"

"It will not be today, or tomorrow, or even the day after," said the boy.

"Well, whenever you decide to leave, let me know so that I can give you some wisdom to take along," the father said.

On the day he wanted to set out, the boy said to his father, "Dad, I am leaving today."

"Are you leaving today?" asked his father.

"Yes," replied the boy.

"Well," said the father, "if on your outward journey you come across any creatures that speak to you, do not refuse their request."

"What kind of creatures do you have in mind?" asked the boy.

"Anyone, so long as it breathes air in and out as human beings do. It could be an ant, a bee, or an elephant, any kind. Please remember what I have told you. Do not be afraid however frightening the creatures may be."

The boy said, "I won't forget." And he left.

He walked all day long until he entered a little forest where dry leaves formed a carpet on the ground. As soon as he stepped on the leaves a swarm of termites suddenly came to life.

He asked, "What are these?"

And the termites said, "We are the ones. We are coming along with you."

"But how can you come along when you are buried beneath these dry leaves?" He asked them.

"Put down the bag you are carrying," the termites said.

He put the bag down and they trooped into it without his taking any notice. He picked up the bag and continued his journey. As he went along he came upon a tree trunk which had fallen across the path. Just by the trunk lay a huge cobra. The black snake moved its head very slowly. As he tried to jump over the trunk he saw the snake and shouted, "What a snake!"

The snake said to him, "Do not shout 'what a snake'. I am coming along with you."

"But how can you come along, when you are such a terrifying creature?" asked the boy.

"I am not coming near you," the snake said to him. "Put down your bag."

The boy, suddenly remembering his father's words, put the bag down. The huge snake slithered into it. When the boy saw this he was too afraid to pick up the bag. The snake noticed this and said to him, "Pick up the bag and you will discover I am not in it. But I will be going along with you. You are not leaving me behind. If you are afraid of me, just lift up the bag and you will discover I am not in it."

The boy picked up the bag and found that there was nothing in it. He went along with the invisible snake in the bag.

As he continued the journey, he came upon millions of ants in a large nest. As soon as he exclaimed, "What a huge thing this is!" The ants retorted, "Don't say 'what a huge thing this is'. We are coming along with you. Put down that thing you are carrying."

The boy asked them in disbelief, "You mean the whole lot of you?"

They said to him, "Yes. Just put the bag down."

He put it down. He did not see them move, so he asked, "What is the matter? Shall I go?"

They said to him, "We are already in the bag. Let us move along."

He continued his journey until he eventually arrived in a certain town. He went to the chief who was a pagan chief who came to like the boy who was now his guest. Questions were put to the stranger: "Where do you come from? What is your father's name? What is your name?" He answered them all. He also told the chief of his dream and mission.

The chief had a special informant called Gabanyei and he always acted on Gabanyei's adivce. If he should dare to ignore the informant's advice, the chief would lose either his life or the chieftaincy. The chief, however, came to like the stranger so much that he would not have his meals except with the stranger.

Everytime the chief had some food he would send for the stranger to come and have the "guest meal". The chief's informant was usually the one who was sent to call the stranger and Gabanyei did not like him. Until now he had always benefited from the left-overs after the chief had eaten. Now there were no left-overs. So, Gabanyei developed a great dislike for the stranger. He would grumble as he went along to call him, "This is something. One should thank one's stars if one does not grow thin these days! The old man has got a queen."

When he found the stranger he would say to him, "Friend, the old man invites you to have supper. Are you coming? You are already full, aren't you? You want to go to bed, don't you?"

The stranger would always say to Gabanyei, "No, no, my friend. I am coming along." And he would go and eat the food and consequently became Gabanyei's bitterest enemy. Gabanyei started thinking up plans to get rid of the stranger.

One day he went to the chief. It was very early in the morning. Knocking at the chief's door, he said, "Father, Chief, old one, you must offer some sacrifice to save your life. We have consulted the oracles and they say the cotton tree in this town must be removed. This must be done by a stranger living with you. There should not be a single leaf lying about. This must be done by a stranger living with you if you are to enjoy a prolonged and prosperous chieftaincy."

The cotton tree was so huge that four men joining hands together would not cover its circumference! The chief was really worried. He said to Gabanyei, "You, whose advice I must take or else lose my life or the chieftaincy! You say you have consulted the forces of the underworld and they have requested that this great cotton tree be removed by a stranger? Do I have any stranger here, apart from the young man who has been my guest?"

"Have you tried him, and has he said he cannot do it?" asked Gabanyei, "Old one, if you want to take this matter lightly I shall not bother you again."

The chief then said, "If you say so, I shall try and see."

The stranger was sent for, and the chief said to him, "It is this cotton tree we would like … We have to perform some ceremonies and you are the stranger here. It is a stranger who must remove the cotton tree from this town. If he fails he will be put to death." "What!" exclaimed the stranger. "This is going to be terrible. Let me think over it."

He went back to his house. He stood clumsily in the room. The termites noticed his uneasiness and said to him, "We knew this would happen. That was why we followed you. Tell them you can do it. Go and say to the chief, 'Old one, I agree.' If by the break of day you find the cotton tree in the town don't believe that we ever followed you."

So, he went back to the chief and said, "Father, I consent to do what you ask of me."

Gabanyei was in high spirits. He pulled up the sleeves of his country cloth gown and said to the chief, "Father, didn't I tell you? Everyone of us is believing that fellow can uproot the cotton tree; never doubt him!" He had a little broom with which he used to drive flies off his legs.

The stranger went back to his room. That night the termites sent out messages to Makeni, Monrovia, Ghana, everywhere in the world summoning all termites to assemble in this town. They descended on the cotton tree and ate up the leaves and branches, moved down to the roots, and than ran up again. When they had eaten their fill they ran to the forest and deposited their waste there and came back to eat more. They ate up everything.

Not long after, Gabanyei thought out a new plan. He said to the chief, "Chief, you are to perform some ceremonies. It is for your safety that I am concerned. The oracles have pronounced that six bushels of benniseeds be scattered around the town. Thereafter, your stranger should pick up every grain and deposit it in the barrie."

The stranger was sent for again. They said to him, "Young one, this is the task for you."

"Let me think it over," he said.

When he went back to his house he made up his mind to run away, but the ants said to him, "Do not run away. We did not follow you to see this happen. Go to bed."

The barrie was thoroughly swept.

"Tomorrow morning, let the benniseeds be found here," said the elders.

Gabanyei ensured that the seeds were thrown in all directions: in refuse heaps, among rice husks, everywhere. All the six bushels. He was eager to have the fellow killed.

Ants, gracious Lord, ants from away unknown places appeared all over the town. Each of them took only two grains and the six bushels were deposited in the barrie.

Then they went to the stranger to say goodbye. "It was for this task that we followed you. We beg to leave."

"Have you finished already?"

"Yes," they replied. And they left.

The next day, Gabanyei said to the chief, "Initiate your daughter into the Bundo society." It was the chief's favourite daughter. The girl was initiated accordingly. Bundo initiates are usually brought to the barrie at the end of the ceremony and what is going to happen now is the part played by the snake which earned the stranger great respect in the town.

The cobra moved in the cover of darkness, lay waiting at the doorstep of the barrie where the initiates would assemble. Soon they began to arrive. All the initiates, except the chief's daughter, arrived in the barry safely. As soon as the chief's daughter stepped outside, the snake bit her and she fell down and died. The cobra immediately disappeared. It returned to the stranger's room.

What a terrible thing! Gabanyei at once suggested that the stranger should bring the dead back to life. The chief said, "What! You do not believe that this is the work of God?"

"If you say so, I will wash my hands of it," said Gabanyei and he drove flies off with the piece of cloth in his hands.

The chief then said, "Go and call the stranger. If he doesn't perform this task, I shall kill him."

When the stranger came, they said to him, "It is the chief's daughter that has passed away. She has just been bitten by a snake. But you have to do with enquiries we hold with the oracles. It is in the interest of good neighbourhood that we ask you to help us. But in such matters we would kill anyone who failed to help us. This is the only sorrowful part of it. Young man, do your best."

"I am not God," he said to them. "Please give me time; I will be back soon."

As soon as he came back to the bedroom and opened the door, the snake said, "I told you of this a long time ago. Go and tell them you can do it. If they agree, bring the corpse here."

The stranger went back and said, "I can help you, but you must take the corpse to my room."

Gabanyei, walking majestically, led the group with the corpse. All night the corpse stayed in the room with the snake. At dawn the snake blew in the mouth of the corpse and the girl rose up. The stranger sat looking at her.

When the chief learnt of this, he summoned all his subjects to the town. Three hammocks were brought to the center of the feast: one for the stranger, one for the girl, and one for the chief. The chief thought it was time to convey his daughter from the stranger's room to the feast where the chief had summoned all his subjects. When the girl emerged from the room there was such thunderous applause that even today it echoed in the world.

There were Creoles in this town. The Creoles sometimes interfere in other people's matters with good intentions. They had seen and taken note of all that had been going on in this town. They composed a song about it in Krio. They said, "The stranger was nearly disgraced, but the plan did not work. The enemy has been put to shame. The enemy has been put to shame. The stranger has won the case."

They sang this song in Krio.

The enemy has been shamed, the enemy has been shamed;
Oh the enemy has been shamed; daddy stranger has won the case.

饥 荒

从前，有一个国家遇上了饥荒，短尾蜘蛛和短尾兔子也生活在那儿。蜘蛛忍受着煎熬，但是兔子看上去悠然自得，甚至还越来越胖了，蜘蛛也发现兔子的肚子总是撑得满满的，还在一天天地变大。

每当蜘蛛央求兔子带他去找点食物时，兔子都答应第二天一大早带他去。蜘蛛就回到家里耐心等着，等到第二天天还没亮，蜘蛛就到了兔子家里把他叫醒。

兔子蹦起来，满腹牢骚地说："哎呀，这也太早了，六点的时候再说。"蜘蛛就爬到房子的外面，抓起一个桶连敲了六下，然后跑回去对兔子说："六点啦，咱们走吧。""等会儿，我还要给孩子们喂水喝。"兔子又说。

蜘蛛又跑出去，提起一个桶就去井里舀水，高声叫道："第一个来喝水的孩子就是我！第一个呐！你看看你，怎么才来？我是第一个，听见没有？"

"兔子啊兔子！"他边跑边叫。兔子就在那里一动不动站着，告诉蜘蛛等到鸡叫的时候再说。蜘蛛又跑到外面学起了鸡叫。

最后兔子妥协了。"好吧，你实在是太烦了，咱们走吧。"

他们就上路去找吃的了，但在找到吃的之前要先挨魔杖的打。要吃到多少盘米饭取决于他们挨魔杖打了多少下。兔子走上前去讨打，魔杖立即狠狠地打了他两下，然后把两盘米饭给了他，很快就被吃掉了。

蜘蛛眼珠子一转。他问兔子是不是说再大的数都行，兔子说没错。蜘蛛沉浸在喜悦中，想象着他要吃到肚子撑不下。于是，就莽撞地上前去要讨打二十多下。魔杖重重地落下，打在他身上一下又一下，打到十几下的时候，蜘蛛已经疼得满地打滚，死去活来般地号叫着。

那根魔杖像人一样能察觉到周围发生了什么，当他察觉到蜘蛛因剧痛而尖叫时，魔杖就停下来回到原来的位置。这时，兔子冲蜘蛛大喊："说一个小一点的数你就能吃上了！"蜘蛛只好听从，讨了三下打。蜘蛛被打了三下后，汗流浃背地坐下来，得到了三盘米饭。

Famine

The country where Bra Spider and Bra Hare lived was hit by famine. Though Bra Spider was suffering, Bra Hare didn't seem affected. He was even growing fatter and fatter. Bra Spider had been noticing that Bra Hare was always "bellyful"—his belly was growing bigger and bigger.

When Bra Spider asked Bra Hare to take Bra Hare where he got food, the latter promised to do so early the next morning. Bra Spider went home and waited patiently. Well before daylight he arrived at Bra Hare's home and woke him up.

Bra Hare jumped up in protest, "Oh, not so early. Wait until it strikes 6 o'clock." Bra Spider paced out into the neighborhood, and took a big bucket which he struck six times. He then ran back to Bra Hare and announced, "It has struck six. Let's go." "Wait until the children come for water," the Hare again suggested.

Bra Spider went out again, lifted a bucket, hit it against the well and started shouting, "I'm the first! I'm the first! Look at you! Just now that you came! I say I'm the first!"

"Bra Hare! Bra Hare!" he ran back calling. Bra Hare stood his ground, telling him to wait until the fowls crowed. Bra Spider went out and crowed like a fowl.

His friend then yielded. "Okay, you're bothering me too much. Let's go."

They started the journey to look for food; they were to be beaten first.

The number of plates of rice they ate depended on the number of strokes they received from a magical cane. Bra Hare went forward and asked for two strokes. The magic cane immediately started to work. It gave him two solid strokes. He received two plates of rice which he quickly ate.

Bra Spider had an idea. He asked his friend whether he could call for any number. Bra Hare told him he could. The thought that he was going to eat as much as his belly could take overwhelmed him with joy. He boldly went forward and asked for two dozen strokes. The magic cane came down heavily. It gave him and gave him and gave him. Having received about one dozen and six, Bra Spider writhed very loudly as if he was about to die.

The cane was a magical stick which acted as if it was a person capable of seeing what was happening around, for as soon as its victim screamed in pain, it went up on its own to start afresh. In response to Bra Spider's cry of anguish, it stopped and returned to its original position again. At that point Bra Hare then shouted to him, "Call for a small number, so that you can eat." Bra Spider conceded and called for three. He was given three strokes. Drenched in sweat, he went back to his seat. There he was served three plates.

贪婪与懒惰①

这是一个关于贪与懒两位老兄的故事，他们两个都住在一个叫图易尤的村子里。

有一年，村子里突然闹起了饥荒，人们都饿着肚子，水源也干涸了，生活非常艰苦。

贪老兄是一个勤恳的小伙子，他时常在地里连轴干上好几个小时，但他也很贪婪。

懒老兄则相反，他很懒惰。他唯一擅长的就是乞讨，他整天都在乞讨，尤其喜欢向贪老兄乞讨。贪老兄对他这样执着的乞讨有点忍无可忍了。

有一年，贪老兄在图易尤五十英里外的地方开垦了一块稻田。"这下懒老兄该不会来乞讨了吧？"他这样想道，全力以赴地投入稻田的劳作，稻子也长得很好。

几个月后稻子熟了，马上要丰收了。一个星期五，贪老兄一边收割稻子，一边想着："我得好好享受这头一次丰收。我那老婆擅长烹饪，会做丰盛的菜肴，煮一盘美味的卡萨瓦木薯叶盖浇饭，我们得好好享受一下劳动成果了。"

木薯叶汁的香味沿路飘到了图易尤，懒老兄闻到了。他想着："我得尝尝贪老兄家的饭了。没点聪明劲儿，谁都别想拦住我吃东西。"他就这样朝着贪老兄的农田走去了。

贪老兄在两百英尺外就看见懒老兄来了，他对老婆说："老婆，到这来，我现在要平躺下去，用块白土布盖着我。你瞧啊，懒老兄奔着咱的饭菜来了！他来了你就告诉他我死了，让他赶紧回图易尤告诉大伙我死了。"老婆子拿布盖着他。

懒老兄来了，听到了贪老兄和他老婆的对话。

---

① 英文原为"贪婪与乞丐"，译者根据原故事的寓意译为"贪婪与懒惰"。

"嫂子好，贪老兄在哪儿呢？我怪想你们的，过来看看你们。"

"老头子刚刚过世了，麻烦你回去村里告诉大伙。"老婆说。

"别啊！别啊，"懒老兄说，"让我缓缓，我还饿着呢，我得吃点你们的饭才有力气走回去。还有，我现在还是有把劲儿可以挖坟的，到时候大伙来了才好下葬。"说着就去给贪老兄挖坟了。

这时，老婆过去跟贪老兄说："我尽力劝懒老兄回去了，但他不肯回去。"

懒老兄迫不及待要吃饭了，他把贪老兄挪到坟旁重重地摔了下去，又回去跟贪老兄的老婆说："咱吃饭吧，吃完了我回去通知大伙贪老兄死了。"

贪老兄的老婆不肯给懒老兄饭吃。懒老兄就跑回去跟贪老兄说："贪老兄，我知道你没死，我知道，你装死就是为了不让我吃你家的饭，你要是现在还不起来的话，那我就把你活埋了。"

"你饶了我吧，懒老兄！走吧，咱们去吃饭。"

最后，三人一起吃了饭。

> 英文对照

Bra Greedy and Bra Beggar

This story is about Bra Greedy and Bra Beggar. Both of them lived in the same village, Tuiyor.

One year, famine desperately struck Tuiyor. Men lived on empty stomachs. The waters dried up. Life was hard.

Bra Greedy was a hard-working young man. He would spend hours on end working in his field. But he was a greedy man.

Bra Beggar, on the other hand, was very lazy. All that he was good at was begging. Every day he would beg and beg, and beg Bra Greedy in particular. Bra Greedy got fed-up with his persistent and continuous begging.

One year, he reclaimed his rice farm fifty miles away from Tuiyor. "Bra Beggar would not come here to beg," he said. He worked hard and hard and hard, and the rice grew well.

A few months later it was ready for harvest. One Friday, they harvested the rice. "I am going to enjoy my first harvest," said Bra Greedy. "My dear wife is good at cooking, so she can cook a delicious cassava-leaf sauce so that we will enjoy the fruits of our labour."

Way down at Tuiyor, Bra Beggar smelt the sweet cassava-leaf sauce. "I must eat Bra Greedy's rice," he said. "No amount of cunning will prevent me from eating it." Bra Beggar therefore set out for Bra Greedy's farm.

Two hundred yards away from the farm, Bra Greedy saw Bra Beggar coming. The former said to his wife, "Come, Kumba, I am going to lie down flat. Cover me with a piece of white country cloth. Look! I know Bra

Beggar is coming for my rice. When he comes, tell him I am dead and he should immediately go back to Tuiyor to report my death to the people." His wife covered him. Bra Beggar came. He had overheard all the conversation between Bra Greedy and his wife. "Hello my dear, where is Bra Greedy? I have just thought of you and I have decided to pay you a visit." "Bra Greedy has just died, please go back to town immediately and report his death to the people," said the woman. "No! No!" said Bra Beggar. "Give me some time to rest. Besides, I am hungry. I would like to eat some of the rice you are cooking so that I will be strong enough to proceed on my return journey. Moreover, I think it will be wise enough for me to dig the grave; so that when the people come, burial will easily take place." Bra Beggar went and started digging the grave for Bra Greedy.

Meanwhile, Bra Greedy's wife went and stood near her husband and said, "I have tried my best to convince Bra Beggar to go back, but he has cunningly refused to do so." Bra Beggar grew very impatient waiting for the rice. He moved the corpse nearer to the grave and dropped it hard on the ground. Bra Beggar went to Kumba and said, "Let us eat the rice and go to town to report your husband's death."

The woman did not yield to his suggestion. He returned to the corpse and said, "Bra Greedy, I know that you are alive. I know that you are doing all this because you do not want me to eat your rice. If you do not wake up now, I am going to bury you alive."

"Leave me alone, Bra Beggar! Let's go and eat the rice."

Finally, Bra Greedy, Bra Beggar and Kumba ate the rice.

陆上好擒鳄

俗话说得好:"陆上好擒鳄。"这句谚语的起源却鲜有人知。不管你知不知道,我现在都要说给你听。

当一个人对另一个人说"你使的劲儿都够把一条鳄鱼摁在地上了"的时候,他表达的意思必定和这个故事有渊源。

从前有个年轻人活像一条鳄鱼,他常常到河边把自己乔装成一条鳄鱼捕猎人类,然后把抓到的人带到水涡底下的寨子里囚禁起来(每个水涡底下都有个寨子)。

每当他把别人的妻女抓到水涡底下时,人们就会喊道:"鳄鱼叼人了!快跑,快跑,快跑!"

其实,那个人在人间的真实身份是镇上的一个铁匠。他的一个工友的妻子到河边洗碗碟的时候,就被他抓住后带到了水下的寨子里。他交代他的手下:"照顾好我的夫人。"

被抓的女人住在水底,不会被杀害,也毫发无损。一日三餐,晚上沐浴休息,床榻上甚至还铺有被褥。

要知道每个水涡下都是他的寨子啊!

他回到镇上后,发现人们早已经敲响有妇人被鳄鱼叼走的警钟了。

那妇人的丈夫在干吗呢?他正四处寻找他的妻子。

酋长命令寻人队伍到河里去找,但队伍下到水里刨了个底朝天也没找到妇人,在四处都找遍之后,最终还是放弃了。

但丈夫没有放弃,他还在独自搜寻着。每天清晨他都在河边徘徊,左顾右盼,并告诉自己:"溺水孩子的尸首都要很久后才能找到,只要我不停地找,就一定能找到她。"

丈夫锲而不舍地在河边找着。在某个星期五,他沿着河走,又饿又渴,看见一棵酒椰树上长着一只汁液饱满的椰子。他当时实在是饥渴难耐了,于是对自己说:"要不然爬上去吸点椰汁吧,可能再也找不到她了,这个椰子是真主赐予我的,我还是爬上去吸点椰汁吧,这样我就不至于饥渴而死。"

于是他爬上了酒椰树,恰好那个水涡就在附近。

他把盖着椰子的椰叶揭开,然后转身取枝下悬着的一根藤茎做酒杯。这时,他瞥见一条鳄鱼努力朝着河岸游了过来,他一边把手伸向藤茎,一边注视着鳄鱼。只见那条鳄鱼猛地冲上了岸上的沙地,他目不转睛地盯着鳄鱼,这时他看见一个男人从鳄鱼的躯壳下钻了出来,然后把鳄鱼躯壳摊平卷起来。那不是铁匠吗?这事太蹊跷了!铁匠收起鳄鱼壳后,用干叶掩藏起来,然后又跑回河边洗脸。

丈夫目睹了全过程,认出那人就是镇上的铁匠,他还给自己家里打过刀。

他轻轻对自己说:"天呐。"

丈夫顾不上喝椰汁了,从树上下来就到镇上去求见酋长。

他对酋长说:"我现在已经筋疲力尽了,但我还在坚持找我的妻子,要是我能在路上找到她,那是多亏了万能的主。很多人白费了力气后就放弃了,就连我的许多朋友也是这样。但是,要是我再找下去还不见她的话,那我就得另做打算了。"

酋长问道:"说真的,你还有什么其他办法吗?你不是各处都找遍了也没找到她吗?"

丈夫回答道:"没错,但您等着瞧吧。"说完就又回到河边去了。

丈夫拿走了鳄鱼壳,沿着小溪走,采了点车前草罩住鳄鱼壳并结结实实捆好,再用藤条绑着夹在腋下。落日时分,他回到了镇里。

丈夫把鳄鱼壳带回家里后,把它藏在地下,他自言自语道:"既然到处找遍了都一无所获,咱们就走着瞧吧。"

第二天一大早,他跑到酋长跟前说:"老爷,我来是要告诉您,我还会再继续找下去的,要是说咱们最后还是要给她办丧事,那咱们就办了。现在我明白了,我再也见不着她了。但我还是要说,只要我有强大的毅力,我就能在陆上擒住一条鳄鱼。只要我坚持不懈,就会在陆上擒住一条鳄鱼!"

"你说的这些话是啥意思?"酋长问道。

"到时候您就知道了。"他回答道。

第二天,工人们都到铁匠的铺子里开工了,丈夫也去了。

"早啊,伙计们!"丈夫向大家打招呼道。

其中一个工人问他:"伙计,现在情况怎么样了?"

"现在我累了,想稍做休息,我知道我永远也见不到着她了。但我想跟大家说,我跟她一起快快乐乐生活了很久,但现在一条鳄鱼把她叼走了,她再也不会回来了,我也受够了四处寻找她的日子。不过我还是要说,如果有强大的毅力就能在陆上擒住一条鳄鱼。如果再也见不到她,那我就要在陆地上擒住一条鳄鱼。我会去告诉酋长和他的手下这件事,也会把这件事告诉邦多会的长老,见不着她的话,我就在陆地上擒住一条鳄鱼!"

到傍晚的时候,他把话又重复说了一遍。

一夜过后,在第二天的中午时分,他跑去铁匠铺重申了一遍之前说过的话。第三天,他继续老调重弹:"我要在陆地上擒住一条鳄鱼!"

铁匠闻言跑去河边找他的鳄鱼壳,但四处都寻不见,就连他觉得最不可能藏的地方也找了四回,依然不见踪影。

丈夫每天都会照样去铁匠铺慷慨激昂一番。铁匠心里明白,丈夫说的那条鳄鱼就是他。

某天,铁匠自言自语:"我的事败露了,虽然我抓了他老婆,不过只要她毫发无伤,那就没什么好怕的。就算我把人带回来了,最坏的结果无非是承担'伤害妇女'的责任。我那鳄鱼壳肯定是被她丈夫拿走了,我得去会会他,好好地跟他商量商量。"

他走到丈夫跟前问道:"小伙子,你老提'陆上好擒鳄'的俗话,那我问你,你是不是经常去河边的沙地那?"

"是啊。"丈夫回答。

"就那片很偏远的沙地,你真会去吗?"

"是真的,我经常去。"

"那你是不是拿了我的东西?"

"你说的'东西'是什么东西?"

"我就直说吧,你老提'陆上好擒鳄'的俗话,你是不是在那沙地上拿过一张鳄鱼壳?"

"我又没打死过鳄鱼,哪来的鳄鱼壳?"

"我知道你没打死过,但咱俩大男人就别婆婆妈妈了,是你把我的鳄鱼壳拿走的吧?你老婆现在在水涡底下跟我一起生活,安全着呢!我给她吃得很好,昨天我离家的时候,她还在熨着衣服。鳄鱼壳肯定是你拿的,快还给我吧,要不,你现在跟我去看看你老婆怎么样?"

"你说的都是真的?怕不是我把鳄鱼壳还给你之后,你不会让我见到我老婆吧?"

"如果我食言的话,你可以告诉大家我就是世上最恶毒的人,但其实,我的所作所为也不全都是坏的。我想让你和你老婆团聚,你就相信我吧!"

丈夫把他藏在地下的鳄鱼壳,就是铁匠的那副,拽出来,解绑摊开。丈夫说:"你满意了吧?你从这副壳子里溜出来又把它藏好的那天,我也在沙地那儿,没被你发现。我爬上了一棵海椰树,你从底下经过,之后我就下树把它拿回家了,就是这副,但我现在还不想给你。"

"老伙计,你就给我吧!你想见你老婆的话,现在就可以跟我去见。"

丈夫拿起那副鳄鱼壳,夹在腋下,跟着铁匠去了。

"只要我能见到她。"丈夫嘀咕着。

走到河边的时候,铁匠问他:"你胆子大吗?"

"当然!"

"我要躺下溜进鳄鱼壳里,等下我们下河的时候你就趴我背上,可别害怕啊,你看见的那些不是河水而是林子,那些水是林子。"

"走吧,别废话,就算要到天上才能再见到她,我也会去。"

"你可千万别害怕,我们穿过林子的时候你要保持呼吸。"铁匠千叮咛万嘱咐。

丈夫趴上鳄鱼壳的背,然后他们就下河了。铁匠说:"快抓住我的腿,告诉自己这些不是河水,只是些水露而已。"

他们在水里窜得极快,不一会就落到了河床上。丈夫在一堆大石头上着地了。他们又走了一小段路才到达目的地。铁匠告诉丈夫:"你老婆就在这儿。"

丈夫问妻子:"亲爱的,你为什么在这儿?"

妻子回答:"我也不知道我为什么会在这儿,是这个人扯着我的脖子生拉硬拽把我带到这里来的。"

铁匠说:"我俩也没发生什么,我连她的手指头都没碰一下,不信你问她。"

"他说的是真的。"妻子回答。

"看在上帝的面上,现在我恳求你原谅我。"铁匠说,"我有些想法想跟你说说。"

"我本来打算要严惩你的,但既然你说还有些事想告诉我,那我不妨先听听吧。"丈夫回答。

"太好了!"铁匠说,"我想让你和你老婆跟我一起扮演鳄鱼,咱们互相理解,这个地方现在就是我们大家的专属乐园了,千万别告诉其他人。"

"我们同意加入你,不会告诉其他人。"夫妻俩说。

"那我们现在就组成了这个秘密社团。"铁匠说。

"好的。"夫妻俩回应道。

就这样,"鳄鱼"驮着夫妻俩启程回镇子。刚一上岸,铁匠就从鳄鱼躯壳里溜出来。洗过脸后,他问夫妻俩:"这张鳄鱼壳现在是我们仨共有,把它藏哪儿好呢?"他们三人一起商量着,把鳄鱼壳藏好后才回到镇上。

"可是,"妻子问他们:"回去后如果镇上的人问我去哪儿了怎么办,毕竟我被鳄鱼叼走的消息已经传出去了,我该怎么回答?"

"你先说说你会怎么说吧。"其余两人回答。

"我就说我到河对岸那边去找我妈了,听到大家以为我被鳄鱼叼走了的传言我会装作很惊讶。至于你们在河边找到了我的衣物,就说是我落在那儿的,我没有被鳄鱼叼走。"

"行,那咱们走吧。"说完他们就回去了。刚到镇子里,众人看见妻子就大声惊呼:"天呐!他们把人给找回来了!大家快来啊!"

现在,三人都被卷入扮演鳄鱼的事件中了。过了一段时间,妻子爱上了另外一个人,还把他带到水下去幽会。她躲开丈夫和铁匠,把情人带到先前三人共同的巢穴里。

后来,事情败露了,两个男人打算去巢穴里看看。铁匠问:"咱的好婆娘哪儿去了?"丈夫回答:"我也没看见她。"铁匠说:"走,找找去!"

那会儿,妻子早就跟老相好约好到巢穴里见面。因为她把鳄鱼壳的使用方法告诉了老相好,所以那人比她先到了巢穴。不幸的是,那天正好两个男人打算去巢穴里看看。

于是,丈夫、铁匠、妻子和情人在水下不期而遇。情人如坐针毡,看着妻子,不知如何是好,妻子也看着他,有话不能说,因为丈夫就在边上呢。情人坐下良久,最后起身离开,跃出水面,远走他乡。他对自己说:"要是被别人发现我在这儿,那我就死定了,那个女人也会向乡人告发我。还是从此消失好。"

那年,妻子在她邦多会的入会仪式上唱着:"昔有四人,而今余三;如意郎君,各奔前程。"

Detaining a Crocodile on Land

Do we all know the meaning of this proverb "That will detain the crocodile on land"? There are not many people here who know the origin of this proverb. Well, whether or not you know it, I am going to tell you.

When a man tells another, "What you have done to me can detain a crocodile on land", he means something which has its roots in this story.

There was a certain young man who used to live the life of a crocodile. He would go to the riverside, turn himself into a crocodile and catch people. Then he would take them to the bottom of a whirlpool where there was a village. Every whirlpool has a village.

There he would detain his victim. And there would be shouts, "A crocodile has caught a human being; kpo, kpo, kpo."

This man was in fact the blacksmith in the town. It was he who caught the wife of a colleague when the woman went to the riverside to wash dishes. As soon as he grabbed her, he took her down to the village and said to the others, "Take care of my wife."

He never killed the woman. He did not harm her in any way. The woman lived under the water, had food regularly, bathed at night and went to bed. She even slept in a bed between sheets.

Every whirlpool is a village, if you did not know this!

When he returned to the town he found that there was already an alarm raised about the woman who had been caught by a crocodile.

What was the husband going to do about it? He was searching and searching for her.

The chief told them, "Go down to the river and search for her." They went down to the river and combed everywhere, but they never saw the woman. They looked everywhere. At last they gave up.

But the husband never gave up. It was he alone who continued the search. Every morning he would walk about slowly, looking around and saying to himself, "Those whose children have got drowned search for a long time. Maybe, if only I continue to search, I will find my wife."

He concentrated his search along the banks of the river. One day, it was a Friday, he became very hungry. He walked up the river until he found a raffia palm with a gourd full of coconut milk. He was very hungry and thirsty and he said to himself, "I shall climb up and drink some coconut milk. Maybe I will never see my wife again. What God has given, only he can take away. I shall climb up and drink some coconut milk, so I won't die of hunger and thirst."

And he climbed the raffia palm. The raffia palm was just by the whirlpool, and he climbed it.

He had just taken the lid off the gourd as he opened it and turned to take the cane cup which was hung on a branch, when he spied a crocodile racing towards the bank. His hand was stretched towards the cup as he looked attentively at the crocodile. The crocodile sped towards the sandy bank and landed. He did not take his eyes off it and he saw a man emerge from beneath a crocodile mask. The man put the mask aside to form a heap. It was the blacksmith! Wonders never end! The blacksmith took the mask and hid it beneath dry leaves. Then he returned to the river to wash his face.

The husband saw it all. It was really the blacksmith in their town; the very one who made their machetes.

He said quietly to himself, "O hoo."

He did not drink the coconut milk. He came down the tree and went to the town to see the chief.

He said to the chief, "I am now worn out with hunger, but I haven't given up the search. If I am lucky to find her in my wanderings, I will say thanks to the Lord. Many people have tried in their own little way and given up; even many of my friends are tired. However, if I don't see my wife after further search, there is something I plan to do."

"Frankly, what else can you do about it? You have already said that you have looked for her everywhere and not seen her," asked the chief.

"Yes, but you just wait and see," the man said. And he went back to the riverside.

He took the crocodile mask down the stream, cut out some plantain leaves and wrap-ped it up neatly. He tied it with some rattan, put it under his arms and headed for town at dusk.

He carried it into his house and dropped it on the ground. "I have searched everywhere in vain. Let us now wait and see," he said to himself.

Early the next morning, he went to the chief and said, "Chief, I have come to tell you that I am now tired of searching around. If we are going ahead with her funeral ceremonies, let us do so. I now know I will never see her again. However, I would like to say this: that sort of behavior can detain a crocodile on land. It will detain a crocodile on land."

"Is that proverb insinuating something?" asked the chief.

"Yes; but you will know later," he replied.

The next day, when a crowd had gathered at the blacksmith's, he went to join them.

"Good morning, friends," he said to them.

One of them asked him, "And how do things stand now, friend?"

"I am now tired and wish to take a rest. I know that I will never see my wife again. However, I have this to say to all of you: For a long time I lived a happy life with my wife … and now a crocodile has snatched her away … if it does not bring back my wife … I am now tired of searching. But let me tell you that that kind of behavior can detain a crocodile on land. If I don't see my wife, a crocodile will be detained on land. I am going to let the chief and his speaker know this. I shall also let the Head of the Bundo Society know this. If I don't see my wife, that is going to detain a crocodile on land."

In the evening he said the same thing.

He slept, and the next day, by noon, he went to the blacksmith's and said the same thing. He said it again the following day, this proverb about the crocodile being detained on land.

The blacksmith then went down to the river and searched for the crocodile skin. He searched everywhere but could not see it; even in places where he would not normally hide the skin. He went down to the river four times and searched in vain.

And every day the young man would come to the blacksmith's workshop and make insinuations about the crocodile being detained on land. And the blacksmith knew that he was the crocodile in question.

One day, he said to himself, "I have been outwitted by this man. I know that I am the one who has captured his wife, but as long as she is safe and well I have nothing to fear. If I bring back his wife, the worst that can happen to me would be to pay for 'woman damage'. But he is certainly the one who has taken my crocodile outfit. I shall meet him so that we may both talk on friendly terms."

"Young man, you always refer to a proverb about a crocodile being detained on land. Tell me, do you usually go to the sandy beach?" he asked the husband.

"Yes," the man replied.

"Do you really go as far as the large sandy beach?"

"Yes, of course. That's where we frequently go," said the man.

"Did you take anything that belongs to me?"

"What sort of thing are you talking about?" asked the man.

"Let me come out plainly; this proverb of yours, about a crocodile being detained on land ... did you not take the skin of a crocodile from the beach?" the blacksmith asked him.

"How can I take a crocodile skin away when I haven't killed any crocodile?" the husband replied.

"I know you haven't killed one. However, as we are both men, let us talk as men do. You are the one who took the skin away. Your wife is with me at the bottom of the whirlpool. She is in a house, safe and sound. She eats well. Even yesterday, when I left her, she was ironing clothes. Give me back my crocodile skin. You are the very one who took it. If you wish, you can come along to see your wife."

"Are you telling the truth? Suppose I return your skin and you do not produce my wife?" asked the husband.

"If I fail to, tell everyone that I am the most evil man on earth. In fact, I have something good in mind for you. I would like to have you and your wife in a partnership. Please do what I have asked of you."

The husband got up and pulled out the crocodile skin which he dropped on the ground. He loosened it. It was the same skin. Then he said, "Are you satisfied? You didn't notice, but I was on the beach that day when you came out of the skin and deposited it on the ground. I was in the palm tree, and you passed just under me. When you left I came down and took it and brought it home. This is it, but I won't give it to you."

"Please give it to me, dear colleague. But if you prefer, you may come along to see your wife," the blacksmith said.

And the man took the skin, put it under his arm and followed the blacksmith.

"As long as I am able to set eyes on my wife …" he said. When they got to the riverside the blacksmith asked him, "Are you brave?"

The man said, "Yes."

The blacksmith said, "I am going to get into this skin and lie down here. You will then get on my back before we take off. But don't be afraid. This is not water that you see, it is all forest. What you see there is all forest."

"I am ready," said the husband. "If I have to go into space to see my wife, I will do so."

"Please do not be afraid. You will continue to breathe as we go through the forest," the blacksmith assured him.

He got on the blacksmith's back and they were set to take off. The blacksmith said, "Hold on to my legs fast, if you are afraid. What you see is all dew, not water."

They sped off. Soon they landed and the man jumped on to a refuse heap. They landed on a refuse heap and walked a little way. When they arrived at their destination, the blacksmith said, "Here is your wife."

"Why are you sitting here, my dear?" the husband asked her. "I really don't know how I got here. It was this man who brought me here. He just grabbed me by the neck and brought me here," she replied.

"There is nothing between us. I have not even touched her finger. You may ask her," the blacksmith said. "That is true," confirmed the wife. "But I would plead with you to forgive me, in the name of God," the blacksmith said. "I have something in mind for you." "I really mean to disgrace you, but since you say you have something to tell me, I shall listen and hear," the man said.

"Well," said the blacksmith, "I want you, your wife and I to be partners in this crocodile game. Let there be an understanding between us that this place is now our common resort. But, please, don't tell anybody else. Don't tell anyone else."

"We agree to join you. We will never tell anyone else," the couple said.

"It is now a secret society we have formed," the blacksmith told them.

"We agree," they said.

So, the three people returned to the town. The man and his wife sat on the back of the "crocodile" during their return journey. When they landed, the blacksmith came out of the skin and put it on the ground. He went to wash his face, after which he said to them, "This skin is now collectively owned by the three of us. Where can we hide it?" It was the three who now jointly agreed to hide it. They had formed a society. They then set out for the town.

Oh women! It was the woman who now asked them a question. She said, "If we arrive in the town and people ask me where I have been to since news had spread that a crocodile had carried me away, what should I say to them?" "You first tell us what your answer would be," they said. "I will tell them that I went across the river to visit my mother, and I am really surprised that there is hearsay of a crocodile having snatched me away. As for the clothes you found at the river side ... I simply forgot them there. It was never a crocodile that took me away."

"Well, let us go," they said to her. And they went. They arrived in the town and as soon as people saw the woman there were shouts of "Hurray! They have found the woman! They have found the woman, my people!"

The three people were now involved in the crocodile game. After a long time, the woman picked up a new lover and started going to the whirlpool with him. She would hide from her husband and the blacksmith and take her lover to their common hide-out.

One day she was exposed. The group decided to go to their hide-out. The blacksmith asked about the woman, "Where is our wife?" The husband replied, "I haven't seen her yet." And the blacksmith said, "Go in search of her."

In fact the woman had previously arranged for her lover to meet her at the very hide-out. The lover had accordingly gone ahead to wait for her there. He had been taught by her the art of using the crocodile outfit, so he could go there all by himself. Unfortunately, the day they agreed to meet was the very day the group decided to have a meeting.

The four people met under the water: the husband, the blacksmith, the wife and the lover. The lover sat a little off and looked intently at the woman, and she looked at him. They could not exchange words, as the husband was next to her. The lover sat for a long time and then got up and left. He came out of the water and went away to a different country. He said to himself, "If those people find me here they are going to kill me. That woman will tell them about me." So, he left.

When the women had their Bundo Society initiation ceremony, the woman sang this song: "There were three of us, there were four of us, but my companion has gone away."

那丁与孜克雷

从前有一个镇子，里面住着两个同一天出生的人，他们的家相隔不远，门对门。他们一起长大，小时候一起恶作剧，其中一个叫"那丁"（克利奥语"无事"的意思），另一个叫"孜克雷"（在《圣经》里一般写作"扎卡利亚"）。那丁家里很富有而孜克雷家里很贫穷，但家境的差距并没有妨碍他们做朋友。他们经常互相拜访，生活过得悠闲自在。只要是孜克雷想要却负担不起的东西，那丁就会主动赠与他。两人眼看就要到而立之年了却还没成家。

那丁的家很大、很高，从楼顶往下吐一口口水，在到达地面前就蒸发了，而孜克雷的家只是一座很矮的小屋子。

有一天，两人在一起闲谈。孜克雷对那丁说："老伙计啊，我发现我们还没结婚就要老了，再不结婚的话，以后恐怕就娶不到合适的了！"那丁表示赞同，并且表示他们应该马上行动起来。

在离他们住处不远的地方有一个镇子，那里的女性人数是男性人数的三四倍，或者是五六倍。

方圆几千里的人都知道那个镇子里盛产美女，世界各地的单身汉都到那里去找媳妇，但由于那里的姑娘们都太漂亮了，没有谁出了城后敢说自己娶到的是最漂亮的媳妇，因为每个姑娘都非常漂亮！凡是来到镇上的外乡人，都会被他见到的第一个姑娘迷得神魂颠倒，而见到第二个后就会把第一个又忘到九霄云外，见到第三个就会被迷得彻底癫狂。当全镇的姑娘都聚到一个地方的时候，世上没人能挑出最漂亮的是哪一个。所以，到那个镇子上找媳妇的人往往都眼花缭乱，无功而返。为了改变这种情况，姑娘们商议后达成了一致意见——改由她们来挑选丈夫。因此，当有意结婚的男士到访镇上的时候，看上他的姑娘就会告诉她的母亲，由母亲邀请那个幸运儿到家中见面，并为他们举办婚礼。

带着结婚的意愿，那丁和孜克雷离家去了那个美妙的镇子。那丁精心打扮了一番，当他们走到半路的时候，孜克雷坐到路边的一块石头上，看起来很苦恼，他拒绝再往前走。那丁对孜克雷的举动感到很奇怪，就问他怎么了。孜克雷回答说："老伙计，我发现我不过是来给你做陪衬，而且我也觉得整件事挺别扭的，啥样的女人才会看上我这样寒酸的人啊？"为了安慰孜克雷，那丁脱下他的衣服给了孜克雷，然后穿上孜克雷的衣服继续赶路。

一到那个镇子，天呐！满镇子都是漂亮姑娘！有七个姑娘立马就看上了孜克雷，但是只有一个姑娘看上了那丁。婚礼结束后，两人就带着各自的新婚妻子回家乡了。

到达他们镇上后，新婚妻子发现要经过一条草木丛生的崎岖小路才能到孜克雷的家，而去往那丁家的路又平坦又干净。当七个新婚妻子到达孜克雷家时，世界上找不到任何语言可以表达出她们的厌恶与悔恨：既没有吃的，又没有穿的，连满足基本生存的物资都没有。那丁的妻子不得不接济她的同乡一些钱，以及吃的、穿的。

日子就那样一天天过着，直到有一天，孜克雷由嫉妒生出了仇恨，打算杀害他的好友。在一个伸手不见五指的夜里，孜克雷雇了几个人在那丁的房前挖了一条又宽又深的沟，又找来些用草药制成的润滑剂涂在通往那丁家前门的楼梯上。

凌晨四点半左右，孜克雷跑到那丁房前的马路中央又哭又喊："老天！着火了！那丁你赶紧出来啊！"那丁从温暖舒适的床上蹦起来，他的妻子抓住他央求他别管，但那丁从她手中挣脱，从房里跑出来到前门廊，穿过前门，刚一踏上楼梯，他就从楼梯上滑倒了，从楼梯上一阶阶滚了下来，最后重重地摔在房前的沟里，当场就摔死了。

那丁的妻子哀恸不已，哭干了眼泪，哭哑了嗓子，直到失声。从丧夫之痛中恢复过来后，她把丈夫农场里所有的农作物都收来，烹调后分给世界各地的孩子，让他们替她为"那丁"而哭（"无事"而哭）。

从那以后，世界各地的孩子就常常"无事而哭"了。

你听到孩子在哭，问他："孩子，你为啥哭啊？"

"为'那丁'而哭（'无事'而哭）！"

"孩子，你为啥哭啊？"

"为'那丁'而哭（'无事'而哭）！"

下次再看见在哭的孩子，就不用担心了。

孩子们会记得那丁妻子的嘱咐——"为'那丁'而哭（'无事'而哭）！"

英文对照

Bra Natin and Bra Zikray

Once upon a time there lived in a town two men. They were born at the same time in opposite houses on the same street. They grew up together, and played many boyish pranks together. One was called "Natin" (Krio for "Nothing"), the other was called "Zikray" (biblical "Zakaria"). Mr. Natin was very rich while Mr. Zikray was very poor. But the difference in monetary status did not affect their friendship. They lived very happily and visited each other regularly. Mr. Natin gave Mr. Zikra whatever he wanted and could not afford. They almost reached middle age without marrying.

Mr. Natin was living in a large house. The house was so large and high that if someone should spit from the top storey, the spittle would be evaporated before reaching the ground below. Mr. Zikray was living in a tumble-down hut.

To cut long matters short, as the two men were conversing one day, Mr. Zikray said to Mr. Natin: "My friend, I have just come to the realization that we have grown old without having wives. If we do not make an effort now to get married, we will not have suitable women in the future." Mr. Natin agreed with Mr. Zikray and decided they should take immediate action.

At that time, there was a town not too far from the town in which the two men lived. The women population of that town was three or four times that of their men if not even five or six times more.

It was a known fact for thousands of miles around that no ugly woman lived in that town. Men came from all corners of the world to choose wives, but the women were so beautiful that no man had come out of the town with a woman he could boast of as the most beautiful. Every woman was a perfect beauty. A stranger to the town would fall head over heels for the first women he saw; by the time the second came along he would completely forget the first, and when he saw the third he would almost go mad with admiration. No man on earth had ever chosen the most beautiful even when a thousand of the town's women were assembled in one place. Men who went to the town to choose wives usually ended up in total confusion and came out without. To change the situation the women came to the common understanding that they would do the choosing. So when a man with the intention to marry visited the town, the woman that liked him would tell her mother and the mother in turn would invite the lucky man and arrange the marriage.

Mr. Natin and Mr. Zikray left their town to visit the wonderful town with the intention to get married. Mr. Natin was well dressed. When they got halfway between the two towns, Mr. Zikray sat on a stone by the wayside looking very miserable and refused to continue the journey. Mr. Natin was surprised at Mr. Zikray's behavior and asked what was the matter with him. Mr. Zikray replied, "My friend, I realize that I am only accompanying you but I am not pleased with the whole affair. What woman on earth would fall in love with a man wearing the clothes that I now wear?" To comfort Mr. Zikray, Mr. Natin took off his clothes and gave Mr. Zikray, and wore Mr. Zikray's clothes and they continued the journey to the town.

When they arrived at the town, Hell was let loose! There where beautiful women all over the town; seven women immediately fell for Mr. Zikray and only one fell for Mr. Natin. After wedding ceremonies were completed, the men returned to their homes with their wives.

When the two men arrived in their town the women observed that they had to go through a bushy unmade road to Mr. Zikray's house while they walk a clean well-made road to Mr. Natin's house. There were no words in all the known languages to express the feelings of disgust and remorse of

Mr. Zikray's seven wives. When they arrived at their marital home, there was no food, no clothes, nor anything to satisfy the basic needs of life. It turned out that Mrs. Natin's wife had to provide almost everything for her fellow townswomen—money, food and clothes.

Life went on like that for a long time until one day Mr. Zikray became very jealous of Mr. Natin. When the jealousy grew into hatred, Mr. Zikray decided to kill his friend. One starless dark night Mr. Zikray hired some men to dig a very wide and deep ditch before Mr. Natin's house. After the ditch had been dug, he collected a lot of herbs and made them into a slimy and slippery paste which he then rubbed all over the steps leading to the front entrance of Mr. Natin's house.

About half-past four o'clock in the morning Mr. Zikray went to the middle of the street in front of Mr. Natin's house and started to shout, at the same time pretending to cry. "Lord has Mercy! Fire, Fire, Oh! Fire! Natin, please come out at once!" Mr. Natin leaped out of his warm and cosy bed, his wife grabbed him and pleaded with him, "Natin, please don't go!" But Mr. Natin freed himself from her and ran out of the room into the parlour, then through the front door on to the front steps. Before he could complete a wink, he had slipped down the flight of steps with lightning speed-knocked himself over once, twice, thrice and with a very heavy fall he ended in the ditch in front of the house and died instantly.

Mr. Natin's wife mourned and cried until her eyes stopped producing tears. She cried until she lost her voice and became totally dumb. When she recovered from the effects of her husband's death, she ordered that all the yams, coco-yams, potatoes, and cassava should be collected from all her husband's farms and brought to her. She then cooked them and gave them to children everywhere in the world and requested the children to help her mourn "For Natin"!

Since that time, children everywhere in the world cry "For Nothing"! So when you hear a little child crying, you ask, "Little boy, what's the matter?" "Natin ma!" ("Nothing mum!")

"Little girl, why are you crying?" "Natin ma!" ("Nothing mum!") The next time you meet a little child crying, do not be worried.

The child remembers Mrs. Natin's request and it is crying "For Natin!" ("For nothing!")

老鹰和母鸡

很久以前,缝纫机还没发明出来,针线是缝纫衣服的主要工具,但只有老鹰有针,老鹰一族是世上唯一能为鸟兽做衣服的裁缝。那时雷鸟和老鹰的关系很要好,因此,老鹰就教会了雷鸟缝纫衣服。

他们的友谊一直持续着,直到有一天,雷鸟的一个亲戚要结婚了,雷鸟的家人们就委托老鹰做婚礼上用的所有礼服。正当老鹰要开始做礼服的时候,她病倒了,为了不耽误婚礼,雷鸟就从老鹰那里借来了针自己做礼服。

婚礼的日子渐渐临近,休息了一段时间后的老鹰也从病痛中恢复过来了。但是这时雷鸟不愿意把针还给老鹰了。婚礼结束很久也不见雷鸟把针还回来,老鹰便打算找个时间去拜访雷鸟,顺便把针拿回来。老鹰见到雷鸟后,雷鸟为没及时还针道歉,并解释说她忙着张罗婚礼忘记把针放在哪儿了,但她一定会尽全力去找回那枚针,一旦找到就给老鹰送去。

半年过去了,一年过去了,一年半过去了,两年过去了。老鹰为要回针不断来回,但每次都无功而返。两年很快就过去了,雷鸟还没有把针还回来。当老鹰已经快要放弃,笃定雷鸟根本没有还针的意思的时候,他要求雷鸟赔偿自己。雷鸟同意了,请求老鹰给她些时间长好身体好开始工作,等赚够了钱就会赔偿她。

老鹰等了十年才再去找雷鸟要赔偿,每次老鹰去要钱的时候,雷鸟都央求她等自己长好身体再去工作。每次都是同样的说辞,老鹰终于不耐烦了,就向认识雷鸟的人抱怨这件事,他们都劝老鹰:"雷鸟是你的好朋友,再耐心等等吧。"老鹰还是不断抱怨,直到他偶遇了母鸡,把他和雷鸟之间的事告诉了母鸡。母鸡问他是否去过雷鸟家里,他说去过,母鸡又问他是否还见过雷鸟的其他家人,老鹰说没有,每次他去找雷鸟的时候,雷鸟就出来和他在大门口谈事情。雷鸟从来不让他进屋子里,母鸡就建议老鹰下次要进到雷鸟家里去看看,还强调等老鹰见到雷鸟的家人后,他就知道从雷鸟的亲戚里搞清楚长幼顺序有多难了。

老鹰采纳了母鸡的建议。一天早上，他趁雷鸟一家还没醒就去了，进到围墙里后老鹰开始敲门。从里面传来一个声音问道："谁啊？"老鹰回答说："是我，老鹰。"雷鸟听出是老鹰的声音，就向门口跑去，但在她还没到门口之前，她的家人就开门让老鹰进来了。在门廊上，老鹰见到了雷鸟的曾曾祖父母、各个表亲和堂兄弟、侄子和侄女，还有其他家人——都是同样的身材、样貌和身高。老鹰把雷鸟拉过来说："你今天要么还针，要么赔钱！"

雷鸟央求老鹰再给她一些时间，等她再长大些就去工作然后赔偿老鹰。

老鹰反驳说："我还要等多久？多亏了母鸡告诉我，我现在才能见到你，你要不还针要不赔钱，不然我就不走！"

雷鸟很好奇母鸡到底说了什么。老鹰告诉她，母鸡说雷鸟都长得差不多，很难分辨各自的年龄。老鹰那天果然印证了这个说法。

雷鸟佯装惊讶地问："那就是母鸡说的吗？"

老鹰确定是，说道："我跟母鸡抱怨的那天听到的就是这个。"

雷鸟重复问："你确定说的就是这个吗？"

老鹰肯定地说："就是因为母鸡告诉我了，我才会一大早过来验证。"

雷鸟对老鹰说："天呐，这叫朋友吗？既然母鸡给我使坏，那作为朋友我就告诉你实情吧：我把针借给母鸡，针被她弄丢了，因为她和我也是朋友，我不敢把事情告诉你，母鸡很嫉妒咱们的友谊，就使坏离间我们。"

老鹰听后，突然觉得母鸡很令人讨厌，就告别雷鸟，飞快地去找母鸡了。

一见到母鸡，老鹰就向她要针："把雷鸟借给你的针还给我！"

"我可什么都没跟雷鸟借！她没借针给我！"

老鹰火冒三丈，没等她把话说完就下了最终警告："你不把针还给我的话，我就捕食你的子孙，把他们一只一只地带走，直到你还给我针！"

从那天开始，母鸡就为她多管闲事付出了代价，于是每次老鹰来要针的时候，母鸡都要在地上找一番，请求老鹰再等等，而老鹰会告诉她他已经做出最后警告了："我早就告诉过你不还针的话我会做什么！"然后他就会抓走一只小鸡。

英文对照

Fowl and Hawk

A long time ago before the sewing machine was invented, the common needle and thread were used to sew clothes and only Hawk had needles. Hawk and his family were the only dressmakers for animals and birds the world over. Well, it happened that Tender Bird was very friendly to Hawk, so Hawk taught Tender Bird to sew clothes.

Their friendship lasted until it came to a time when one of Tender Bird's relatives would get married. So the family entrusted Hawk to prepare all the dresses for the wedding. About the time when Hawk began to sew the dresses he fell seriously ill. To avoid delaying the wedding, Tender Bird borrowed the needle from Hawk to do the sewing.

By and by, the wedding date came and went. After some time Hawk recovered from his illness and until then Tender Bird did not return the needle. Hawk waited for a long time after the wedding but still Tender Bird did not return the needle; so Hawk decided at a certain time to visit Tender Bird and collect the needle. When they met, Tender Bird apologized for not returning the needle and explained that during the very busy time she had prepared for the wedding she misplaced the needle, but she would definitely make an effort to search for it and as soon as she found it she would take it to him.

Six months went by, a year, a year and six months, two years. Hawk went to and fro to collect the needle, but Tender Bird could not produce it. The delay went on for another two years. Tender Bird was unable to return the needle. When Hawk convinced himself beyond all doubts that Tender

Bird had no intention of returning the needle, he told Tender Bird that she should pay for the needle. Tender Bird agreed but requested Hawk to give her time to grow up and start to work; when she began to earn money she would pay for the needle.

Hawk waited for ten years before he visited Tender Bird for the money. Every time Hawk went for the money Tender Bird would beg him to wait until she grew up and began to work. It went on and on like that until Hawk became impatient and started complaining to people who knew Tender Bird. They would say to Hawk, "Tender Bird is your friend, so be a bit patient." He continued complaining until once he met Fowl and told Fowl what had transpired between Tender Bird and himself. Fowl asked him if he had ever gone to Tender Bird's home. He said he had. Fowl enquired further if he had ever seen any of Tender Bird's relations. Hawk replied he had not because whenever he visited Tender Bird, Tender Bird would come up to the gate and there they transacted business. Tender Bird had never allowed him to go her home. There and then Fowl advised Hawk to go into Tender Bird's house and remarked that when Hawk met with Tender Bird's family then he would know how difficult it was to ascertain the old from the young among Tender Bird's relations.

Hawk took the advice and went to Tender Bird's house early one morning before the household was awake. He got into the compound and knocked at the door. Voices came from within asking, "Who are you?" Hawk answered, "It is me, Hawk!" Recognizing Hawk's voice, Tender Bird ran to the door but by the time she reached the door they had let Hawk in and he was in the middle of the parlour. Hawk met Tender Bird's great-great-great grandmother and grandfather, great-great great aunts and uncles, great-great cousins, Tender Bird's nephews and nieces and the rest of her relations—they all were of the same size, same face, same height. Hawk grabbed Tender Bird on the spot and told her, "You will return my needle today—this moment—or pay for it."

Tender Bird began to beg for a little more time explaining that as soon as she grew up and started to work she would pay everything.

Hawk retorted, "For how long should I continue to wait? Thanks to

Fowl for what she told me! Now that we have met, I will not quit this place without my needle or the money for it!"

Tender Bird was curious to know what Fowl told Hawk. Hawk replied that Fowl said that one could not determine the age of Tender Birds because they all looked alike and Hawk had proved it that day.

Tender Bird pretended to be surprised and asked, "You mean to tell me that was what Fowl said?"

Hawk assured her, "That was exactly what Fowl told me when I complained to her."

Tender Bird repeated the question, "Are you sure Fowl told you that?"

Hawk assured her that it was because of Fowl told him that and that was why he had come this morning to prove it.

Tender Bird said to Hawk, "Ah! Those are the people we call friends. Hawk, because Fowl has done this to me I will tell you the truth as a friend. I lent Fowl your needle. She lost it. But as she and I were as good friends as you and I, I was afraid to tell you. Fowl is jealous of our friendship and she is bent on doing something to spoil it."

Hawk became very annoyed at Fowl and left Tender Bird and sped on to meet Fowl.

When they met, Hawk demanded his needle, "Fowl, I want my needle that Tender Bird lent you!"

Fowl replied, "Borrowing and lending do not exist between Tender Bird and me! She did not lend me your needle."

Hawk was very angry with Fowl and did not wait for her to complete her explanation but gave her an ultimatum, "If you do not return my needle, I will prey on your children and carry them away one by one until you return my needle."

Until this day Fowl is paying the price for being too forward. Any time Hawk comes around for his needle Fowl will be searching the earth for it and requesting Hawk to wait a moment. Hawk will remind her of his ultimatum, "I have told you what I will do if you do not return my needle!" And he will take a chick away.

为何鸟儿有多彩的羽毛

很久以前,全世界的鸟儿都在互相争夺霸主地位,获胜条件是从巴弗迪亚飞到世界的尽头再飞回来,谁先飞回来谁就获胜。那时候巴弗迪亚正被饥荒所笼罩,因此,大多数起飞的鸟儿都在航行路上被遇到的各种各样的食物分心了。

它们起飞后不久,秃鹫们就遇到一个动物尸体。它们将尸体团团围住,开始抢食起来,而其他鸟儿则忙着赶路。飞了几英里后,鸡群遇见了些米粒,它们像秃鹫一样围成一圈,啄食地上的米粒,把比赛的事忘得一干二净。

其他鸟儿继续飞行,不久后看见一片野果林,"可多鸟"被深深吸引住了,它们放慢了飞行速度去吃野果子,而其他鸟儿继续飞着。一般而言,"科玛鸟"的飞行速度是所有鸟中最慢的,但这次最先飞到世界尽头,赢得了霸主地位,奖品就是成百上千件五彩缤纷的衣裳。它们返回的途中将一部分奖品——五彩衣裳分发了出去,只把最好的一些留给自己。

这就是为什么鸟儿都有缤纷多彩的羽毛,而羽毛最美、最为珍贵的"科玛鸟"成为百鸟之王的原因。

英文对照

Why Birds Have Different Colours

Once upon a time, all the birds in the world competed for a chieftaincy. The requirement was to fly from Bafodea to the end of the world and back before all the other competitors. Bafodea was struck by famine. So when they set out most of the birds were distracted by the different kinds of food they came across in their flight.

No sooner did they take off than the vultures came across a carcass. They crowded around it and started to eat while the other birds continued on their journey. Some miles away, the hens too came across some rice. Like the vultures, they came together and started to peck the rice and forget all about the competition.

Others continued with the flight and soon came across some wild fruits which attracted the "Kodo-Kodos". They stayed behind eating the fruits while others continued the flight. The "Koma" birds which are normally very slow, slower than all the other birds, were the first to reach the end of the world. At the end of the competition, the "Koma" won the first prize, that is, a gift of many beautiful clothes. On their return journey they gave out some of the clothes to the other birds, leaving the best ones for themselves.

That is why all birds have beautiful feathers but the "Koma" is the most beautiful and precious and the king of the birds.

女仆的仆人

大千世界,容易聪明反被聪明误,现在讲的故事大伙可得牢记在心里。

从前有两位富有的酋长,其中一个酋长的女儿要嫁到另一个酋长的家里,而那个女孩自从出生后就生活在高楼里,从来没有下过楼。

人们常说,"送姑娘到夫家得找个靠谱的人陪着",这句话实际也警醒人们要常到新婚对象家里查查家风,了解清楚情况。

婚事定下来后,女孩的父母过了几天就派人把女儿送去了夫家,派了一个侍女陪行。让一个漂亮姑娘夹在你跟你爱人中间可不明智,何况那个侍女娇媚罕见,而女孩本人姿色平平。

出发前,女孩被打扮得花枝招展,还围了一段绸缎在腰上,所有嫁妆装在盒子里顶在头上,就这样前往夫家。酋长听说新娘子已经在来的路上的消息,就命令他的族人们把从他家至博城①大概80英里的路上,铺上了最豪华的棉布来迎接。

由于女孩从没走过这么远的路,刚出自己的寝宫没几步,不到半英里,她就开始喊累了。她不小心踩到了一队军蚁,有一只咬了女孩的脚趾一口,女孩疼得叫起来:"老天爷,看哪!什么东西咬我了。"

侍女对她说:"我早就说过,你的裙子迟早会拖累你。咱俩互换衣服吧。"

"为啥?"

"这样蚂蚁就咬不到你了。"侍女撒谎道。

于是,女孩脱了腰上的绸缎给侍女穿。"嫁妆盒也交给你了。"女孩把嫁妆盒也给了侍女。

她们到了后,人们把侍女错当成了新娘。接新娘的人用花轿把侍女抬回了酋长的庭院里。歇息片刻后,他们让女孩端水给侍女洗浴,侍女接过水盆,试了试水温后就开始洗浴,然后被送入洞房舒舒服服地歇着。

第二天清晨,有人交给女孩一些稻谷让她去舂米。她一边舂米一边唱着一首悲伤的歌。第二天，她在舂米时仍然唱着同一首歌，这被偶然路过的酋长的一个传令官听到了，并报告给了酋长。酋长一听，就亲自去了女孩舂米的地方看个究竟。只见女孩一边舂米一边唱着：

（合唱）天呐！
我本是女仆的主人，
如今却成了女仆的仆人。

酋长听到这歌声后，返回住处叫了一个信使赶紧去把亲家酋长叫来。在去镇子的路上，酋长看到了正在舂米的女儿。女孩的父亲一到，径直去了女婿的卧室。在那里，酋长看到侍女正躺在女婿床上。他顿时火冒三丈，狠狠踹了侍女一脚。如今，打雷时你听到的声响就是那一脚的余音。侍女被狂风刮到天上，头磕到天堂里的一座金屋又弹到另一座，就这样天堂里的每座金屋都被她磕了个遍，而她眼里淌出的泪花就形成了我们现在的雨，所以下雨天总让人感觉阴郁。

注释 ① 博城，塞拉利昂第二大城市，距首都弗里敦300多千米，是塞拉利昂南部的行政中心，同时也是塞拉利昂国内的交通运输、商务、教育中心。博城于1889年铁路出现时开始了现代化进程，它曾是塞拉利昂为英国保护国时的首都。博城人以友好、善良、纯真著称，因此，博城有"甜蜜博城"的美誉。当地的曼迪族人对中国人尤其友好。据说，"博城"这个名字源自当地人的慷慨。一天，猎人射杀了一头大象，周围村庄的村民们都跑过来分领象肉。由于象肉很多，猎人花了几天时间才把象肉分完，并且不停地对来领取的村民说"Bo-lor"（这是给你的）。当地的老人及一些游客于是决定将此地取名为"Bo"（博城）。

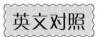

西非民间口头文学作品欣赏（塞拉利昂篇）

英文对照

The Maid's Maid

Heh, too much craftiness is not good in this world. I am going to tell you about it so that you can store it in your mind.

There were two rich chiefs. One got married to the daughter of the other. The bride was born, bred and nurtured in a multistory building. She had never put her feet on the ground below.

It is advisable that when you are sending a bride away to her husband, you make sure that a reliable person accompanies her there. It is also advisable that a relative visit the couple occasionally.

After the marriage had been contracted, the bride's parents sent her away to her husband after a few days, with a maid to accompany her. It is never good to use a beautiful woman as a mediator between you and your lover. The maid was a rare beauty, and the chief's daughter was not.

Before they set out, they dressed the bride gorgeously and wrapped just a satin around the maid's waist, put all the loads on her head, and off they went. When he got the news that his wife was on the way, the chief asked his subjects to spread the largest cotton clothes on the path over a distance as long as from here to Bo, about 80 miles.

Because the bride had never walked long distances before, except to move about in her palace, she started to get tired before they had covered even a quarter of a mile. They stepped on some driver-ants. One of them bit the bride on her toe. "Kwo-oBoi-Joe, look! Something has bitten me," she cried.

"I told you before that that dress would eventually become a bother to you. Give me the dress you have on," the maid requested.

"Why?" the chief's daughter asked.

"If you do so, the ants will not bite you again," the maid lied.

She took off all that she had on and gave to the maid to wear: "Now you carry the box." The maid put the box on her mistress' head.

As they arrived in the town, it was the maid whom the people mistakenly regarded as the bride. She was soon carried in a hammock to the chief's compound accompanied by a hornman. After they had rested, they asked the chief's daughter to go and fetch water for the bride to bathe. She fetched the water, warmed it, the maid bathed and was led to a comfortable bed to rest.

The following morning the chief's daughter was given some husk rice to pound. While pounding she began to sing a sorrowful song. The following day when she was pounding again and singing the same song, one of the chief's informants overheard her and alerted the chief. Soon, the chief himself left for the farm where the chief's daughter was pounding and singing.

Chorus: Yayamingo yamingo-o.

I, the owner of the maid

Have become my maid's maid.

When the chief heard the song, he went back to his palace and sent a messenger to call his father-in-law. As the girl's father came, he went straight to his son-in-law's palace where he found the maid on the chief's bed. On his way to the town he had found his daughter pounding rice. In a rage, he kicked the maid. All the thundering sounds that we hear today are as a result of that kick. There was no zinc house in heaven that that maid's head did not knock against. Her head went knocking a zinc house in heaven, "gbubum, gbubum". The tears that rolled down her eyes are what we call rain today. Those tears were a very sorrowful sight.

披着羊皮的狼

从前有个叫辛巴克罗的村子，大猫住在那里。大猫生性狂野，面容可怖，和老鼠一族是死对头，每当他见到一只老鼠就会抓住吃掉，以此来表达他对世上所有老鼠的不满和敌意。因为吃了太多，老鼠几乎要被他灭族了。

一天傍晚，全部老鼠都聚集到辛巴克罗，想找到摆脱他们的死对头大猫的方法。

鼠群里，最矮小但也是最聪明的凌迪站出来说："兄弟姐妹们，欢迎大家前来开会，找出最佳方案脱离窘境是我们的当务之急。咱们去找大猫，让他在咱们向真主祷告的时候在一旁听颂，让唤礼之声来感化他这个吃鼠的恶魔，咱们或许能免于屠杀。"

老鼠们认为可行，就派遣了一对使者去找大猫。见到大猫后，使者们说明了来意，恳请大猫在他们祷告的时候在一旁听颂。听到这些祷告，无论是怎样的人都会被感化，放下屠刀。这样一来，就能减少他们的伤亡。

大猫听后，回答说："伙计们，很抱歉告诉你们，我是屠戮过你们的同胞，但既然你们都求我了，我就该同情一下你们。我衷心认同我们该向真主祷告来让我克制住杀伐的行为。我会去麦加圣地，加入圣徒的队伍，向真主祷告，这样或许更加行之有效，也显得更虔诚。"

但大猫言行不一，他只是想找个借口让老鼠们察觉不到他们将要遭受的灾难。大猫也明白，等他从麦加回来，老鼠的种群早已成倍地壮大了。

老鼠们收到大猫的回复，松了一口气，他们很开心，大猫终于答应不再屠杀他们。为此，他们为种族屠杀的告终大摆筵席，以示庆祝。到了大猫启程朝圣麦加的日子，世上所有老鼠都带着从圣地回来后的大猫将不再杀伐他们的期盼为他的朝圣筹集路费。

大猫去了麦加，在那儿待了近一个月。快要回去的时候，大猫给老鼠们寄了一封信，这样老鼠们就能满心欢喜地迎接他回家。老鼠们也正准备为即将朝圣归来的大猫办一场盛大的宴席。老鼠收到大猫的信后，花了好几个钟头清扫辛巴克罗，然后准备了一顿豪华大宴席：有白米饭、甜蔗汁、果酱，只要你能想到的美食，应有尽有，他们还组建了车队去机场迎接大猫回来。那天，大猫一到机场就受到了老鼠们簇拥而至的迎接。刚下飞机就被套上了圣徒的长袍，头上的头巾也显得金灿灿的，还有老鼠乐师们为他演奏，在宴席上，大猫也坐在上席，俨然成了焦点人物。

凌迪看着已成圣徒的大猫，左看看右看看，都快把大猫印在眼里了。接着，他小声地跟同伴说："大猫真的是从麦加回来的吗？他真的心地变善良了吗？我咋不太信呢？但不管咋说，咱们走着瞧吧。"其他老鼠没把凌迪的话太当回事，他们沉浸在狂欢和喜悦中，大吃大喝着，以为大猫再也不吃他们了。

凌迪还是担心，他把不同家族的老鼠长老一个个叫来，提醒他们不要对大猫放松警惕。"我看大猫没一点圣徒的样子，我总感觉他还是不怀好意，你们还是小心为妙。""你就别拿这事烦我们了，我们到这来是享受的，不是找罪受的，咱们都知道大猫已经去过了麦加，向真主发过誓，再也不捕杀咱们了，他会信守承诺。咱们现在自由了，好好享受漫长余生吧！"凌迪和大伙就这样不欢而散。

有些老鼠正围着大猫转悠，甚至会坐到他的头和肩膀上，但大猫面不改色。后来，"圣徒"还是出手了。他先从醉倒在他袍子底下的老鼠开始，抓住一只老鼠就拧断脖子，直接在宴席上大快朵颐。没过一会儿，有些老鼠也发现情况不太对劲，自己的同伴越来越少了。而机智的凌迪早已远离了大猫，对他持敬而远之的态度，并且惋惜同伴不听他话。不一会儿，老鼠们发现大猫正在一个个地屠杀他们，就一个个都跑走了。大猫也察觉事情败露，便恼羞成怒，扯掉头巾，撕开袍子，扑向鼠群。老鼠们争相逃命，远在辛巴克罗百里外的地方都能听到他们的呼救声。凌迪躲在角落目睹了这一切，有些老鼠死于了大屠杀，有些也死里逃生了。从那天起，猫和老鼠就成了不共戴天的仇人。

时至今日，像这样的事还在不断上演。亲爱的朋友们，请多多留意那些自称"圣人"的人，他们可能像大猫一样有着狼子野心，却是披着羊皮的狼。他们满口伦理道德，用身份来掩饰自己。

{英文对照}

A Wolf in Sheep's Clothes

There was a village called Simbakoro. In this village lived Bra Cat. He was wild and fearful. Rats were his enemies. Anytime he saw one he would catch one and eat one. He ate so many rats that he nearly finished that rat family. This incurred the wrath and animosity of all the rats in the world.

One evening, all the rats assembled at Simbakoro to find ways and means of getting rid of their enemy, Bra Cat.

In the meeting, Lendii (the smallest but cleverest) of the rats stood up and said, "My dear brothers and sisters, I welcome you all to this important meeting. It is indeed necessary that we find the best solution to our problems. Let us meet Bra Cat and ask him to join us in offering prayers to the Almighty God to appeal to the evildoer to stop killing and eating us."

All the rats agreed and they sent a delegation to meet Bra Cat. The delegation met Bra Cat. They explained their problem to him and appealed to Bra Cat to join them in offering prayers so that whoever is responsible for their death will stop killing them.

Bra Cat said, "My friends, I am very sorry to inform you that I have been killing your fellow rats. But since you have pleaded to me, I greatly sympathise with you. I agree with you wholeheartedly that we should all pray to God to help me to resist from such practices. To make my prayer quickly and more acceptable to God, I am going to proceed to the Holyland in Mecca to join other holy Muslims to offer prayers to God for you."

Bra Cat did not mean what he said. He was finding a way to divert the rat's attention from their calamity. He also knew that if he went to Mecca, by the time he would have returned rats would have multiplied in size and number.

The rats accepted Bra Cat's message in good faith. They were happy that their tormentor would stop tormenting them. They therefore made a great feast to mark an end to cannibalism. Bra Cat fixed the date for his pilgrimage to Mecca. All the rats in the world made financial contributions to the pilgrimage in the hope that when Bra Cat returned from the Holyland, he would not eat them again.

Bra Cat went to Mecca. He spent almost four weeks in Mecca. When he was about to return, he sent a letter to the rats so that they could happily welcome him back home. They were to hold a great feast for Bra Cat. The rats conceded to Bra Cat's request. They spent hours on end keeping Simbakoro clean. They prepared a splendid feast. Everything, rice, rum, sauce, you name it—was there in abundance. A long motorcade was set to bring Alhaji Cat from the aeroplane field. The day arrived. All the rats assembled at the airfield to welcome Alhaji Cat. When he landed from the plane, he was well clothed in the Alhaji attire. His turban was shining like gold. He was welcomed by the best musicians of the rats. In the party, he occupied the high table, at the centre of all the rats.

Lendii looked at Alhaji. He looked and looked and looked. He looked deeply into his eyes. He whispered to his friends, "Do you think that Bra Cat is from Mecca? Do you think that he has changed his ways? I doubt it very much. Anyway, let's wait and see." The other rats did not take Lendii seriously. They were overjoyed with happiness. They ate, drank and danced to the end of cannibalism in the rat kingdom.

Lendii was worried. He called all the different rat families one by one and warned them against Alhaji Cat. "I am not satisfied with Alhaji," he said. "I have a feeling that all is not well with us. So please be on your guard," he concluded. The other rats told Lendii, "Please don't disturb us. We have come here to enjoy ourselves but not to talk about evil things. We know that Cat has been to Mecca and he has taken an oath before the

Almighty Allah that he will not kill us again. He will keep to his promise. Freedom is ours. Long life is ours." Thus they did not listen to Lendii's advice.

Some of the rats would run around, sit on his turban, but he didn't do anything. At last Alhaji decided to play his game. He started with those who were drunk and who were under his gown. He would catch a rat, twist its neck quietly and eat it whilst the party was going on. With time some rats became conscious of what was going on. The number of rats started to diminish. Lendii, the cleverest of them all stayed far away from Alhaji and watched everything with admiration for Alhaji and contempt for his fellow rats who had not listened to his advice. Soon all the rats realized that Alhaji was killing them. Alhaji too knew that the rats had known what he was doing. The rats decided to stay away from him. He became annoyed, threw off his turban, threw off his big gown and pounced on the rats. The rats ran for their lives. Their wailings were heard 100 miles off Simbakoro. Lendii hid himself in a corner and enjoyed it all. Some rats got killed in the process and others escaped. Since then rats and cats have been enemies.

Is the same thing not happening today? My dear people, be aware of some of these Alhajis and Alhajas. They could behave like Alhaji Cat. They never leave their bad games. They always hide under the name of Alhaji and Alhaja.

杜果名字的由来

从前,邦特有个白人要步行去一个很远的村子。那时候的路还不能通车。走了很远一段路后,干粮都吃完了,可离那个村子依然很远,路边不见有人烟,他饿得都快要走不动路了。就在他坐下来休息时,他看到在离他几码远的一棵树上挂着一些奇怪的水果。

他走到树前,发现果实已经成熟,于是决定尝一尝,就爬上了那棵树。

那时,人们对这种水果还一无所知。尝了一个后,他发现果子味道非常鲜美。于是他吃了很多,还摘了一些,准备路上吃。吃饱后,他说:"(肚子)满裹(杜果)。"就这样,人们就开始用"杜果"来称呼这种水果。

英文对照

How the Mango Got Its Name

There was once a white man from Bonthe who had to walk to a distant village. At that time, there were no motorable roads. Having to walk a very long way, his food supply finished while he was still a long way from the village. There were no houses along the road. The man became so hungry that he could go no further. As he sat down resting, he saw strange fruits hanging from a tree, a few yards from him.

He walked up to the tree and then noticed that the fruits were ripe. He decided to taste some and he climbed the tree.

At that time men didn't know anything about this fruit. After tasting one he realized that it was very delicious. He ate a lot and took some with him. When he was well-fed, he said, "Now, MAN GO." And it was from those words that the name "mango" came to be used.

穷小子与坏人

从前有个坏人喜欢欺骗穷人。有天坏人雇了个穷小子到他家里干活。坏人对穷小子说:"要是你干得好的话,我月底就付你两英镑,但有个条件,付工钱之前,我要你给我拿回两样东西来。你要是拿不回来的话,那我就一分钱都不会付给你,你觉得怎么样?"穷小子一听,一个月能赚两英镑,高兴坏了,想都没想就答应了这个条件。

穷小子连续工作了整整一个月,到月底最后一天时,他跑去跟雇主说:"我把活干完了,您还满意吧?"这个坏人说:"我挺满意的。"穷小子又问:"您告诉我,给我付两英镑工资前,要我拿回来的那两件东西到底是啥?"坏人邪恶一笑:"把'嘻'和'哈'带给我,我就会给你工资了。"听到这个,穷小子仿佛遭到了晴天霹雳,自言自语到底什么才是"嘻"和"哈"呢?但他是个聪明的小伙子,不一会就想出了一个好点子。

他跑到森林中一个黑漆漆的山洞里,他对那里很熟悉,摸索了一阵后,在里面抓了一只大蜘蛛,又抓了一只蝎子。他用钳子把蜘蛛和蝎子放到一个黑瓶子里,把它密封好带回给了雇主。

"这里面就是'嘻'和'哈'。"穷小子说。

穷小子的坏人雇主往黑瓶子里面看了一眼,问穷小子:"你往里边放了些什么?"

穷小子回答:"把手指伸进去,'嘻'和'哈'就出来了。"说完,他把瓶塞打开了。

坏人雇主把手指伸了进去,蝎子狠狠地蜇了他一下,疼得他"哈呀哈呀"地叫了起来。穷小子大笑了起来,说已经给他"哈"了。"现在把你另一个手指伸进去,你就能拿到'嘻'了。"但坏人雇主已经被吓怕了,赶紧付给了穷小子应得的两英镑。

西非民间口头文学作品欣赏（塞拉利昂篇）

英文对照

A Poor Boy and a Wicked Man

Once upon a time there lived a wicked man who liked to cheat poor people. One day he engaged a poor boy to work for him in his house. "If you work well," he said to him, "I will give you two pounds at the end of the month with on one condition. Before paying you, I shall send you to fetch me two things. If you do not bring them to me, you will not get one penny of your wages. Do you agree?" The boy, pleased at the idea of earning two pounds a month, accepted his condition, without further reflection.

Throughout the month the boy worked conscientiously, and when the last day of the month arrived, he went to his master and said, "I have finished my work. Are you pleased with it?" "I am very pleased," said the master. "Well, tell me what the two things are before you give me my two pounds," said the boy. Then the wicked man replied with an evil grin, "Bring me Hi and Ha and you shall have your pay." The poor boy was thunder struck at this, and asked himself what on earth Hi and Ha might be. But he was a very cunning lad and he soon had a bright idea.

So he went away into the forest to a very dark cave that he knew of, and there he caught a huge spider. After looking around for a while, he also found a scorpion. With the aid of some pincers, he put them both into a black bottle, which he carefully corked and carried back to his master.

"Here," he said, "are Hi and Ha."

The boy's master looked at the bottle and asked the boy, "What have you got there?"

The boy said, "Put your finger in and you will bring out Hi and Ha," and he uncorked the bottle.

The master thereupon put his finger in, and the scorpion gave him such a sharp bite that he cried out "Ha-a-a". Then they boy laughed aloud and said, "You have got Ha. Now put your other finger in and you will get Hi." But his master had had enough and paid the poor boy his two pounds.

西非民间口头文学作品欣赏（塞拉利昂篇）

以德报德

  邪恶存在于世上不是一天两天了，它的存世之久是无法想象的。但可以肯定的是，邪恶是和人类一同来到这个世界的，因此，它总是处处与人相随。
  很久很久以前，有条鳄鱼住在溪流里。那条小溪是他的固定居所。但有一年天气异常反常，雨迟迟不下，所有溪流都干涸了。那时的人们还会捕猎鳄鱼作为食物，所以鳄鱼担心会有人类来捕杀自己，于是苦苦寻人将自己从干涸的小溪里救出来，带到河边。几近绝望时，他看见一个天真的小女孩经过。那个女孩正要去另一个村子，给她母亲的友人送垫子。当小女孩走到离他不远的地方时，他扑到小女孩面前。女孩走近鳄鱼，问他是否需要帮忙。鳄鱼对她说："好姑娘，过去二十年来我一直生活在这个地方，没吃的也没人来帮我，我现在非常虚弱也非常饿，希望你能把我带去最近的河边，把我留在那里。"
  小女孩说："可能有点难，先生，妈妈派我把这个垫子送到隔壁村子的朋友那去。我很赶时间，再说，我也抱不动你呀？"最后，鳄鱼还是说服了小女孩帮助他摆脱险境。
  鳄鱼对她说："好姑娘，如果你把我留在这里，我就会被杀掉，你不妨把我严严实实裹在你的垫子里，把我带到最近的河边，我非常渴，求你了，好姑娘，救救我吧。"
  小女孩答应了。她铺开垫子，把鳄鱼严严实实包好，顶在头上。一路上她遇到了很多人，但她都没有透露自己头上顶着什么东西。她走了很远才来到一条河边。她告诉鳄鱼，到河边了。鳄鱼央求小女孩把他放到河中央，女孩就把他抱到河中央，说："好了，我得走了。"鳄鱼转向她说："好姑娘，我得跟你说实话，我说过我非常饿，因为我已经好几年没吃东西了，现在我必须吃了你，若放你走，那我就是对不起自己了。"
  小女孩无法相信，目瞪口呆。她对鳄鱼说："我救了你的命，还耽搁了我自己的事,就为了把你顶在头上扛到了这里,我本以为你会以德报德的。"

鳄鱼告诉小女孩别说胡话了。她的"以德报德"理论在世界上的任何地方都站不住脚。小女孩告诉他,她从小就这样对别人,也期待别人回报。鳄鱼完全不能理解这种"迟钝"的生活哲学。这个小女孩恳求鳄鱼饶了她,但鳄鱼不肯。最后,鳄鱼对小女孩说:"那我们问三个路人你的善举是否值得回报,如果他们都觉得值,你就自由了,但如果他们都说不值,那我就只好吃了你。"

小女孩同意了。几分钟后,马来到河边喝水。鳄鱼对他喊道:"马先生,您帮我们琢磨琢磨,'以德报德'有道理吗?"马转过身来对他们说:"不管是谁跟你们说的这些,他一定是个疯子,创造世界的时候可没按照这个理论。瞧瞧我,我曾经背着我的主人越过高山,跨过平原,穿过荆棘丛生的灌木,做牛做马不知付出了多少,可现在我老了,主人一家子都不想管我了,你也瞧见了,我是孤孤单单地来喝水的。所以说善有善报是假的。"

鳄鱼转身对小女孩说:"听见了吧?"不久,牛也来喝水了。鳄鱼又问牛:"'以德报德'有道理吗?"牛慢慢地抬起头来,嘲笑他们说:"你们疯了吗?竟然会相信以德报德。我年轻的时候是主人的财富来源,但他卖了我的孩子,卖我的乳水,主人也因此变得富有。可现在,我老了,有人说还不如把我卖给屠夫。你能想象吗?谁说善有善报?"鳄鱼转身对小女孩说:"听见了吧,你还是放弃吧,你的'以德报德'理论已经被驳斥两次了。"但是,小女孩坚持要等第三次。

第三个经过河边的是"勒姆"先生,一种极具智慧的动物。在非洲的文学作品里,"勒姆"是所有动物里最聪慧的。他一来,鳄鱼就问了他同样的问题。勒姆回答说:"在没了解事情原委之前我通常不会下结论,那么,能告诉我是什么导致您问我这个问题吗?"

鳄鱼把事情的来龙去脉都告诉了勒姆。说的也都是实话。勒姆对他说:"朋友,首先我不太相信,一个小女孩竟然能把你顶在头上带过来。我想亲眼看看,你俩能从河里出来一下吗?"鳄鱼于是又说服小女孩,叫她答应再把自己顶在头上带出河里,证明给勒姆看。勒姆又对鳄鱼说:"你躺到垫子上,让小女孩把你包裹好,再让她顶到头上让我看看。"

小女孩再次放开垫子,再把鳄鱼包裹好了。然后,勒姆让小女孩拿来一根绳子把鳄鱼绑了起来。小女孩照做了。小女孩刚把鳄鱼顶到头上,勒姆就走近去跟她说:"姑娘,难道你是'舍塞斯'人吗?"(舍塞斯人就是那些不吃鳄鱼的人。) 现在鳄鱼对你欲行不轨,倒不如以其人之道还治其人之身,把他带到你村子里去,把他烤着吃了,他心地太坏了,把他带走吧。"

鳄鱼嘶叫着,但因为被绑着逃不了。小女孩就这样把他带到了村子里。你能想象鳄鱼的下场会是什么吗?恩德终究还须以恩德相报啊!

One Good Turn

Ungratefulness was not born yesterday. I cannot even hazard a guess at his age. All I know is, it came to this world the same time man entered this world. So it has always lived with man.

In the very distant past, a crocodile was living in a stream. This was his permanent abode. But there was a particularly bad year when rains refused to come. So all the streams dried up. This crocodile was marooned in this dried-up stream. He was there fearing that some human beings would come and kill him. This was the time when people ate crocodiles and were in constant search of them. The crocodile was looking for a friend to rescue him and took him to a river. He was almost going to give up when he saw an innocent young girl passing by. This girl was sent to another village to carry a mat for her mother's friend. When the girl came near where he was, the crocodile beckoned to the young girl. She went near him and asked what she could do for the crocodile. The crocodile said to her, "My little girl, I have been living in this place for twenty years without food and nobody to help me. I am terribly feeble and hungry. I would like you to carry me to the nearest river and leave me there."

The young girl said, "Well, sir, I was sent by my mother to take this mat to a friend in the next village and it is urgent. How can I carry you?" The crocodile persuaded the young girl to help him out of his precarious situation.

He said to her, "My girl, if you leave me here, I will be killed. I want you to wrap me neatly in your mat and carry me to the nearest river. I am extremely thirsty. Please my girl, do this for me."

The little girl consented. She rolled out the mat for him, she wrapped him neatly and carried him on her head. On her way, she came across many people but she did not disclose what she was carrying on her head. She walked a very long distance before she could come to a river. When she came to the river, she told the crocodile that she had come to a river. The crocodile asked the little girl to leave him in the middle of the river. The girl took him in the middle of the river and said, "Here you are. I must go." Then the crocodile turned to her and said, "My girl, I must be frank to you. I told you I was terribly hungry since I have gone without food for years. Now I must eat you. If I let you go, I will be doing injustice to myself."

The little girl could not believe this. She was dumbfounded. Then she said to the crocodile, "Do you mean you are going to eat me? I saved your life. I even had to forget about my errand, carried you on my head to this place. I would have thought one good turn deserves another."

The crocodile told the little girl that she was talking nonsense. That her "one good turn" philosophy was not tenable anywhere in the world. The little girl told him that this was what she was brought up to do to others, and to expect from others. The crocodile completely dissociated himself from such "obtuse" philosophy of life. The little girl pleaded with him but he would not let her free. Finally, the crocodile said to the girl, "Now, we are going to ask three people who pass by whether one good turn is bound to deserve another. If all of them say yes, then you will go free; but if all of them say no, I will eat you."

The little girl agreed to this. A few minutes later, a horse came to the river to drink. The crocodile called to him and said, "Mr. Horse, could you please help us here? Is it true that one good turn deserves another?" The horse turned to them and said, "Whoever told you that must be mad. The world is not created on that principle. Look at me! I used to carry my owner on my back through mountains, plains, thorny shrubs, etc. Now when I am old, neither his children nor he cares about me. Don't you see I come alone to drink water? So it is not true that one good turn deserves another."

The crocodile turned to the little girl and said, "Did you hear that?" Shortly after, a cow also came to drink from the river. Again the crocodile asked the cow whether it was true that one good turn deserved another. The cow slowly raised his head and laughed at them. He said to them, "You must be crazy to believe that one good turn deserves another. When I was young I used to be a source of wealth for my Master. He would sell my children, he would milk me and sell the milk. He became rich from this. Now that I have grown old, there is talk about selling me to the knacker. Can you imagine that? Who says one good turn deserves another?" The crocodile turned to the little girl and said, "Did you hear that as well? You had better give up because already two people have refuted your 'one good turn' theory." The little girl insisted that the third person came.

The third person to come to the river was Mr. Lem. This was an extremely witty animal. In fact, in the African context, he is the most intelligent of all the animals. When he came, Mr. Crocodile posed the same question to him. Mr. Lem said to them. "Well, I don't normally give a verdict until I know the background of the case. May I know what happened that now leads to this question?"

The crocodile explained what transpired between him and the little girl. He spoke the truth. Then the Lem said to him, "My friend, in the first place, I don't believe that the young girl carried you on her head. I want to see it with my eyes. Can both of you then come out of the water?" Fully convinced that the girl carried him on her head, the crocodile agreed to come out of the water and prove it to Mr. Lem. The Lem said to the crocodile, "Now let me see you lie down on that mat, wrapped and carried on this little girl's head."

The little girl rolled out her mat again and wrapped the crocodile. Then the Lem asked the girl to bring a rope and tie the crocodile. She did. When she put the crocodile on her head, the Lem came close to the little girl and said, "My little girl, are your people SESAYS by surname? (The Sesays were the people who did not eat crocodiles.) This crocodile was going to be ungrateful to you; now pay him in his own coin. Take him to your village and roast and eat him. He is a damned ungrateful wretch. Now take him along."

The crocodile was wailing but he could not escape because he was tied. So the little girl took him to the village. You can guess what happened to Mr. Crocodile. One good turn deserves another.

狗与影子

从前有只贪吃的狗,无论吃多少也填不满肚子。那时正值丰收时节,食物充足。贪吃狗的主人是个有名的猎手,每天都能带着猎物回家。那只狗就每天不停地吃啊吃,有好几次它都因为肚子吃得太饱而无法呼吸。贪吃狗从不让其他狗靠近它的食物,有猫、狗或母鸡胆敢靠近它吃东西的地方,它就会把它们撕成碎片。

有一天,狗主人在狩猎后满载而归,那是它主人在猎人生涯中最大的一次收获。通常所有的猎物都会和着米饭一起烹饪。当主人坐下来吃的时候,汤勺里最大的一块肉从他手里滑落到了地上。主人还没来得及眨眼睛,贪吃狗叼起那块肉就跑了。它一直跑到了镇子边缘的一座桥上。它在桥上望了望水面,看到了水里自己的倒影。贪吃狗以为那是另一只狗叼着一大块肉。它就一直这样看着,并还想要得到那块肉。它不知道那是它的影子。它告诉自己,水里的狗叼着的肉比它的还要大,所以它必须拿到那块肉。

它冲着倒影吠叫,想着水里的狗听到它的吠叫会吓得把肉松开。但它一叫,它自己嘴里的肉就掉到水里沉了下去。它再往下看着水面,只见水里还是有只狗,但肉不见了。它不停吠叫着,直到累了才回家。回到家,贪吃狗挨了主人无情的一顿鞭打。这只贪婪的狗赔了夫人又折兵,既没吃到肉,又因为擅自叼走肉挨了顿打。这就是为什么当你什么都想要的时候,却往往什么也得不到。

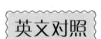

The Dog and His Shadow

Once upon a time, there lived a very gluttonous dog. He would never go satisfied however much he ate. He would eat for years continuously without going satisfied. This was the time of harvest when there was enough food in the land. The owner of this greedy dog was a hunter, and was a well-known hunter. He would bring home games every day. This dog would eat and eat and eat. There were times when he could not even breathe because there was no space left for breathing. He would not allow any other dog to even come around. If any dog or cat, or even a hen came near where he ate, he would tear him to pieces.

One day his owner got a very big game, the biggest one he ever got since his career as a hunter. As usual, all of it was cooked with plenty of rice. When the hunter sat down eating, the biggest lump of meat in the soup dropped from his hand on to the ground. Before the hunter could wink his eyes, the dog had grabbed the meat and run with it. He ran and ran until he came to a bridge in the outskirts of the town. When he came to the bridge, he looked in the water, and he saw a reflection of himself. The greedy dog thought this was another dog with a big lump of meat in his mouth. He looked, and looked and looked; he wanted that meat too. But this was only his own shadow. He convinced himself that the lump of meat he was seeing in the water, in the mouth of his fellow dog, was bigger than his. So he must have it as well.

He barked at the reflection in order that the dog he was seeing in the water would drop his meat and he would take it. When he barked, his own meat dropped from his mouth and went deep down the river. He looked down again in the river and saw that the dog in the water too did not have meat any more. He barked and barked and barked until he was tired. He then returned home. When he got home his owner flogged him mercilessly. So the greedy dog lost on both sides—he could not eat the meat and he was beaten for taking it away. This is why you end up missing all if you want all at the same time.

老鹰与麻雀

从前，麻雀找到老鹰，想借一头牛为他去世的父亲举行某种仪式的葬礼。在把牛交给麻雀前，老鹰坚持要签署一份协议。

协议的第一部分是，每当鹰来接牛时，他不能发现麻雀闲着。如果发现麻雀无所事事，麻雀就要当场把牛还给老鹰。协议的第二部分是，如果麻雀像其他鸟一样身体会长大，那麻雀就要偿还债务。老鹰不知道麻雀和其他鸟类不同，麻雀体型总是很小。

一年后，老鹰来接他的牛。麻雀说："你也看到了，我正忙着偿还借牛的债务，所以我没有闲着。"于是，老鹰回家了，第二年他又回来取牛。麻雀说很忙，他告诉老鹰，他正在尽最大努力筹集资金来偿还债务。

第三年，老鹰又去麻雀家里。在路上，他遇到了母鸡。母鸡问他要去哪里。老鹰回答说："我要去麻雀那里取回一头牛。麻雀的父亲去世时，麻雀向我借了一头牛来举行一个仪式。"老鹰把他们达成协议的事告诉了母鸡。母鸡说："告诉你吧，麻雀是一种不安分的鸟，他总是动来动去永不停歇，而且，如果你想知道他会不会长大，只要看看他父母就行了，你会发现他们外表体型都很相近。"

因此，老鹰再去找麻雀时，他就要求见见麻雀的父母。麻雀进到房子里，和父母一起出来了。他们长得实在太像了，老鹰根本分不清谁是谁了。他很生气，一把抓住离他最近的那只麻雀，要求把他的牛立刻要回来。老鹰说："有人告诉我了，你们这种鸟永远不会长大。"恰巧，老鹰抓住的那只就是欠债的麻雀。麻雀问老鹰他是怎么知道的。老鹰回答说，是母鸡告诉他麻雀的体型都是一般大小。于是麻雀问老鹰："这么说，是母鸡泄露了我们族群的秘密？""是的。"老鹰回答说。"那好吧，"麻雀说，"无论什么时候，只要你看到了母鸡，就立刻抓住她，撕开她的肚子，你会发现她肚子里的东西和牛肚子里的东西是一样的。"

于是老鹰就飞去找母鸡。时至今日，老鹰还会搜寻母鸡，以验证麻雀的话是否属实。

英文对照

Hawk and Sparrow

Once upon a time Sparrow went to Hawk to borrow a cow in order to perform a certain ceremony for his late father.

Before handing over the cow to Sparrow, Hawk insisted that they sign an agreement.

The first part of the agreement was that whenever Hawk came to collect the cow, he should not find Sparrow idle. If he found him idle, Sparrow should refund the cow on the spot. The second part of the agreement was that Sparrow would repay his debt if he grew in size like other birds. Hawk did not know that Sparrow, unlike other birds, is always small in size.

After a year Hawk came to collect his cow. Sparrow said to him, "As you can see I am busy working to refund your cow, I have not been idle." So Hawk went home and returned the next year to collect his cow. Again Sparrow was busy and told Hawk that he was doing his best to raise money to repay the debt.

In the third year Hawk set out again for Sparrow's house. On the way he came across Hen who asked him where he was going. Hawk replied, "I am going to collect a cow from Sparrow who borrowed it to perform a certain ceremony when his father died." Hawk told Hen about the agreement they had made. Hen said, "Let me tell you the truth: Sparrow is a restless bird. He is always on the move. Moreover, if you want to know whether he will ever increase in size, just ask him to show you his parents. You will find out that they are so much alike."

So when Hawk visited Sparrow again he asked to see Sparrow's parents. Sparrow went into the house and came out with his father and mother. They were so much alike that Hawk could not tell them apart. In anger, he seized the bird that was very close to him and demanded his cow, saying, "I was told that you belong to a group of birds which never grow in size." Fortunately the bird Hawk seized was the debtor. Sparrow asked Hawk how he got this information. Hawk replied that it was Hen who told him about the normal size of Sparrows. Then Sparrow asked Hawk, "So is it Hen who revealed our family secret?" "Yes," answered Hawk. "Well," said Sparrow, "whenever you see Hen, arrest her immediately and tear her stomach open, there you will surely find something similar to your cow."

So Hawk flew off in search of Hen; even today Hawks are still looking out for Hens to discover the truth of Sparrow's statement.

长毛的青蛙

从前有个农夫住在一个叫罗斯卡的村子里。那个村子之所以会叫这个名字,是因为地里有很多石头。

尽管土地存在这种问题,农夫还是打算在上面种点什么,于是决定在地里大规模地种植花生。他犁好几百英亩地,在地里下好花生种子后,心中开始满怀期待。不久,花生发芽了。每天早晨,他都要在农场巡查,以确保害虫和老鼠不会破坏庄稼。庄稼丰收时,大家纷纷给他竖起了大拇指。

一天,鼠王召集会议。在这次会议上,鼠王跟他的臣民们谈到了人类的邪恶。他告诉他的臣民,有些人类是因为吃多了老鼠才长得肥头大耳,于是提议向人类复仇。一只老鼠站起来说:"陛下,人类会吃老鼠是事实,我们的种群有一天可能会因此而灭绝。但我有一种预感,目前我们还不能对人类发动战争,因为我们连一根棍子都拿不住。"鼠王和其他老鼠也表示同意。另一只老鼠站起来说:"既然人类都穿着衣服生活,我们为什么不干脆在他们睡觉的时候偷他们的衣服呢?"鼠王回答说,这很难,因为我们甚至不知道究竟有多少人类。正在开会时,一只老鼠气喘吁吁地跑了过来。显然,他要给大家带来些好消息。

他上气不接下气地说:"陛下,我发现了一大片花生田,就在几英里外,现在向您报告。"老鼠们听到这个消息很兴奋。鼠王当即宣布,战争的消耗会从掠夺人类的成果中赚回来。于是,花生田就这样被毁了。那天晚上,老鼠们去了花生田里,毁掉了一部分庄稼。第二天早上,农夫如往常一样下田巡查。他意识到肯定是某些动物在头一天晚上来田里毁了庄稼,但究竟是什么动物他就不得而知了。因此,农夫决定晚上留守在农田查个水落石出。农夫在农场待了一整晚,但没有看到任何动物。接下来的两个晚上依然一无所获。其实,老鼠们也在监视他,所以他们不去花生田里。正当农夫放弃时,老鼠又来了,破坏了农场的另一部分。农夫决定去拜访先知解惑时,老鼠几乎要把庄稼摧毁殆尽了。

  农夫先去拜访了一只叫露露的聪明的鸟。他向露露说明了来意。露露拿出一张垫子和一个又旧又脏的袋子，这两件东西看起来起码有二十年没洗过了。袋子里装着珠子和其他物品，露露用它们咨询神谕，并对农夫说："到农场周围筑一道篱笆，留下一个小缺口，你可以坐在那里观察，这样你肯定能抓住罪魁祸首。"农夫答应了。先知还告诉农夫，要远离农场，并雇一个人专门看着。露露推荐了一条叫"辛"的蛇。

  农夫接受了这个建议。他辞别了先知露露。回到农场后，按照先知露露的指示去做。然后，他又去跟"辛"商量雇佣服务的事。辛同意了。于是，他们就一起来到农庄。蛇对农夫说："你到田的另一端找个地方守着，我就留在这一端，运气好的话，谁是肇事者今晚就见分晓了。"

  农夫在另一端坐了好几个小时也没见一只动物。蛇就让他回家，自己继续看守。

  夜深了，老鼠们来到花生田，甩开膀子拼命吃啊吃。有些吃饱后就离开了。但有一只特别贪心的老鼠，想要在那天晚上吃完整个花生田。其他老鼠都走后，只有他留了下来。

  不幸的是，辛就在一旁静静等候着这只贪婪的老鼠。肚子填饱后，老鼠打算走了。在回去的路上，辛一口逮住了他，用鼠族的语言问他："你是谁？"老鼠回答："我是只青蛙而已。"老鼠这样说是为了吓住蛇，因为他知道蛇是惧怕蛙毒的，这样他就会马上被放开。蛇又问道："难道青蛙会长毛吗？"

  辛被自己的笑话逗得合不拢嘴，一张嘴，老鼠伺机逃走了。老鼠回到自己的族群后，把自己被蛇逮住的事告诉了大家，并警告大家今后要远离花生田。这样花生田才没有被洗劫一空。

The Frog That Grows Hair

A farmer once lived in a village called Rosar. The village was so called because its fields were extremely stony.

In spite of this natural problem of the land, the farmer was prepared to make something out of it. He decided to cultivate groundnuts on a very large scale. He was able to plough hundreds of acres. When he completed planting, he was hopeful. The groundnuts started nicely. Every morning the farmer would inspect his farm making sure that pests and rats did not destroy the crop. The crop started to flourish and everybody was praising the farmer.

One day, the King of the rats summoned a meeting. At this meeting the King of the rats addressed his subjects. He spoke about Man's wickedness. The King of the rats urged his subjects to be aware of men who grow fat by eating rats. He also suggested that they should take revenge on man. One rat got up and said, "My Lord, it is true that man eats rats and that our society might one day be ended by such an act. But I have a feeling that we cannot wage a war against man since we can't even hold a stick." This was well taken by the King and the other rats. Another rat got up and said, "Since man wears clothes to walk around, why can't we simply steal each man's clothes while they are asleep?" The King replied that this was difficult since they didn't even know how many human beings were there. While the meeting was going on, a young rat came panting. He apparently had some good news for the community.

He started: "Hm, K-k-king, I h-have just stumbled upon a very vast farm of ground—nuts some miles from here. I came to inform you about it." This news was received with tremendous joy. The King of the rats then told his subjects the war against man was to be waged against man's efforts. The groundnut farm was therefore destroyed. That night the rats went to the farm and destroyed a part of the farm. The farmer as usual visited the farm the next morning. He realized that some destructive animals must have visited his farm the previous night. He could not tell which animals must have done the damage. The farmer decided to keep watch at the farm that night. He spent the whole night at the farm but could not see any animal. He spent two subsequent nights to no avail. The rats were watching him and so kept away from the farm. When the farmer discontinued the watch, the rats came again and destroyed another section of the farm. They were almost going to destroy the whole farm when the farmer decided to see the seer.

The farmer went to Pa Lulu, a small but clever bird. He explained his problems to Pa Lulu. Pa Lulu brought out a mat and an old dirty bag that looked unwashed for twenty years. The bag contained beads and other items. In the manner of a seer, Pa Lulu consulted the Oracle through these beads and other items, and said to the farmer, "Go to the farm, and make a fence right round the farm. Leave a very small opening where you will sit and watch. If you do that then you are sure of getting hold of the culprit." The farmer agreed. The seer further told the farmer to even keep off the farm and employ a special watch, "Employ somebody to keep the watch at the small opening. I would recommend Pa Sheen—a snake."

The farmer agreed to this suggestion as well. He left the seer's place. He went to the farm and did exactly what he was told by Pa Lulu, the seer. He then went to hire the services of Pa Sheen, the snake. Pa Sheen agreed and they went. When they arrived, the snake said to the farmer: "You take a place at the other end of the farm while I remain at the exit. We might be lucky to know the culprits this night."

The farmer sat for hours on end but could not see any animal. So the snake told him to go home while he would continue the watch.

Very late at night, the rats came to the farm fully convinced that they would again have a free-for-all kind of loot. They ate and ate. Some had enough and returned. There was a particularly greedy one who was bent on destroying the whole farm that night. He stayed behind while the others went away.

Unfortunately for this rat, Pa Sheen took a quiet posture at the exit waiting for this greedy rat. After eating to his satisfaction the rat now decided to go away. On his way out, Pa Sheen arrested him with his mouth and asked in the rat's language, "Kende dukla?", meaning "who is this?". The rat replied in the same language, "Dukla makende, kure kure ma roto", meaning "It's me the frog". The rat said this to scare the snake as he knew the snake would be afraid of the frog's poison, and so would have released him immediately. The snake said in the same language: "Hm, roto di fon-i?", meaning "Does a frog grow hair?".

This made Pa Sheen laugh his sides out and the rat had a chance to escape. When he got back to his comrades, the rat explained what transpired between him and Pa Sheen, and warned every rat to keep off the farm. This was how the farm was saved from total destruction.

忘恩负义的男孩

从前在一个村子里住着一个喜欢钓鱼的男孩。一天早上，他像往常一样去钓鱼，运气不错，他钓到了许多。他高兴坏了，想一整天都待在那里钓鱼。但幸福是短暂的，一场暴风雨袭来，他赶紧把所有钓到的鱼都收起来装进袋子里走了。

他途经一片开阔的田野，看到一堆熊熊燃烧的火，挡住了他的去路。为了找另一条路出去，他放慢了速度。正当他要离开时，突然被某个东西吸引住了。他发现在熊熊燃烧的大火中有条蛇。蛇对他说："孩子，看在上帝的分上，我希望你把我从火中救出来。"男孩很善良，拿起钓竿，救下了蛇。

蛇向他表示感谢。把蛇放下来之前，男孩想把它移到远离火的地方。蛇抖个激灵，让男孩放下他。男孩把蛇放下来。蛇立起身子说："虽然你救了我，但我还是要咬你，你看不到明天了。"男孩很害怕，问蛇："这就是你回报我的方式吗？求你了，不要杀我，我求你饶了我。"

蛇说："要我饶了你，须满足三个条件。我问一个问题，必须由三个路人回答。这个问题就是：如果有人帮助了你，你会怎么回报？"男孩又困惑又担心，不知道说什么。不久一只狗过来了，问发生了什么事。男孩就把事情的经过悉数讲给狗听，包括他是如何遇到蛇的以及蛇提出的问题。

狗讲述了自己的人生历程："我从小就从母亲身边被带走了，监护人疼爱我，一日三餐喂我，允许我在家自由活动，当他出去散步时，我就照看房子，没有人敢进去，有人来了，我也必须先确认身份，才能让他们进来。"

"现在我老了，"狗继续向小男孩解释他的处境，"喉咙也哑了，监护人不再关心我了，他们不让我进院子，也不给我吃的，我就只能吃些臭鱼烂虾，这是他们对我所有付出的报答。"蛇让狗先走，并对小男孩说："听见了吧，现在谁也救不了你。"

不久，一头老奶牛出现了，但她头上没有角，甚至不能正常走路，她已经很久没有干活了。男孩又把遭遇告诉了奶牛。他问:"奶牛,如果有人对你好,你会怎样报答他呢?"奶牛毫不犹豫地回答说:"我出生的时候是我主人的宝贝。我被照顾得好,吃得也好,现在我老了,不能生育了,他们不再照顾我了。就算我死了,他们也不在乎。我给他们生了许多牛犊,现在我工作效率低,他们就不那么关心我了。"蛇听得一肚子火,仿佛随时要爆炸。他警告男孩说,如果最后一个路人还与狗和牛说的类似,那他一定会杀了男孩。

蛇威胁男孩的时候,兔子出现了。他刚醒来,在四处寻找吃的东西。蛇向兔子讲述了他和男孩之间的事。兔子觉得男孩太冤枉了,于是想到了一个拯救他的计划。

兔子问小男孩,他是怎么把蛇从火中救出来的,男孩解释了他如何用一根棍子救了蛇,然后把他放进了自己的袋子里。兔子打断了他的话,说蛇不可能钻进男孩的袋子里去。

"我能钻进去,是的,我真的钻进了他的袋子里。"蛇说。兔子要求蛇再回到袋子里,眼见为实。

蛇跳进袋子里,把身体的一部分留在外面。但是兔子说:"除非整个身体都在里面,否则我不会相信你。"蛇整个儿钻进了袋子里。兔子立刻用绳子把袋子紧紧绑住,不让蛇出来。他让男孩用救蛇的棍子打蛇。男孩用力把蛇打死了。

就这样,男孩被兔子救了。他赶紧跑回家,向妈妈讲述了他遇到蛇、狗、牛、兔子的经历。他的母亲给他买了一只狗。妇人对他说:"孩子,你带着这条狗去打猎。"

有一次,男孩带着狗去打猎。在路上,狗看见一只老鼠,就追赶它。老鼠飞快地跑进一个洞里。突然,狗看见了兔子。这正是将男孩从蛇手中救出的那只兔子。狗追赶兔子并抓住了他。男孩把兔子带到他妈妈那里。兔子自言自语道:"这就是我欺骗蛇所付出的代价,如果我没有从蛇手里救下这个男孩,他今天就没有机会抓住我了。"

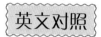

The Ungrateful Boy

Once there lived a boy in a village who loved fishing. One morning, as usual, he went to fish and was lucky to catch many fishes. He was so happy that he wanted to stay there the whole day fishing. But his happiness was short for a heavy storm started blowing. He hurriedly gathered all what he had caught, put them in his bag and left.

On his way he came to an open field and saw a fierce fire burning, blocking his way. He slowed down in order to find another way. As he was about to divert, something caught his attention. Snake was right in the middle of the burning fire. Snake called on to him saying, "Boy, I want you in the name of the Lord to save me from this fire." The boy was very kind-hearted. He took his fishing stick and with it he was able to save Snake.

Snake thanked him for saving him. The boy wanted to remove Snake far away from the fire before putting him down. Snake had an idea. He asked the boy to put him down. Then he put him down. Snake stood up on his tail and said, "Now that you have saved me, I am going to bite you and you will die tomorrow." The boy became afraid and asked Snake, "Is this how you are going to pay me for saving you? Please don't kill me. I beg you spare my life."

Snake said, "I will only forgive you on three conditions. I am going to ask you one question and the question must be answered by three witnesses. The question is, 'If someone does any good for you, what will be his reward?'" The boy became confused and worried and didn't know what to say. Soon Dog came by and asked what was wrong. The boy explained everything to Dog—how he had encountered Snake and the question posed by Snake.

Dog narrated his life history thus, "I was taken from my mother when I was young. I was loved by my guardians. I was fed regularly and I had access to everywhere in the house. When my guardians went for a walk I would look after the house and no one dared to enter it. Even when they were in, visitors had to be identified before I would allow them in."

Dog then went on to explain his plight to the boy. "Now I am old," he said. "I have lost almost all my voice. My guardians don't care for me any longer. They don't allow me into the compound. They don't feed me. I only feed on decayed food and faeces. This is the reward for all my kindness," Dog concluded. Snake asked Dog to go, and said to the boy, "Have you heard what Dog has said? Nothing will save you now."

Soon old Cow appeared. She did not have any horn. She could not even walk properly, and had long since stopped producing. Again the boy told Cow how he came in contact with Snake and the question posed to him by Snake. The boy asked, "Cow, if anyone does good to you, how will you reward him?" Without hesitation Cow replied, "When I was born, I was the darling of my owners. I was well looked after and properly fed. Now that I am old and sterile, they do not care for me. Even if I die, they don't care. I have produced many calves for them. Now that I am unproductive, they care less about me." Snake became angry and dangerous. He warned the boy that if the last witness came and gave the same answer as Dog and Cow, he would surely kill him.

No sooner had Snake threaten the boy than Rabbit appeared on the scene. He had just woken up and was roaming about finding something to eat. Snake explained everything between him and the boy to Rabbit. Rabbit at once felt sorry for the boy and immediately thought of a plan to save the boy.

Rabbit asked the boy to explain how he managed to save Snake from the fire. The boy explained how he used a stick to save Snake and later put him in his bag. Rabbit interrupted and said that it was not possible for Snake to go into the boy's bag.

"I went into it. Yes, I really went into his bag," Snake said. Rabbit demanded that Snake should go into the bag again so that he could see with his own eyes and indeed believe Snake.

Snake jumped into the bag leaving some part of his body outside. But Rabbit said, "Unless the whole body is in it, I will not believe you, Snake." Snake went right into the bag. Immediately, Rabbit took a rope and tied the bag strongly so that Snake could not come out. He asked the boy to beat Snake with the stick that saved Snake. The boy beat Snake, and beat Snake, and beat Snake, until Snake died.

Thus the boy was saved by Rabbit. He ran home quickly, and narrated his experience with Snake, Dog, Cow and Rabbit to his mother. His mother gave him a dog which she had bought for him. She said to him, "My son, take this dog, and go with it whenever you go hunting."

Once the boy went on a hunting expedition and took the dog with him. On their way, the dog saw a rat and chased it. The rat quickly ran into a hole. Suddenly the dog saw Rabbit. It was Rabbit who had rescued the boy from Snake. The dog chased Rabbit and caught it. The boy took Rabbit to his mother. Rabbit said to himself, "This is the prize I have to pay for being ungrateful to Snake. Had I not saved the boy from Snake he would not have caught me today."

为什么动物会怕猎人

动物都想不明白,为什么猎人手里只拿着一根木棍,却很容易将他们捕获。实际上,动物们误以为猎人手里的枪只是一根木棍。

一天,动物们在丛林里开会。狐狸因为机智和狡猾备受动物们的推崇。其他动物让狐狸告诉他们,在这个世界上,他们应该害怕什么。而狐狸认为,每只动物必须先说出在世界上自己最害怕的东西。兔子说:"我害怕狮子。"所有其他较弱小的动物也都说出了各自认为害怕的动物。有些说是大象,有些说是狼,还有些说是鲸鱼。当问到狐狸害怕什么时,他说:"真的,你们提到的所有动物我都不怕;我最怕的是穷人,一个衣衫褴褛,手里拿着一根木棍的人。"狐狸告诉他们害怕穷人的原因。他说:"我害怕穷人,因为穷人一旦哪天向别人祷告了,哪天就会有一个人死去。"

经过一番准备之后,动物们商定了一个公开见面的日子。这样,每一个动物都有机会登场来展示他们的实力,以此证明为什么其他动物必须或有必要害怕他们。这次盛大的见面会马上就要到了,所有的动物都将面对面交流。狐狸邀请了乞丐——一个衣衫褴褛、手里拿着一根木棍的男人。所有的大型动物,如大象、鲸鱼、狮子都来了,各自炫耀他们的力量。

动物们抽签决定由谁先展示力量。抽中首签的是大象。于是,大象先被邀请表演,以向其他动物证明他的可怕之处。大象优雅地腾挪跳跃着,一边跳跃,一边舞蹈。尽管当时还是雨季,一瞬间,整个场地都被一层厚厚的烟雾和灰尘笼罩,所有的动物都惊叹于大象的威力。动物们认为,他们中的任何一个都不是大象的对手。大家既佩服大象,又害怕他。这时候,狐狸问动物们这是不是他们害怕的,动物们齐声回答:"是的!"响声不绝于耳。

接下来轮到狮子了。狮子只是一声吼叫,就震得树木颤抖,树枝摇晃,一个抱杀就能同时抓住好几棵树。动物们又惊又怕,四散躲避。当他们再集中在一起时,想起了狐狸说过的关于穷人的事情。"我说,狐狸,"其中一只动物说,"你现在能不能请你最害怕的那个乞丐过来?让他向我们展示展示,让我们看看他到底有什么可怕的。"

这时,乞丐还躺在竞技场附近的一棵树旁边。他从那里悄悄钻了出来。他刚现身,豹子就咆哮着问动物们是不是该害怕那个人,反正自己是不会怕的。乞丐被要求证明他的本事,让动物们看看为什么他们必须害怕他。乞丐瞬间化身成了猎人,接受了挑战。他站起来,绕到一棵树的背后,拿出他的那根木棍。他给他的枪上了子弹,瞄准了大象,然后扣动了扳机,正好击中大象的牙。大象受了致命伤,站在原地,像喝醉了一样。他挣扎着在那个位置站了许久,但最后还是伤痛难忍,摔在地上,死了,像石头一样僵硬。

在此期间,其他动物开始变得焦躁不安。他们发现大事不妙,发生在大象身上的事是他们一辈子都不曾见过的。一招杀死大象更被认为是不可思议的事,尤其大象刚刚才证明过他是最强壮的动物。

这件事发生前,原本地球上所有动物都生活在一起的,但从那天起,事情变了,所有的动物都分开了。每一个种群都找了一个安全而隐蔽的地方来防御人类。猴子们也第一次爬上了树顶。

这就是为什么直到现在动物都会害怕猎人的原因。

Why Animals Fear Hunters

No animal knew what it really was; they took it for a mere batten that the hunter carried in his hand, so they felt easy prey to hunters. Indeed, they mistook the gun to be a batten.

One day, the animals held a meeting in the bush. Because Bra fox was held in very high esteem by all the animals for his wit and craftiness, he was asked to tell the animals what they should fear in the world. Bra Fox however suggested that it was necessary for each animal to tell the others what he feared most in the world first. Hare said, "I fear Lion." All the other less powerful animals showed what each of them personally feared. Some named Elephant, some Wolf and others named Whale. When Bra Fox was asked to tell them what he feared, he said, "Really, I do not fear all the animals you have named; what I fear most is the pauper—a man dressed in tattered clothing who carries a log in his hand." He told them the reason why he feared the pauper. He said, "I fear the pauper because when the pauper prays to anyone, one will die on that day."

After this preliminary, the animals agreed on a date for a public exhibition so that every animal could perform to confirm his claim why other animals must fear him. Indeed, the date for that great exhibition came to pass; all the animals met. Bra Fox invited the pauper—the man in tattered clothing and with a log in his hand. All the big animals such as Elephant, Whale, Lion came, showing off.

The lot was drawn, and it first fell on Elephant. Elephant was then invited to perform so as to prove to the other animals reasons for fearing him. With elegant prance, the elephant sprang to his feet and started dancing. Soon, the entire arena was taken over by a very thick envelope of smoke and dust. It was in the rainy season, so all the animals marvelled at the great feat of the elephant. They concluded that Elephant was even capable of eating up any of them. They admired and feared him. Bra Fox then asked the animals whether that was what they feared; there was a resounding echo of "Yes, yes" from among the animals.

The lot next fell on the lion. As soon as the lion brayed, the vibration in the trees caused the boughs to sway and overlap one another. In a single sweep, he would grab at seven or ten trees together. The animals were so amazed and frightened that they started to run away. When they assembled again, they recalled what Bra Fox had told them about the pauper. "Please, Bra Fox," said one of the animals, "will you now invite the pauper—the man you said you fear most? Let him show us how powerful he is and why we should fear him."

At this time, the pauper was already couched by a tree near the arena from where he quietly emerged. No sooner had the pauper arrived than Leopard growled and asked whether that was the man they should fear, and retorted that it was not for him. However, the pauper was asked to prove his mettle and show the animals why they must fear him. The hunter accepted the challenge. He got up and passed behind a big tree and later emerged with his batten. The hunter loaded his gun to capacity. He took his aim at Elephant, the biggest of all the animals. He aimed and aimed and aimed and fired at the elephant. The bullets caught Elephant right in his tusk. Indeed, Elephant had received his fatal wound. Elephant stood in one place looking like someone getting intoxicated. He stood in that position for a long time; but at last, the wound got the better part of him and eventually he was dead, as stiff as a stone.

During the interim, however, the other animals became restive and supposed that a very bad thing was about to happen, a thing they had never seen in their lives—what happened to King Elephant. This was all the more considered an impossible feat especially when King Elephant had just performed to prove that he was the strongest of all the animals.

Originally, before this incident took place, all the animals on the earth were living together, but from that day this incident occurred, all the animals separated. Each group found a safe and secluded place in defence against man. The monkeys, for the first time climbed to the tree tops.

This was how it came about that all animals fear hunters today.

三个朋友

从前,有三个朋友——鳄鱼、山羊和狗,他们住在一个村子里。三者当中,鳄鱼是个货真价实的损友。他们来到河边,决定在河上筑一座拦河坝,这样捕鱼就会变得容易多了。

鳄鱼请狗和山羊在一边唱歌助兴,这样干活效率就高多了。鳄鱼自己先唱起了歌,歌词大意是:

不管抓没抓到鱼,我肯定不会空手回去。

然后他请狗来唱。狗就唱道:

上帝保佑,我可是个跑步能手。

狗唱完歌后,鳄鱼示意山羊,现在轮到他唱歌了。山羊明白了前面两首歌的意思,也唱了起来:

稳重的人都善于掩饰情感。

山羊和狗都明白鳄鱼歌声背后的含义。因此,山羊决定一旦看到鳄鱼追狗,他就躲到河里的淤泥中去。鳄鱼的歌让山羊和狗都提心吊胆,生怕逮不到鱼,自己会遭殃。三个朋友把网放进水里。过了一会儿,他们注意到网里网住了三种不同的生物。一条是"弓弓"鱼,另一只是螃蟹,还有一条是叫"本特"的小鱼。当他们把网提起来时,山羊请鳄鱼先把网上来的鱼进行分配,但鳄鱼有不同的意见,他表示现在捕到的东西太少了。鳄鱼就让山羊来分。山羊一听不知所措,他担心若分配不合鳄鱼的意,自己就可能会被他吃掉。

正讨论着,狗显得不耐烦了,因为他急着想要自己的那一份。于是,狗上来三下五除二就把捕到的鱼分了。他把螃蟹给了山羊,把一条叫"本特"的小鱼给了鳄鱼,把那条叫"弓弓"的大鱼留给了自己。狗刚拿到自己的那份,就发现鳄鱼正两眼瞪着他,他赶紧放下东西逃跑了。鳄鱼起身追赶狗,边追边大喊,要是让他抓住,他就把狗和鱼都吃掉。狗听到他这样说,跑得更快了,到后来鳄鱼连狗的影子都看不见了。鳄鱼看到自己已经没有机会抓住狗了,就回到他们捕鱼的地方,想在那里找到山羊,可他四处找都找不到山羊,因为这时山羊已经把自己埋进了淤泥,只剩下鼻子和角露在外面。但是鳄鱼没有放弃寻找,因为他知道山羊是非常聪明的。他告诉自己,山羊一定还躲在这条河的某个地方。鳄鱼放下渔网,把它扔到深深的泥坑里,这样才能网到大鱼,也可能网到山羊。他拉网的时候,发现一个奇怪的东西,看起来像一根棍子。山羊因为被网碰到了,就往后退。但是鳄鱼要把这个看起来像棍子的东西拿过来,觉得下面可能有一条大鱼。

鳄鱼一拿到那根所谓的棍子,山羊就大叫起来,鳄鱼高兴得笑了。山羊这时意识到自己有生命危险了。他恳求鳄鱼说:"在吃我之前,我有一个很好的建议。你也知道,我的肉很香甜,但在吃之前,请把我洗干净。"鳄鱼同意了。洗干净后,山羊请求鳄鱼在他的身上撒点盐,再放到石头上晾干后再吃掉也不迟。

山羊的所有要求鳄鱼都接受了。这时,山羊认为他可以开始咬绳子了。鳄鱼看到很惊讶,就对山羊说:"你已经被涂上了盐,都快成了我的盘中餐了,现在还在吃什么呢?"山羊听到这个提问心里一阵兴奋,因为他已经想好了怎么回答。山羊告诉鳄鱼,他正在嚼他踩着的那些石头。鳄鱼问山羊:"那你吃了石头后还会吃什么?"山羊回答说:"我吃了石头后,就把周围的东西都吃了。"鳄鱼听了山羊的回答后,心里一惊,打算马上离开山羊。鳄鱼担心如果山羊吃完石头和周围的东西,他就会成为下一个受害者,因为他就躺在山羊的旁边。

鳄鱼撒腿就跑,还以为山羊在后面追呢。山羊看到鳄鱼仓皇逃走,也决心离开这个地方。感谢上帝,山羊最终得救了。后来,山羊来到了城里。

这个故事告诉我们,害人之心不可有,防人之心不可无。

Three Friends

Once upon a time, three friends—Crocodile, Goat and Dog used to live in a village. Of the three of them, Crocodile was the bad friend. When they got to the river, they decided to dam the river so that the fish could easily get in.

Crocodile asked Mr. Dog and Mr. Goat to sing so that the work could be done faster. Crocodile first sang his own song which went thus:

Whether I catch or not, I know that I will not go home empty handed.

He then asked Dog to sing his own song. Dog sang:

Bless me, I am able to run.

After Dog had finished singing, Crocodile told Goat that it was his turn to sing. As Goat understood the meaning of the two previous songs, he also went on to sing:

Older people keep their senses inside their stomach.

Both Goat and Dog knew the meaning behind Crocodile's song. Thus, Goat decided that as soon as he saw Crocodile chasing Dog, he would hide himself in the mud. This made both Goat and Dog alert in case no fish were caught. The three friends lowered their net into the water. After some time they noticed three different fish in the net. One was bow-bow, one a crab and another a small fish called gbenthe. When they removed the net, Goat asked Crocodile to share the first among the three of them, but Crocodile was thinking differently as what they caught was too little. Crocodile then told Goat to do the sharing. Goat was very confused because he was thinking that if he did not share the way Crocodile would like, he might be eaten by him.

During this discussion Dog became annoyed because he wanted his own share. He then shared the fish with them. He gave the crab to Goat, the small fish called gbenthe to Crocodile and the large fish called bow-bow was left for himself. As soon as he got hold of his share he saw Crocodile looking at him and decided to run away from Crocodile. The latter then chased Dog. While chasing Dog, he shouted at him saying that if he caught Dog, he would eat both Dog and Fish. When Dog heard him, he ran much faster until Crocodile could not see him any more. As soon as Crocodile saw that there was no chance of getting hold of Dog, he then decided to return to where they had been fishing hoping to find Goat there. On his arrival, he searched for Goat but it was difficult to find him as Goat had already buried himself in the mud, leaving out only his nose and horns. However, Crocodile did not give up his search since he knew Goat was very clever. He then said to himself, "I am convinced that Goat must be somewhere in this river." He brought down his fishing net and threw it very deep into the water by the mud so that he could get big fish, or Mr. Goat. While drawing the net, he noticed a strange object which looked like an old stick. Since Goat was touched by the net, he decided to move backward. But Crocodile had made up his mind to remove the object that looked like a stick as there might be big fish underneath it.

As soon as he got hold of the so-called stick, Goat gave a very loud cry which made Crocodile laugh for joy. Goat then knew that his life was in danger. But Goat pleaded with Crocodile saying, "Please, before eating me, I have a very good piece of advice to give you. As you see me now, my meat is very sweet to eat but before you eat me, you should wash me well." Crocodile agreed. After washing, Goat told Crocodile to put salt on his body and then place him on top of the stones to get dry before preparing him to be eaten up.

Crocodile accepted everything that Goat requested him to do. The thought then came to Goat that he should start chewing the cord. Seeing this, Crocodile was surprised and said to Goat, "You have already been salted for my food. What are you eating?" Goat was very pleased to hear this question as he had already decided what to answer. He then told Crocodile that he was chewing some of the stones that he was standing on. Crocodile asked Goat, "What will be the next food for you after eating the stones?" Goat answered, "After eating the stones, I will then eat everything that is around me." After having heard this answer, Crocodile decided to go away from the Goat fearing that if Goat decided to eat stones, and everything that was around, then the next victim would be him since he too was lying by.

He started running, thinking that Goat was behind him. When Goat saw Crocodile running, he decided to leave the area and said thanks to his gods that he was saved. He then went to town.

This story tells us that you should not be a wicked person to your friend and a heart of defense is indispensable.

后　记

互学互鉴：让民间口头文学
　　　助力中非民心相通

——写在纪念中非开启外交关系 66 周年之际

2022 年是中非开启外交关系 66 周年，66 这个数字在中国意味着"吉祥顺利"，预示着中非合作的美好前景。

"根之茂者其实遂，膏之沃者其光晔。"2018 年 9 月，习近平主席在中非合作论坛北京峰会开幕式上的主旨讲话中引用了唐代文学家韩愈《答李翊书》中的诗句来比喻中非关系要从根基上下功夫。这句诗的意思是："有了茂密的树根，才会有丰硕的果实；有了充足的灯油，才会有明亮的灯光。"那么，中非关系的根基究竟指的是什么呢？回顾 66 年来中非交往的历史脉络，在笔者看来，中非双方相似的遭遇和共同使命，相互尊重、同心同向、守望相助、合作共赢的发展理念和实践正是中非关系的良好根基。要贯彻落实习近平主席在中非合作论坛第八届部长级会议开幕式上主旨演讲中所提出的"四点主张"和"九项工程"，共同构建新时代中非命运共同体，就必须进一步筑牢新时代中非民心相通的友谊桥梁，夯实中非关系的民意基础。

当前,面对百年未有之大变局和复杂多变的国际形势,中非合作也面临诸多挑战。要夯筑新时代中非民心相通的友谊桥梁,要求我们在外交、人文交流、教育、经贸合作等各个领域,以习近平新时代中国特色社会主义思想为指导,主动契合中非合作大局,增进理解,弘扬好中华语言文化,有序推进中非人文交流、加强互学互鉴,在发展中切实增强中非双方人民的获得感,促进民心相通,扎实筑牢中非关系的民意基础。

(一)弘扬中华语言文化,促进民心相通

世界文明正是在不同语言文化的交流融通中相互碰撞,激荡出灿烂的文明之花。正所谓"美人之美""美美与共""和而不同"。习近平主席在提出"四个自信"时强调指出,文化自信,是更基础、更广泛、更深厚的自信。在五千多年文明发展中孕育出来的中华优秀传统文化,积淀着中华民族最深层的精神追求,代表着中华民族独特的精神标识。坚定的文化自信是我们在实施文化"走出去"战略中的底气和定力。

时至今日,中国在非洲的48个国家中共建有62所孔子学院,48家孔子课堂(含下设孔子课堂)。孔子学院(课堂)深度融入当地的大学、中小学、职业技术学院及社区等,通过教授汉语,传播中国传统文化,为中非民心互通打下重要基础,是弘扬中华语言文化的重要平台,在促进中非民心互通上功不可没。孔子学院(课堂)在开展教学和文化活动之外,还积极服务当地,比如举办人才招聘会,开展"中文+职业技能"培训等,不断深化、拓展服务领域,为中非人文交流、经贸合作搭建语言沟通的桥梁,为中非的共同发展默默贡献力量。比如,塞拉利昂大学孔子学院建立的"武术太极俱乐部"不仅成为当地民众交流、健身和学习了解中国文化的平台,受到了当地民众的欢迎,还丰富了当地社区和学校体育教育的内容。塞拉利昂弗拉湾学院附中的校长莱比女士说:"孔子学院的武术太极教学,填补了我们学校体育教学的空白,不仅强身健体,还富有趣味性,深受学生欢迎。许多学生就是从武术太极开始了对中国的了解。"又比如,因为非洲当地网络、电视普及率不高,大部分人仍采用无线广播和收音机来获取信息,塞拉利昂大学孔子学院创办了"中国之声"汉语空中教室,推出《跟我学汉语》《中国音乐》《中国新闻》《我眼中的中国》等栏目。由当地的汉语教师担任节目主持人,邀请曾经赴华学习或交流的学者、学生现身说法,介绍在中国的所见所闻和切身感受。每周播出两期,每期听众过万人,扩大了影响,加深了当地人对中国的了解。

后记

语言文化的交流不是单向的。文明因交流而多彩，文明因互鉴而丰富。文明交流互鉴，是推动人类文明进步和世界和平发展的重要动力。在向世界传播中华语言文化的同时，我们也在吸收其他民族文化的营养，这是一个不同文明互学互鉴的过程，世界文明正是在这样的交流互鉴中得以传播、传承和发扬光大。

非洲的民间口头文学来源于非洲丰富的民间传统文化和民族文化，非洲大陆民族的多样性，也使得非洲的民间口头文学呈现出文化的多样性。它们是当今非洲文化和精神气质的直接来源和重要体现。因此，要读懂今天的非洲，我们非常有必要从这些田间地头的口头文学作品去着手了解，唯有如此，我们才能真正理解非洲普通民众的行为方式和非洲文化的深刻内涵，不断增进国际理解，促进中国与非洲各国之间的民心相通。

（二）推动中非人文交流，促进民心相通

中非教育合作是中非全方位友好合作关系的一项重要内容。从 20 世纪 50 年代至今，中非教育合作走过了从无到有，从互派留学生的单一形式到多层次、多领域、多形式的教育合作三个不同阶段。2020 年 6 月 18 日，教育部等八部门印发了《关于加快和扩大新时代教育对外开放的意见》（以下简称《意见》）。《意见》指出，教育对外开放是教育现代化的鲜明特征和重要推动力，要以习近平新时代中国特色社会主义思想为指导，坚持教育对外开放不动摇，主动加强同世界各国的互鉴、互容、互通，形成全方位、宽领域、多层次、更加主动的教育对外开放局面。新时代的中非教育合作要秉持《意见》要求，主动服务国家外交战略，实施积极的国际化发展策略，助力非洲的人才培养，进一步提升中非教育合作的规模、培养层次、交流渠道与形式等，促进中非多元文明的互学互鉴。

教育是人文交流的重要基础性领域，人文交流赋予了教育合作交流新的属性和新的使命，为教育合作交流提供了更大的平台和空间。在中非合作论坛这个大的合作框架下，目前，我国已经建立了中非教育合作论坛、中非教育部长论坛、中非文明对话等合作和交流机制。在这些机制之下，中非教育开放与合作有了更多深度探讨和开拓实践的平台，人们对新时代的中非教育合作寄予了全新展望。

非洲是中国对外教育交流合作的重点对象之一，双方在双向留学、合作办学、人员交流等领域取得了诸多合作成果，为中非教育合作与人文交流做出了卓越贡献。开展中非教育合作交流可以有效推动中非高校之间的学科建设与合作,也在教育层面进一步增进了中非之间的相互理解和包容,搭建起了一座沟通与合作的友谊桥梁。

总之,中非间的深度理解需要长期的相互交流才能发展为深度互信,对此我们应有充分的心理准备。这需要社会各界和驻非各行各业的广泛参与和锲而不舍的努力,持之以恒,久久为功,扎实夯筑中非民心相通的牢固根基,为共同构建新时代中非命运共同体做出积极贡献。

我们深信,西非的民间口头文学作品将会让我们穿越时空看到非洲大陆过去的许多东西,帮助我们更好地了解非洲的文化,促进中非之间的合作交流和民心相通。

何明清
2022 年 12 月 30 日于赣州